A CALAMITY OF WINGS

Sharon Marie Brasher

For Julia and Michael

PROLOGUE

LONDON

A black van waited in the shadows just outside the elite neighborhood of Kingsbridge. It was 4:00 am.

Except for the smoky grey Persian that perched upon a stone garden wall, the street was completely deserted.

"I fucking hate those things." The driver, known only to his partner as B.K, glared at the cat as it licked its paw and kept a watchful eye on them.

He picked a piece of fuzz off of his exquisitely tailored, cobalt blue suit and then pretended to resecure the clasp on his lapel pin. It was a blue orchid, set with stunning blue diamonds.

To wear this pin, meant he had been vetted and was a bona fide, card-carrying member of the Order. And he'd taken that moment to fiddle with it, more as a show of superiority than for any other reason.

"Do you think it's weird the way it's looking at us? It makes me nervous," the younger man said.

"It's just a fucking cat. Are you sure the flight was today, Scruffy?"

"Positive."

Scruffy was not his real name. B.K had taken one look at him and decided that was what he would call him. It was embarrassing and mortifyingly demeaning. He hated it. He also hated being laughed at, especially by someone who was high-born.

But he kept his mouth closed, concealing his true feelings behind a congenial smile. He knew better than to risk rubbing someone of a higher rank with all sorts of family connections, the wrong way.

The younger man also wore a suit, a less expensive and slightly more wrinkled one. He did not wear any mark of distinction.

He regretted the red silk tie his wife had lovingly tied around his neck this morning. It stood out too much. He also regretted the black suit which he felt made him look like an undertaker.

Unlike the driver, the man was nervous. Even the tiniest mistake could lead to centuries of unacknowledged grunt work and he was not about to let that happen, not after he'd been invited to join this organization.

It was an honor to even be considered for the Order, and almost unheard of for one not of noble blood.

He'd done his homework. He'd researched the exact streets the mark would take. He knew the intended target's routine backward and forward, etched in his memory as surely as the curves of his wife's breasts.

And he knew the precise moment to strike.

The target should have already been enroute to Heathrow International.

Where was he?

B.K. glanced down at his partner's leg which bobbed up and down erratically. "Relax, Scruffy. You act like this is your first time or something," he said, then chuckled. "Oh, right."

Then they spotted the car.

"See. Nothing to worry about," B.K said.

They pulled behind, following at an inconspicuous distance for nearly eight miles.

"X marks the spot," Scruffy said.

The reinforced van began to pass, and when the vehicles were nearly parallel to one another, took a sharp, violent plunge into the driver's door.

The car flipped into the air, landing upside down on the shoulder of the road.

They pulled over just ahead of the wreckage and got out to surveille the damage. The victim hung from his seat belt, confused, but still alive.

"You know what to do," B.K. said.

In a matter of seconds, the car and the man inside were doused in gasoline. Scruffy struck a match and tossed it inside.

It was chilly outside, and he rather welcomed a little bit of heat on his cold fingers as the flames rose higher.

He didn't mind the screams of the man who burned inside. In fact, he hardly even noticed them at all. The adrenaline pumped furiously through him.

His first hit was a success. Things had gone exactly according to plan.

"What about the other matter?" he asked.

"It's been taken care of."

The two men piled into the van and waited as long as they dared.

"He should be good and dead by now," B.K. said.

There had been no witnesses, or at least that is what they thought. Neither of them had noticed the same cat from Kingsbridge looking on from an adjacent field.

They pulled back onto the road, their taillights disappearing as the fabric of space around them distorted and the night swallowed them whole.

PART ONE

CHAPTER ONE

THE DRAGON'S NECK

It was entirely too early for dinner, but I was starving.

It had been nearly seven hours since I tried to choke down a piece of dry toast and I salivated over everything on the menu.

Little bits of heaven wafted out from the kitchen provoking my stomach into an outright rebellion. It growled threateningly, *feed me, damn you, or else!*

Mary's Diner had a dimly lit 70's vibe, booths covered in well maintained, orange vinyl and Tiffany-style light fixtures that hung low over white laminate tables.

A counter with stools ran beside the register stopping short at a glass display case full of gorgeous cakes, éclairs, and Italian cookies.

I considered ordering one of everything and then unconsidered it. I could feel the pounds settling on my thighs just from thinking about it.

5

From my seat by the window, I took in my surroundings. There were three other customers besides myself.

A white-haired gentleman pretended to read a book, but lowered it enough to study me suspiciously when he thought I wasn't paying attention.

The couple in the back, brooding youths with electric blue hair, huddled close together and stared longingly at one another.

I wondered if any of them were locals. There had been no traffic in or out of Glenhaven. It hadn't even appeared on my map or GPS.

The only way to get here was a white-knuckle drive along the Dragon's Neck, a treacherous narrow road of undulating curves and nothing at all to stop a car from careening over the side of the cliff.

The moment I'd reached the edge of town I'd known this place was different.

There was something completely Brothers Grimm about the way its intertwining trees pressed together from opposite sides, enshrouding the covered bridge into town in complete and utter darkness.

It was so dark inside of the tunnel and the amplified roar of the creek passing beneath it, made me wonder if I'd unwittingly driven into the mouth of a cryptid creek monster.

The air, layered with multitudes of flora and fauna, had been both sweet and bitter sour. But there was an unknown element that penetrated my inner being, vibrating the hairs on my neck and arms and making me light headed.

There was an energy here that was as elusive as my knowing. It informed the nature of everything around me. It hung heavy, yet, was nowhere.

It had nothing at all to do with being so high up in the mountains and more to do with the reason I'd ended up here to begin with on this late September day.

Realizing I'd found this place, didn't make it any easier to understand why I'd been pulled here to begin with.

A slim fifty something woman in jeans, a white T-shirt, and a red and white checkered apron approached my table.

Her sandy brown hair with few visible strands of silver was only just long enough to fit inside her scarlet scrunchie, but her eyes stood out the most.

They were strikingly blue, peering into me as if she were capable of ripping intimate details out of my psyche.

However, this wasn't conveyed in the friendly tone of her voice, "Hi there. Can I get you something to drink while you make up your mind?"

I noticed the nametag pinned onto her shirt. *Mary*.

"A coffee would be nice. And I think I'll have the lasagna." I folded the menu and handed it back to her. "Is this your restaurant? I'm Helene Parish."

When I extended my hand, she stared at it as though inspecting for razor blades before slipping her own work calloused one into mine.

"Mary Romano. Yes, this is my place. Nothing much, but it keeps me busy. What brings you to our neck of the woods?"

I'd worn way too many layers of clothing and sweated underneath her probing gaze.

I wiped tiny beads of perspiration off of my forehead and decided to keep my answer as vague as possible, "I found Glenhaven by accident. I was just exploring and ended up here. I'm also really intrigued by a town that technically doesn't exist, at least not on a map."

My answer caused something to shift in her. She relaxed and broke into a smile, "Map or no map, you found us just fine."

Mary left and returned with a steaming hot mug and an enormous rectangular portion of lasagna.

"Is there a motel here or a bed and breakfast where I could find accommodation?"

"I'm afraid the only thing we have to offer is the old cottage. Dr. Richter rents it out to hikers and such."

"Do you know how I can get in touch with him about it?" I asked.

"No need for that. I keep the key here for him. Would you be staying just for the night?"

Without even thinking, I heard myself say, "I might stay a few weeks. I mean, if it isn't already booked."

Mary's eyebrows flew up at this. Then she wrinkled up her nose, "We don't get many long-term guests. You didn't rob a bank or kill anybody, did you?"

I laughed at this, "No heinous crimes. Nothing any shadier than a transcendental crisis, I'm afraid."

Again, I felt the powerful sting of Mary's blue eyes. "Should I be worried about you?"

It took a second for her meaning to sink in, that I might have chosen Glenhaven as a final destination.

"Oh! Gosh, no. I promise. I really just need some peace and quiet."

This was true. I did need this. And I couldn't very well tell her that I had no fucking idea why I'd come here, that I'd had an irrational, unshakeable pull to this place.

And I definitely couldn't tell her I had no plans to leave until I figured this out.

Again, Mary disappeared through swinging doors where I heard the clinking of pots and pans.

She returned, took a pen out of her pocket, and handed it to me along with a short-term rental agreement. "Fill this out. I'll also be needing a copy of your driver's license."

I fished my ID out of my wallet. She took her time looking back and forth between it and me. Then she pursed her lips and peered out the window, "Is that your Civic?"

I nodded and she jotted down the number from the front license plate.

"Washington state, huh? You're really far from home."

It felt like she could look straight through me, all the way down to the pain caused by everything I'd lost.

I found myself opening up to her, "Funny, it doesn't feel like home anymore. I don't have any family left. It's just me."

Mary's face softened. It was as though she had made a decision about me and I'd passed a secret initiation known only to her. "Then maybe it's about time you found a new one, Helene."

I almost told her that things never seemed to end well for the people who loved me. But instead said nothing, not that she'd expected a reply.

"Just need to make a copy of this. Let me know if you need anything."

While savoring all the flavors of my first decent meal in days, I filled in my personal information on the form.

When Mary came back, I settled up what I owed in exchange for the key and directions.

"Welcome to Glenhaven. Here's my number. Don't hesitate to call if there are any problems," she said.

I was anxious for a shower to wash away the road grime, not to mention how exhausted I was.

Outside the grey sky gave way to a fine mist. It settled over the downtown casting its charming brick buildings and square with its white gazebo into an ominous sepia hue.

It took only a few minutes to reach the cute cottage, isolated off of a gravel road and surrounded by woods.

It was freshly painted, white with black shutters. There was a wooden porch big enough to fit a red Adirondack chair and a concrete urn that someone had filled to the brim with yellow mums.

I jiggled the key in the lock and attempted several times before it sprang open. It wasn't as primitive as I'd been expecting it to be.

The walls inside were also white, brightening up the interior and balancing the dark hardwood floors that had been beaten up with time.

There were three rooms; a living room that included a wall designated as kitchen space, a tiny bathroom with a claw foot tub and rain shower, and a bedroom large enough to hold a full-size bed, dresser, and wardrobe.

I opened up the windows to let in some fresh air and took advantage of a break in the rain to unload the car.

The trunk was crammed to capacity with clothing, edge worn documents I might need, and random things that had no rhyme or reason and just wanted to fit inside the leftover space.

I'd left without having any idea of where I would end up or how long I would be gone.

It had the mark of madness.

Sane people didn't abandon their jobs and leave their lives in the pursuit of intangible ideas. They didn't trot off to regions unknown, racing toward whatever invisible thing that was that was beckoning to them.

I was sure any armchair psychiatrist would tell me that my recurring nightmares were just more evidence of this irrational self-delusion.

But they hadn't lived what I had, had they?

I would never make sense to anyone who hadn't seen into the future, who hadn't smelled the illness in their partner before the doctors even knew the cancer was there.

I would never make sense to anyone who hadn't killed another person with a mere thought.

No, there was no explanation in their Diagnostic and Statistical Manual of Mental Disorders to explain me.

At twilight, I had just enough energy to shower and climb into bed. But I didn't want to sleep. I didn't want to dream.

Dreaming opened the door to nightmares.

They were always the same, not the details of them as much as knowing that I was viewing snapshots of the same event from different geographical locations.

But the faces of the people, marred by wide-eyed terror, their blood curdling screams when they realized they were going to die, that never changed.

Sometimes right before the moment of impact, an acceptance fell over their faces and they gently braced for it. I admired the grace in that.

Then the disturbing event happened, even more disconcerting because of the suddenness with which it rushed in.

I woke up trembling, every time, never dulled to the horrors of what I witnessed.

The one that had haunted me most was the woman holding her son's hand as they walked down an urban street. She laughed at something he said and tossed her dark, glossy mane behind her shoulder.

The child was no more than five years old, a contrast to his mother with his mop of unruly brown curls, chocolate ice cream stains on his collar, and a constellation of freckles across his chubby cheeks.

In his free hand, he dangled an action figure of some kind and as he spoke, he flew it up through the air in steady orbits.

Others passed around them, not paying attention to the boy or his mother. And why would they, really? It was ordinary.

Then the earth shook beneath them. Buildings around them swayed. People scattered, looking up, aware of the threat the tall buildings posed.

When a huge chunk of a building's façade pulled away and fell through the air, it was in the perfect shape of a butterfly, as if it had been cut from the plaster with a giant cookie cutter.

It was strangely beautiful, until it struck.

The shockwave of the impact blew parts of the boy in all directions. Flesh and blood splattered indiscriminately.

It had missed his mother. Tossed face down onto the pavement, blinded by dust and disoriented, she called out for her son.

Then the atmosphere ignited. And everything was gone.

Another night I had a bird's eye view of a small coastal village.

At a fish market, men smiled and joked as they toiled away in the heat of the day, an easy-going familiarity among them as they chewed and spit tobacco, and bragged about their sexual prowess.

The wall of water cast a shadow over their corrugated metal shack, but it was no defense against the millions of tons of sea water.

Bodies and buildings were ripped off of their fragile foundations, right before their world, one that had been filled with routine and tradition, evaporated into ash as if it had never existed at all.

There was a deep fear that these dreams were warnings of things to come, like they had been so many other times.

And If I didn't sleep, I wouldn't dream these things into being.

It was a sort of Schrodinger's cat concept. If I didn't see these possible outcomes, they couldn't exist. I'd developed a whole strategy around this avoidance of sleep: midnight trips to the grocery store, binge watching series, walks through the town at 3 am.

You'd be amazed at what you could learn about a town at this time of day when the invisible came out of hiding, pushing carts laden with their most valuable possessions.

A thriving community of the lost and wandering gathered mere steps from posh shops and microbreweries.

You could learn how hard life was for some. You could see with your very own eyes those society had turned their backs on, and how the city's finest, brave police officers, bound to protect and serve, harassed the most vulnerable without mercy.

And you could discover that beneath all the charm and surface glitter, the heartless pulse that kept this illusion going.

I had shared this observation with a coworker.

"A woman alone at that time of day is just asking for trouble. Aren't you scared?" Anita worked as a teller.

I was a mortgage broker with my own office. We only rarely rubbed elbows, but my sleep aversion, fed by an uncontrolled caffeine addiction, made it inevitable that we would eventually run into one another in the break room.

"Not at all. If anything, they should fear me," I'd said.

Her laugh had been prissy and condescending, "Right. Because you're like a secret ninja or something." She had rolled her eyes before taking a bite of stale donut leftover from a staff meeting two days before.

I had let this slight roll off. I hadn't cared whether or not she believed me. It was true. And at the close of the day, I'd leave my signed resignation letter on my desk and never see her again.

Even after all the real tragedy that had happened in my life, I'd never been prone to bouts of anxiety or depression. I'd always been able to push through whatever situation presented itself.

But the dreams were something I couldn't shake, dragged behind me in every waking moment with heavy chains I couldn't break.

And if the world was going to end in the near future, my last moments wouldn't be spent hunched over stacks of paperwork.

I couldn't shake the sense that Glenhaven was an insular chrysalis, that maybe by entering through the dark abyss, I'd unwittingly set into motion some kind of metamorphosis.

For so long I'd been running, from heartache and the parts of myself I'd never understood that were so alien from others.

What would happen now that I had stopped?

What would happen if I let her loose, this fiery spirit who could bend the world to her will and had no qualms about doing so, the girl who looked into the truth that others tried to hide.

Was she powerful enough to stop these horrible things from happening?

And if not, what good did it serve to see anything at all?

CHAPTER TWO

THE ELUSIVENESS OF IT

It was nearly noon when I awoke to bright light flooding in and realized I had slept undisturbed throughout the night. It was the first sleep in a long time that had not been a hard-won battle.

Disoriented, I could make out a distinct scratching sound coming from the front door.

A white Siberian Husky peered back at me with curious grey eyes.

He didn't look like a stray. The salt and pepper hair along his back was shiny and well-groomed, and he wore a collar.

Once again, the dog lifted his large white paw to gently scratch at the door.

I cracked it open and cautiously extended my hand, "Hello, there."

He licked my fingers, and since he hadn't tried to eat me, I opened the door wider so that I could pet him.

His tag was fairly new and I could easily read his name. No address. No owner. All in all, it was a pathetically useless name tag.

"Did you escape, Rogue? Where do you live?"

Just as quickly as he'd come, Rogue sprinted down the steps and into the thicket of trees.

Because I was starving and in desperate need of coffee, I dressed quickly. After I had food in my stomach, I would deal with buying groceries and supplies.

I found an empty parking spot in front of City Hall and walked down to Mary's where I slid into the same booth by the window.

As if reading my mind, she plopped a cup down in front of me and poured it full of coffee as a man walked in with a crate of milk cartons.

Mary met him with hands on her hips, "I needed a crate of buttermilk this week, Lester. I was going to add cornbread to the menu to go with the pinto beans. You know everyone will be expecting that. Now what do I tell them?"

The man sat the crate on the floor and threw his hands up in frustration. "You tell them I have no control over how much milk my cows can produce, and that is just the way it is."

"Well, if it isn't within your control, it just isn't," she finally said. "But you'd better bring it next week, or there might not be any of that pound cake you like so much. You get my drift?"

"That's mean, Mary. Just plain mean," he said.

I got the feeling this was a conversation that got repeated on a regular basis.

"Sorry," she said when she returned. "What would you like?"

"Grilled cheese and a salad with vinaigrette, please."

"How was everything with the cottage?"

"It's perfect. But I do need to get some provisions."

"Houston's right across the street there. If they don't have it, you probably don't really need it. I'll be back with your food soon."

She made her rounds to the other tables, and came back with my order. "I hope you'll enjoy your time here, Helene. There's not much night-life, but I do push the tables back on weekends for dancing. And on Wednesday nights, we have an open mic. It can be anything from flute playing to poetry readings. You should come by tomorrow night."

"I might do that, Mary. Thanks."

After lunch, I ran into the Houston General Store which was owned by James and Irene Houston.

Their whole family helped out with the business which included a farm where they grew vegetables, tended bees, and raised chickens.

This included their two sons, the oldest, Harry, along with Harry's wife, Tracy, and their youngest, Mark, who I guessed was in his late twenties.

James and both of his sons had been blessed with fiery red hair. The entire family was unusually tall. Irene Houston was beautiful, nearly 6 feet herself, with shaggy blonde hair.

This made Harry's petite brunette wife stand out. I was only 5'6", but even I towered above her.

Mark was a bit of a flirt in spite of our age difference.

I was used to this kind of attention from men, but it wasn't because I was particularly beautiful. Honestly, I never understood what it was that they found so alluring. I chalked it up to my having an unusual aesthetic.

I was thin, yet curvaceous. My eyes were light hazel, appearing either green or amber, depending on the colors surrounding me or how the sunlight hit them just so. My strands of the deepest, darkest brown were thick yet as fine and soft as goose down, and as unruly as weeds, growing unnaturally fast.

And then there was the inch wide streak of pure silver that ran down the right side of my hair. I had always hated it, not because people were always touching it, random strangers, young, old, and in between.

I hated it because it was a reminder, appearing overnight the day after my sweet sixteen. The day after my world changed forever.

"I can show you around anytime you like. I know where the best trails are for hiking," he said.

Mark was extremely charming, easy going with the gift of gab. I knew he would be fun to hang out with. Still, I didn't want him to get the wrong idea about where this could lead.

"It would be nice to have a *friend*."

He smiled brazenly at the not subtle emphasis and nodded. "All right then. *Friend*. How about early in the morning? I like to get out before work, plus it's nice and chilly then."

"Sounds great. I'm staying at this address." I tried to show him the piece of paper but he waved it away.

"Only one place to stay in Glenhaven. I'll be by around 7:00."

"Right. Then I'll see you in the morning."

Mark disappeared to the back, and I continued with my shopping. What the market lacked in variety, it certainly made up for in quality. I dropped honey and way too many locally made jams in my basket.

All the produce smelled fantastic, every bit of it organic. I couldn't get over the enormity and brilliant color of everything.

I noticed Tracy on her tiptoes dusting a nearby shelf and said, "I've never seen vegetables like these before. They're almost too beautiful to eat."

She laughed, "James swears it's the heirloom seeds he uses, but I say it's something in his hands. I've planted those same seeds and they didn't turn out anything like that."

"Maybe he's the plant whisperer," I said.

"It's not a joke. He definitely is."

"Bread?"

"I'll show you. Mary Romano brings it over during the week. By the way, you don't have to worry about Mark. He a good guy but he can charm the fleas off a dog. It's just his nature."

"I did get that impression."

I followed Tracy to the front of the store. "Looks like we have ancient grain and sourdough left."

"Sourdough works for me."

She handed over the brown paper bag. "So...what's your story?"

Where did I begin? And what could I tell her without making her mistrustful of me?

I settled on, "Things haven't gone the way I've wanted them to in my life. It's forced me to reassess what I need to do next. I thought the fresh air might help me gain proper perspective."

"Careful. That's kind of why I came here. And I never left. It's like this place draws the people here who need to be here, you know. That probably sounds weird."

The idea that I could belong somewhere, that there was a place where I fit in, a place where I made sense, a place that wanted me, struck an emotional chord within me.

The real question was, why? What did Glenhaven want with me?

"I don't think that's weird at all."

"Whatever the reason, I'm glad you're here, Helene." I knew that she was being sincere.

I left with the warm feeling clinging to me, the cozy aftermath of my instant connection with her and the entire Houston family.

As I placed my items inside the car, Rogue came bounding out of nowhere again and burrowed his nose in the crack of my ass.

"Hey! Boundaries, dude." I rubbed the top of his head and he panted appreciatively. "Should I be worried about you?"

A whistle shrilled in the distance and the dog charged off in its direction.

"Guess not."

The rest of the afternoon was spent organizing my things in the cottage and exploring the woods behind it.

I breathed in the clean air and marveled at the calmness and clarity of my thoughts here.

I'd been able to sleep without nightmares. I couldn't remember the last time that had happened. And I didn't have the lingering images trailing overhead today like an angry doom cloud.

I navigated the slippery layer of decaying leaves carefully. Somewhere along the trail, I realized the sounds of birds and insects had ceased.

I pondered the stillness, but it wasn't completely silent.

The humming tone dwelled here, vibrating my eardrums and forcing the fine hairs along my arms to stand on end, just as they had when I'd approached the town.

The smell of it, the elusiveness of it, was like a word that lingered on the tongue but never came.

Under the cover of trees, twilight swept in, threatening to plunge me into shadows.

I turned back the way I came in and recognized the haze of light that rose like a faint beacon from below the tree lined ridge.

Its tendrils reached up and spilled into the starless sky above.

Perhaps people lived down there. I imagined it could be house lights or street lamps. But this felt wrong. It was something else.

This knowing made me pause and search my feelings.

I had the urge to go toward it, to recklessly cut down the hillside, through tightly woven branches until I'd found what was waiting there.

It was the snap of a twig that brought me back to my senses.

Something large was here with me. I panned the surrounding area. I could see nothing, but I felt its eyes boring into me.

I shivered at the sudden coolness in the air, contemplating my next move. This place butted up against the Appalachian Mountains.

I knew black bears roamed this area, but were they known for stealth?

Wouldn't that be something? To journey all this way on a quest only to become part of a statistical anomaly of people eaten by bears.

From behind, I was startled by the flapping of wings as whatever it was took flight. It was massive enough to momentarily blot out the sky.

A bird of prey, maybe? A turkey roosting in a tree for the night?

It was gone now. Along, with my desire to explore these woods without as much as a flashlight.

The creature had saved me from doing something extremely stupid. I quickened my pace until I'd made it back to the safety of the cottage.

My shakiness over the encounter lingered while I prepared a peanut butter sandwich and poured myself a glass of port wine, which I enjoyed while wrapped up in a blanket on the porch.

By my second glass, the feeling of uneasiness was replaced by one of tranquility. I wondered if this was because of the remoteness of the town providing a much-needed buffer from the outside world.

Regardless of the reason, I welcomed a break from the feeling that disaster lurked just around the corner.

CHAPTER THREE

IF EYES WERE FLYING DAGGERS

The next morning Mark arrived promptly at 7:00 am as he'd promised.

"I hope you haven't eaten yet. I packed some waters and breakfast for later." He stepped over the threshold and patted his backpack.

"I haven't. That's nice of you. Sorry, can't remember where I put my athletic shoes. Give me a couple of minutes."

I found where I'd tossed them into the bottom panel of the wardrobe and quickly slid them on.

In the other room, I heard Mark pilfering through the refrigerator. When I rejoined him, he closed the fridge and tossed a strawberry into his mouth.

"Just make yourself at home," I smiled.

"Sorry, you must think I am completely uncivilized. I forget that it is not a normal thing to walk into someone's house and head to the fridge. Also, I am always hungry. Always. Ready?"

"I am."

He pointed to a trail to the right of my cottage that wasn't as well maintained as the one from yesterday.

I got a feeling that most day hikers would have overlooked it completely.

"This is the path the men used to take to get to the coal mine. There used to be twenty houses or more like yours before they fell into ruin. The Richter family owns this town, bought the land for a song in 1945 from the Tennessee Coal, Iron, and Railroad Company after the company basically abandoned this place."

Richter. Why did that name sound familiar?

"One of them is a doctor or something?"

"Yes, Amsel is the town doctor. He took over the practice from his father."

"Interesting that they would choose such a remote location to settle in."

"The Richters consider themselves to be good stewards. They bought it with the intention of protecting it and helping it recover."

"That or they don't like people very much."

Mark laughed, "I don't think that's true. They've devoted their lives to helping people."

The path rose at a steady ascent. A thick canopy of trees made the crisp air feel much cooler.

Not far into the trail, it began to slope off again and twist. Ten minutes later we were standing at a small lake.

"This is Misty Lake."

"Looks like a nice place for a swim," I said.

"Sure is. And for catfish. We have a fish fry every summer. Invite everybody in the town."

Misty Lake was overlooked by the ridge line I'd been on the night before. Dense vegetation climbed all the way up to the higher elevation. A waterfall ran through angular rocks and flowed down the cliff face.

With the faint sun just beginning to turn the lake's surface into an enormous reflecting pool, the view was stunning. "It takes my breath away," I said.

"All the water to Glenhaven flows down that mountain. I may be biased, but I would be willing to wager this is the purest water in the world."

"You might be right. Do people live close to here?"

"No, not at all. The mining left behind some hazardous pits. There are certain areas we're not allowed to venture into."

"I thought I saw some lights through the trees last night."

"Maybe some hikers had a fire out there. Common sense can come in short supply with those folks. Like I said, it's dangerous. I wouldn't go beyond the signs that are posted."

"Thanks for the warning," I said.

Mark glanced at my legs and did a double take before he tried to hide the huge grin that broke out. "Helene, you might want to move. You're standing in poison oak."

I leapt backward, "Crap!" It was not good considering that I was highly allergic to the stuff.

I was annoyed with myself for not paying better attention to where I'd been standing.

In between his chuckles, Mark managed to pull out a bottle of hand sanitizer from his backpack which he rubbed all over my leg and scrubbed vigorously with a bandana.

He spread on a salve that wreaked of foul-smelling herbs and looked like poo. "This may not stop the rash entirely, but it will definitely help."

"What is that stuff?"

He handed the tube to me, "Not sure, exactly. The pharmacist mixes it with local plants and who knows what. It works like magic, though."

"Well, I'm going to smell lovely."

"Yeah. Try to keep a good five feet between us," Mark joked.

I threw the salve at him, harder than I'd planned.

He caught it easily and only laughed harder, pointing to his red hair. "Now, now. I'm the one who's supposed to have the temper."

"You're like the annoying brother I never wanted." His laugh was infectious and I couldn't help but join in. "You're terrible."

We worked our way around, west of the lake, until we reached the opening of a cave. It was a relatively easy climb up the rocks.

Once we made it, Mark plopped down, pulled out a thermos of coffee, and poured it into cups.

I sat down next to him, and bit into the cranberry muffin he offered. "It's delicious. How long has your family lived in Glenhaven?"

"Always," he said.

"But your family must have roots somewhere else."

He shook his head, "As far as my parents are concerned, nowhere else matters. This place gets into you. It flows through your blood like it's part of you. People may come off like they'd like to be anywhere but here. But they don't leave. Why?"

"I don't know. Why do you think?"

"Because they figure out that they don't need all those things they thought they did. They realize this place is about as good as it gets."

"How deep does this cave go?"

"I don't know exactly, for miles, then branches off in different directions, into tight crannies that I'm not too keen to go into. Makes me claustrophobic."

For a while, we sat in comfortable silence taking in the scenery below us.

"So do you have a boyfriend back home?"

"I had a husband. But he died of stomach cancer three years ago."

Suddenly, all the characteristic humor faded from Mark's eyes, "I'm sorry, Helene. That must have been hard."

"Thank you. Yes, it was pretty devastating." Or would excruciating or unbearable have been a better way to describe the way it ripped out my heart?

Brian was everything that I had left. When disease swooped in like a thief with a knife, carving away at him, what remained was a person I hardly recognized.

He'd become a skeleton with sallow skin clinging to it. Even the light in his eyes, in the end, it took that too.

Not wanting to delve into this pain any longer any longer than I had to, I asked, "What about you. Is there someone special in your life?"

"There's one girl. She works at the antique store. Our families have been friends forever, but I don't think she sees me as anything more than a friend. We're too close, I guess."

The girl I'd seen at the antique store when I'd peeked in earlier that day was named Sadie. She was an attractive woman who wore stylish cat-eye glasses and Converse shoes.

I remembered thinking that she would blend right into a big city.

"She looks a little out of place here. Perhaps she has ambitions beyond Glenhaven."

"Sadie graduated from Brown with a degree in psychology a few months ago and came back home. She doesn't seem to be in a hurry to leave again either. I don't think she knows what she wants."

"Then there's still time," I said.

"Time for what?"

"Time to make her fall in love with you."

He stared straight ahead, seeming to ponder this.

When he noticed my attention drawn below us, Mark said, "They cleared everything out for the mining operations. All this time and the land hasn't fully recovered."

My ears buzzed from the steady discharge of energy all around us. I could smell ozone in the air. Mark didn't seem to notice this, or perhaps he'd lived here too long and was desensitized to this phenomenon.

I was on the verge of asking him, when he said, "We should probably head back. I promised to pick all the ripe vegetables before I head to the store."

Mark helped me climb down from jagged rocks.

Half an hour later, we were back at the cottage. "You should come out to the diner tonight."

"That's right. Mary said something about Wednesday being open mic night. Maybe I will."

"You won't regret it," he said before pulling away in his pickup truck.

I spent the rest of the day curled up with a book.

At some point, I'd dozed on the sofa and woke when it was nearly dark to find it had fallen open on the floor.

A long shower helped to get rid of the grogginess. I scrubbed the salve off with soap and remarked that there was no sign at all of a rash from my poison oak exposure.

I thought about Mark's invitation. An evening at the diner might actually be a good opportunity to mingle with the town folk.

I threw on a pair of jeans, a purple blouse, and some comfortable flats, and combed out my shoulder length of wavy hair.

The only jewelry I wore was a large piece of jade that hung from a thin leather cord.

Mary's diner was packed when I arrived, and I didn't recognize anyone right off.

"Helene!" Mary waved from a table in the back. "You made it. Have a seat." She flipped over a clean glass and poured in cabernet sauvignon.

"Thanks." I studied the people around us, recognizing Sadie leaning on a pool cue.

Before, I hadn't realized there was a section in the rear of the restaurant with a stage, a pool table, and three dart boards. Tonight, it was lit up like the Vegas strip.

"Is it always like this?" I asked.

"Yep. Like one gigantic family reunion every Wednesday, Friday, and Saturday night."

Mary grabbed the arm of a dark-skinned woman who wore oversized blue jean overalls over a white tank top.

Her shiny black hair was coiled into miniature Princess Leia buns. She had a young girl with her that I guessed to be seven or eight who was almost her exact doppelganger.

"I'd like you to meet Helene Parish. She's going to be with us for a few weeks," Mary said.

"Yes. I heard we had a new addition. How do you do? I'm Georgia Ellwood. This is my daughter Alexia."

"It's nice to meet you both."

"Georgia is an amazing artist. She has the art studio a few doors down," Mary said.

"I would love to see your work. When would be a good time to visit?" I asked.

"Any day before two. I like to keep my afternoons free for painting."

I smiled at Alexia who didn't seem to like the attention and slipped fully behind her mother.

When they had gone, I took another sip of wine. "Her accent? Is she French?"

"French Canadian," Mary said. "Showed up here when she was pregnant with the wee one. Never seen the father. If you ask me, he's the reason she stayed. You know what I mean?"

"You think she ran away from him. Why?"

"She was afraid of something. And I'm almost 100% positive judging from the bruises she had when she arrived that she was not too interested in being found."

Feeling uncomfortable gossiping about Georgia, I changed the subject. "What do you have planned for tonight?"

Mary waved her fist at someone across the room. "Looks like the entertainment finally drug his sorry ass in here."

Mark shrugged his shoulders apologetically. A guitar case hung at his side.

"Mark? He's the entertainment?"

"He's darn talented. I keep waiting for him to realize just how talented and take his show on the road."

From what he'd told me today, I couldn't see that ever happening. Mark had his roots firmly established in Glenhaven and didn't seem to have any interest in finding a bigger pot.

He turned on the microphone, and plugged his electric acoustic guitar into an amp.

A sudden burst of feedback resounded throughout the diner before Mark adjusted some knobs and it died down.

"Hello," he said. "Were you hoping I wouldn't make it?"

Laughter filled through the room.

"This is a new song. And for that reason, I'd like to dedicate it to a new friend. Everybody, give a hand for Helene Parish."

I felt my cheeks redden and wanted to crawl under the floorboards.

In spite of my embarrassment, I managed an awkward smile and a tiny wave to the crowd.

Mental note, punch Mark Houston in the arm. Hard.

He began to sing a slow ballad.

She rode in with the wind. I'd waited so long for her to return, the girl of my dreams, and if she'd give me the chance, I'd show her how our dreams can match, how our heartbeats can blend together. Anything you want. That's what I'll give, Anywhere you want to go. That's where I'll follow, Cause this life isn't worth a damn without you

It was obvious to me that this song was about Sadie.

I glanced toward the pool table where I'd seen her earlier. But she wasn't watching Mark. She was glaring at me. Staring daggers was more like it.

Sadie thought the song was about me.

In an instant, she recovered and jerked her attention back to her game. If that was any indication of her feelings for Mark, he'd been completely wrong about her not having any.

Again, I felt a stare drilling into me, this time from the table behind. I turned, locking gazes with the man there.

His eyes were unusual, a deep color, not brown, or blue.

Were they violet?

And his hair, it was as white as the driven snow.

There was an intensity to him that was unnerving and I instantly broke eye contact.

I could feel my breathing coming out in short, shallow bursts as my heart pounded in my chest.

I brought my wineglass to my lips and noticed that my hands were shaking. "Who is the gentleman at the table behind us?" I asked.

Mary leaned back so that she could see. "The invisible man?"

I searched among the throngs of patrons, but there was no sign of him.

Mark took a break and headed over with a bottle of beer in his hand, "How did you like your song?"

Since Mary had gone to the back to get more wine and we were alone, I brought up Sadie.

"Impressive. You're very good. But we both know who you should have dedicated that song to, and it certainly, wasn't me."

"Do you think she noticed?"

"Oh yeah…if eyes were flying daggers, I'd be dead."

Mark's smirk disappeared and he was about to press for more information, but Mary returned.

Before going back to the stage, Mark whispered, "We'll talk more about this."

Several glasses later, the wine caught up with me, and not in a good way.

I suddenly realized how tired I was. "I should probably be going."

"So soon?" Mary asked.

"It seems I can't hold my liquor like I used to."

"It must be the altitude. Do you want me to get someone to drive you home?"

"Definitely not! Thank you, though. It's not far to the cottage. I can walk."

The temperature had dropped ten degrees and I wished I'd brought a jacket. I was grateful for the full moon that illuminated the gravel road ahead.

I peered into the trees, looking for the light I'd seen deep in the woods, but there was nothing, just the ebony velvet of night and the throaty screech of a barn owl.

My thoughts immediately turned to the stranger I'd seen earlier.

What had been behind the fierceness in his eyes?

Much like Sadie, I'd caught him off guard, glimpsed something I wasn't meant to see.

Why had the man had such an effect on me?

There was something that was so familiar about him, and yet he was foreign and unreadable.

Those subtle things I could pick up from people whenever I made the choice to really focus in, I could not pick apart from him.

He was a blank page where nothing had been written, no favorite color, no vibes of blatant narcissism, no lingering thoughts or tendency toward good deeds, or weird fetishes.

It was utterly bizarre. It nagged at me for the rest of the walk home.

I was glad I'd left a light on. There was nothing lonelier than coming home alone to a dark house.

I slipped through the door, but not before I noticed a streak of white through the trees. The silhouette was familiar enough to me now.

Had Rogue been trailing behind me the entire time?

He was a free roaming spirit. I wondered what that said about his caretaker as he veered into the dense canopy of trees.

CHAPTER FOUR

CONSUMED BY FURY

It was March 13th, my 16th birthday.

My adoptive parents, Harold and Lela, surprised me with a trip to N.Y.C. and tickets to a musical.

We grabbed an early lunch at a restaurant in Chinatown. We'd taken our time, laughing and talking as we enjoyed dim sum.

Afterward, we strolled through the city.

The place breathed. It had a pulse and an unquenchable thirst for the chattering pedestrians that filled its sidewalks and for its streets to be overrun with the constant blaring of taxi horns.

I felt it down to my bones and we rode upon it, letting it carry us along a jet stream of pure joy.

My mother insisted on taking me shopping. A green leather jacket, perfectly fitting jeans, Tiffany bangle bracelet, and pink frosted lip gloss, before we headed toward Broadway to catch our show.

I remember how we all were together, as if nothing could ever go wrong.

It had been a perfect day and then we caught the last train from Penn Station to the home of family friends we were staying with in Connecticut.

I leaned my cheek against its cold window and watched towns blur by, bound together through a network of power lines and fading street lamps.

Snow began to fall. There was something magical in the whirling flakes, tossed about in the wind before hitting the ground in soft landings.

I remember thinking that we were like those snowflakes. We'd had our celebration. We'd done our dance, and now we were spent, spanning the miles in complete silence.

But it was the most delicious exhaustion, the kind you wanted to bottle so that you could savor it forever.

It was dark when we stepped off the train onto the deserted platform.

We walked toward our rental car in a groggy stupor, my dad carrying the ridiculously large shopping bag, while my mother held my hand.

I don't know why the man blocked our path. Maybe anyone who happened by would have been a target. Or maybe he had studied many people that night before deciding upon us.

The man moved swiftly, holding the knife to Harold's throat, "Stay quiet and nobody gets hurt."

I knew it was a lie. I knew the way I always knew.

There was darkness inside this man. His life had been a series of ill-gotten gains. He'd done bad things to good

39

people just because it made him feel powerful or could earn him a few dollars.

My mother squeezed my hand, so tightly I could feel her nails drawing blood. Her voice shook. It was barely above a whisper, "Please, we will give you what you want."

"Shut up!" The man glared at my mother. "Nobody talks. Okay. I talk."

His focus shifted back to my father. "Drop what's in your hand and turn out your pockets."

The bag fell onto the frozen sidewalk. My father's wallet hit next, followed by loose change that fell with a muted pings against the concrete.

But the man did not release him.

"People like you got it so easy. I take your wallet; you just go out and buy a new one. I take your money; you go to the bank and get more money. It's just a minor inconvenience."

He noticed me and smiled. "Such a pretty little thing. Pick all that up, drop it in the bag, and hand it to me."

I did as he said and his hand grazed mine. The brief contact made my skin crawl.

And then I knew what was inside his mind. I saw a van, duct tape, and rope. I saw a gun hidden underneath his jacket, in the waistband of his pants.

This wasn't just a robbery. He planned to take us with him.

He held the knife tighter against my father's neck, then motioned toward me and my mother, "You two, turn around. And don't look back."

I heard Harold Parish moan in pain before the thud that hit the ground.

I couldn't not look. I had to see what had happened.

There was so much blood gushing from the cut on Harold's neck. He moved his mouth, but only a gurgling sound came out.

I wasn't scared anymore. I was angry. A wrathful vengeance settled inside of me and what followed was calm. I had ice in my veins as I reeled toward the man, shielding my mother behind me.

The man laughed at this, "What are you going to do about it?" He pulled the gun out and waved it around to prove how pointless it would be to go against him.

I took in his black winter cap. How he was stout with a battered face, a nose that had been broken many times, and a scar that ran the length of his jaw.

But I wasn't scared of him or his gun. I was consumed by fury. I felt it boiling over like a volatile and destructive blue flame.

I wished for him to die. I wished for him to be swallowed by the same fire that I was consumed with.

Then he was.

There was no reason behind it.

I knew I'd caused this thing to happen.

And when the man began to writhe within the fire, I'd felt no mercy or remorse.

I'd been satisfied that he had gotten exactly what he deserved.

CHAPTER FIVE

A SIREN'S CALL FROM THE BLACKNESS

Why had the nightmares stopped since arriving in Glenhaven?

Two nights and a couple of daytime naps, and not once had I woken up drenched in sweat, crying out in anguished despair.

But I had dreamed. The memory of it made the color flood into my cheeks.

It had been so sensual and lucid. Lips passionately probed mine. Relentless waves of pleasure washed over my body as I'd moved my hips under the weight of a lover I couldn't see.

And then the dream had shaken me loose.

I'd opened my eyes to the faintest glow of moonlight cast against the bedroom wall, my intense arousal still evidenced by the lingering wetness between my legs.

I'd never had a sexual dream that intense before, not one that left me dizzy with longing.

But after a series of alternating pillow punches and staring in frustration at the clock, I finally fell asleep again, and didn't wake up until nearly noon.

It had to be more than a mere coincidence that the nature of my dreamscape had changed. What was it about being here that had triggered this dramatic shift?

I pondered this as I settled on a can of vegetable soup to appease my growing hunger and rummaged through all the drawers in search of a can opener.

There definitely wasn't one.

But I did find a hammer, a screwdriver, and a relatively sharp knife that I used to, in no time at all, nearly sever my right thumb.

As I stood there, dumbfounded by my own stupidity, with my gushing thumb wrapped up in a paper towel, I decided to look online for ways to open a can without a can opener.

Instantly, a dozen videos queued up waiting to be viewed. It was unfortunate for my throbbing finger that I had not chosen to do this first.

Since the gash was deep and would require a stitch or two, I slid on a light jacket and walked into town, passing my car I'd left parked in front of Brenner Antiques.

I entered Dr. Richter's empty reception room and found a sign in sheet but no receptionist.

While I waited, I sifted through various rugged outdoorsman type magazines and a few celebrity rags before the door finally opened.

I was face to face with the mystery man from the diner.

His white blonde eyebrows rose, but his expression was completely blank.

He read my name off of the clipboard, "Helene Parish? I'm Dr. Richter. Won't you come with me."

For an instant, I considered simply running out the door. I breathed in a fair amount of oxygen to calm myself and followed him down the narrow hallway.

His broad shoulders and impressive height filled it in a way that seemed unnatural, like he was designed to roam beneath cathedral ceilings and within candle lit, gothic rooms of a dreary castle somewhere.

A door was opened to a tiny exam room and he motioned for me to have a seat.

When he smiled, his face softened in a way that made me sure I'd only imagined the intensity last night at Mary's.

"What happened here?"

He moved mere inches from me.

He smelled of Glenhaven, as if this place had been bottled into a fragrance that clung to his skin.

His irises were indeed violet and I felt myself being sucked into their strange and penetrating depths.

Abruptly, I remembered myself and gained control of my senses, "I...uhm...didn't have a can opener. But I did have a can in need of opening."

I unwrapped my bloody towel for him to see. "Then this happened."

He slid large warm fingers around my wrist, holding it as he examined my thumb. This slight contact brought a flush to my cheeks and caused my pulse to reach warp speed.

He gave no indication that he had noticed my reaction to him, except for the twinkle of humor in his eyes that made me wonder if he was keenly aware of how his close proximity was affecting me.

"I'm afraid this will require a few stitches. I'll give you a shot to deaden it and we'll have you fixed up in no time."

He retrieved a syringe from the cabinet and vile of clear liquid that he injected around my cut. "You're the talk of the town."

"Am I?"

"Everyone seems to be completely besotted with you."

It should have been a compliment, but it felt like he'd just thrown shade my way, as if he might have mentally added, *I, however, am still trying to figure out why.*

"I'm sure that's not true. I haven't met *everyone.*" When my attempt at humor fell flat, I studied the plaque that was hanging on the wall and tried to breathe normally.

To Dr. Richter, in appreciation of contributions to Glenhaven
1949- 2009

I pointed toward it with my free hand, "You are remarkably well preserved."

"That was presented to my father. I took over his practice when he died."

"I'm sorry."

"Thank you. It was many years ago."

The doctor's accent was hard to place, as if superimposed with the lyrical qualities of many different countries.

45

He sewed my thumb and I could not bear to look, instead staring straight ahead, "Your accent is different. Did you not grow up here?"

He didn't answer right away, and I wondered if he had heard me properly.

Finally, he said, "I did not. Mostly, my mother raised me. I've lived all over the world. I only came to Glenhaven because I was needed here."

"This must have been a hard transition for your family, coming to such an isolated place."

He wasn't wearing a ring, but then some men didn't wear them.

"No family. It's just me."

The doctor was close enough that I could feel his breath stirring the hairs along my arm. I wondered what his lips would feel like pressed there.

The thought came out of left field and forced the blood into my cheeks again but seconds later he had already let go of my hand.

"You are free to go," he said.

"That was quick and painless. I appreciate you taking care of me."

I stood, tied my jacket around my waist, and searched for my wallet. "I didn't see a receptionist. Should I pay you, then?"

"No charge today. Consider this an apology for not having all the important staples of living at the guest house."

"That's very kind. I'm sure we'll bump into one another again."

"In a place this small, that is a certainty."

I nodded, taking the tube of antibiotic cream he offered, and tossed it inside my purse.

I could feel him watching as I rushed out.

It was not like me to be so flustered. I searched for reasons to explain this reaction to him.

I'd always trusted my instincts, this knowing things about others that I couldn't explain, of knowing who I could trust, and who I could not.

I was drawn to Dr. Richter and at the same time, terrified of him.

The encounter had completely knocked me off my game and I needed something to ground me back in reality. I decided to stop by Georgia's gallery.

I cut through the square that looked so different today than it had when I'd arrived.

Sunlight glinted off of sparkly flecks in its brick paver stones, erasing its dark foreboding mood and transforming it into the perfect spot to conduct an entire bridal shoot.

I entered through the bright red door of the gallery, immediately impressed with the art pieces I saw.

Her style appealed to me the same way that outsider art did, but unlike folk art that denoted a lack of skill, she had tremendous precision, and there was complexity in the themes.

I was drawn to her birds and the flowing lines of her female silhouettes.

One woman in particular, stood outlined against a world of towering ice. Her white head was bent downward, her rounded shoulders, gently curved inward.

Such deep sadness was conveyed in these lines, but there was more going on than that.

The subtle angle of the chin, the certainness of her arms falling at her side, and the way her feet were planted defiantly, captured a moment of strength and resolve with amazing simplicity.

"I really like this one," I said. "The woman carries so much sorrow, yet she endures."

Georgia stood side by side with me, staring as I did. "You see a lot, Helene. Maybe you can empathize with the woman because you yourself have suffered?"

Mary's comments about her sudden arrival in Glenhaven had me wondering if the woman in the painting might actually be Georgia.

"I've had my fair share," I admitted.

Georgia spoke softly, "Let me see your palm."

She cupped my right hand, careful of the small bandage there, and with a swift motion, put on the reading glasses that hung from the colorful beaded chain around her neck.

"Loss is the cross you bear. You drift alone, tormented by visions." Georgia smiled sadly, and peered into my eyes. "You are running away, yet at the same time, you are running toward answers. But what you seek conceals itself from you. It is only by throwing yourself upon the pyre that you will know the truth."

She let go and I pulled my hand away awkwardly.

"You're embarrassed that I see so much."

"No...not at all. I'm just not used to that shoe being on the other foot. It's usually me seeing what others don't want me to. How do you get all that from the lines on my palm?"

Georgia shrugged. "I don't know how. I just do. I imagine you can relate to this."

I nodded, suddenly at a loss for words. I was used to hiding this part of me away from others because it scared them.

But here I was feeling connection and understanding with a person I hardly knew.

As if Georgia understood exactly how unnerving her impromptu reading had been, she instantly lightened the mood, "This painting wants to be with you."

"Yes, I believe you're right. How much?"

"It's $1600. But for you, $555. It's a number of great change and transition. And maybe you could treat me to lunch one day."

"That is a more than generous deal. I'll take it."

She pulled the painting off the wall and began to wrap it in protective layers of paper.

"I don't worry about what is generous or not. Everything I have ever needed has been provided for me. And this painting has been waiting for you to find her."

I touched Georgia's hand, stalling it briefly from tying the package off with a twine handle. "Thank you."

She shrugged in a way that let me know that she would not stand for any more of what she considered to be unnecessary gratitude.

"So where does Alexia go to school?" I asked.

Georgia pointed to the ceiling. "Upstairs. In my office. She attends an online school. They use video conferencing

49

so she can interact with her class. She learns so much. I just wish there were more young children around for her to socialize with."

I recalled how shy Alexia had been at the diner. Glenhaven couldn't be an easy place for a woman of Georgia's age to find companionship either, especially with limited available males to choose from.

"Have you ever thought about moving to a bigger city?"

"I've considered it. But here, I never have to be worried. That offers great freedom and peace of mind. Alexia can roam the hills and be a child without me having to hover over her. There are times, it can also seem more like a fish bowl, you know? But for now. We stay."

I nodded. "Perhaps when Alexia is a little older."

"Perhaps. Here you go. Take good care of my lady for me."

"Promise. I'll cherish it always."

I loaded the painting into the car and looked for Mark but he'd gone to work at the farm. I would have to give him the details about Sadie later.

Back at the cottage, I decided to soak in a warm bath and read the book I'd picked up from the library, while at the same time attempting to keep my injured hand dry.

For some reason I'd chosen a steamy romance novel.

I'd made it to chapter ten and things were just getting good when there was a knock on the door.

I slipped out of the tub and secured the tie to my robe, instantly regretting not putting on clothes when I spied Dr. Richter eyeing me through the window in the door.

The only thing protecting me from his probing eyes was thin, terry cloth fabric.

He held up the tube of antibiotic cream, answering my question of what had happened to it and why he was standing on my doorstep.

Undoubtedly, it had fallen out of my purse in my hurry to make a quick getaway.

Since he'd taken the time to bring it to me, I couldn't very well ignore him, which was exactly what I wanted to do.

"Mystery of the missing cream solved," I said. "Thank you for going out of your way to bring it here."

"Actually, it wasn't out of my way. I live on the road, up on the hill."

Although I hadn't invited him in, the doctor maneuvered effortlessly past me. For a person as large as he was, there was a surprising grace to his movements.

Against my will, I found myself noticing parts of him I had no business noticing.

I resented his laid-back comfort at my expense. Also, I resented that his eyes had briefly settled on my hardened nipples, and that he had witnessed my resulting scarlet cheeks.

"Were you getting ready to go out for dinner?" he asked.

"No. I was just going to make a sandwich. I have a book I'd like to finish.

This was a polite way of telling him to get the hell out. But instead of leaving he plopped down on the couch as if he had every right to do so.

"Why don't you get dressed and come to my house for dinner? Surely, a home cooked meal will sustain you better than a sandwich. Afterward, I'll bring you back here and you can get back to your reading."

As desperately as I wanted to tell him thanks but no thanks, I found myself saying, "Sure. Okay. Give me 15 minutes."

I'd dropped the romance novel I'd been reading on the steam trunk which served as a coffee table. When I left him to change, he had picked it up.

I usually never even read that type of book. Why couldn't I have chosen something more intellectual to read?

Quickly, I pulled the hair tie out and brushed through the tangles. I applied a subtle amount of makeup to bring out the green in my hazel eyes, then selected a simple black sweater dress, thin enough for an evening that was only just a little chilly.

Why not? The dress was flattering and I needed all the confidence I could get in light of how Amsel Richter turned me into a bumbling mass of nerves.

I put on a pair of ankle boots and came back to find the doctor with his head still buried in my book. Since he didn't make an immediate move to close the book, I cleared my throat.

He held up a finger indicating he intended to finish reading the page.

An emotion I couldn't decipher crept into his eyes when he finally looked up at me. But just as quickly, the shield of indifference fell back in place.

"I like your book. Very much," he said.

I was on the verge of saying something sarcastic until I realized he wasn't poking fun. He was being sincere. "Isn't it a little too feminine? I mean, it's a romance. Men usually think they're ridiculous."

I also thought they were ridiculous. That was until I found myself sucked into this one.

"So only women are interested in romance?" he asked.

"No. I just mean…"

"What? That all men adhere strictly to stereo types?"

I'd just been served. "Yeah. Something like that. Sorry." I covered my face with my hands. As a woman I'd spent my entire life fighting stereotypes, just to have committed the same offense.

"I believe stereotypes are destructive to the human endeavor. But if it would make you feel more comfortable, we could stay here and you could make a sandwich for me instead," he taunted.

"To be honest, I don't have mad skills in the kitchen. My sandwiches are mediocre at best."

"As I never would have assumed," he said. It was a last playful poke before he opened the door for me.

To say he lived on a hill was an understatement.

I began to understand the reason he drove a Land Rover. If there was any kind of snow or ice, you'd never make it up or down without four-wheel drive.

The elevation leveled off and we came to a stone wall with a massive iron gate. He hit a remote control and the gate swung open.

Holy security, Batman. In light of Glenhaven being a small town, it was a bit odd to see the security cameras everywhere.

"Fort Knox has got nothing on you," I joked.

He ignored this comment and parked in the circular driveway at the front of the house. It was immense and constructed from the same champagne-colored stones as the wall around its perimeter.

Everything about it, down to the massive doors at the entrance, felt old world, as if the house, and everything inside had been aging on that hill for ions.

"This is amazing. I feel as if I've traveled back in time."

He opened a bottle of chianti and poured it into Baccarat glasses. "Maybe you have."

He slid my glass across the kitchen island and encouraged me to have a seat there, "My father spent his life rescuing old relics from 'the wrong people,' his words, not mine."

Amsel was a competent chef. Hypnotic, that's what it was to watch him sauté vegetables and sear steaks in record time.

I struggled to keep a level head. But a few sips of wine later, I could barely hide the ogling.

54

He carried the plates to a huge covered patio. I had no idea when he'd started the fire in the outdoor fireplace, but I was grateful for its warmth and comfort.

When he held my chair, he draped a blanket across my shoulders.

I smiled thankfully and tried not to react to his fingers sliding across my forearm.

From across the table, he studied my hair. "Your hair, it's unusual. The silver has a sheen to it that is almost metallic. When did it begin to grow like that?"

"I was a teenager. It became this way after my father died."

I didn't correct him, that it had never grown in, that it had happened overnight, that I had simply woke up to it being like this.

It was as if the discharge of energy that night had permanently scarred me.

"A difficult time to lose a father, just as you were on the verge of becoming a woman," he said.

It was a dangerous conversation to be having. I immediately moved the topic back to his family.

"Is your mother...is she still living?"

"Yes. She's in her 70's; last we spoke, she was in South America doing humanitarian work in who knows what kind of conditions."

"She sounds like an incredible person."

He only nodded, as if the conversation bored him.

"You mentioned you mostly lived with your mother. How long were your parents divorced?"

"They were never divorced."

"But they didn't live together? They were estranged from one another, then?"

"No. They loved each other dearly, but were rarely in the same place at the same time," he said this as a matter of fact, as if no other explanation were needed.

"I don't understand. If they loved each other, why didn't they live their lives together?"

"Love and proximity have nothing to do with each other, Helene."

"Of course, it does. If you love someone, how could you bear being separated from them? Time is so precious."

He studied me intently. "Yes, time is precious. Some of us have more. Some have less. But quantity does not always translate into quality. So… you've experienced this intense, passionate type of love, personally?"

"Yes, with my late husband."

He cocked his head and weighed my response. There was a glint in his eye. Did he doubt what I'd told him?

Brian had been a good man, a kind man, but not exciting. He hadn't made my heart leap or turned my legs to jelly.

He'd cooked me omelets and brought me hot tea on a cold winter's day. He was steady like a heartbeat. He was comfort.

A long silence followed before Amsel finally spoke again.

"I really am sorry for your loss, Helene. But my parents believed in the mission work they were doing, and that it was more important than anything, even being together.

No offense, but shouldn't real love be able to survive anything? Even being apart?"

"A love everlasting. That idea is promoted by every fairytale known to man. It's what every girl dreams of finding." My voice was soft and dreamy.

It's what I had dreamed of too. Once.

And then there it was. For a fleeting instant, the look I'd seen at the diner. Something fierce and raw.

I sucked in my breath and averted my gaze.

When I found the courage to meet his eyes again, they were shielded. And I questioned whether I'd seen anything there at all.

"You didn't have this kind of love with your husband, Helene."

"What could you know about me? We've only just met. How could you know what I feel or the depth of the feelings I had for my husband, Dr. Richter?"

"Please, call me Amsel. You hid in that marriage. You did not really live in it."

He leaned in on his elbows and studied me. "Why did you come to Glenhaven, Helene?"

I should have taken offense. I should have put him in his place for overstepping his boundaries. But I didn't. I didn't because there was truth in what he said, even if I didn't want to admit it.

"I don't know," I said.

It took only a few seconds to recognize the canine that ran straight at me and propped his upper paws on my lap.

I rubbed behind his ears. "Hello, Rogue."

"So, you've met the wanderer?"

Rogue went to rest beside the doctor. "You're lucky I saved you a plate. Where have you been, rascal?"

"He's yours," I said.

"Who else would put up with him?"

Amsel Richter left briefly and returned with a plate of raw steak that he placed on the patio. The canine sat up and waited with one ear slightly perked.

The signal was a simple nod from his owner.

Rogue leisurely walked over to his plate and began to slowly consume it as if he wanted to make his scrumptious meal last as long as possible.

Obviously, my worries about him had been unfounded. He was spoiled beyond belief.

"Mark Houston told me a little about Glenhaven, about how your family purchased land from the mining company."

"Yes. My father along with his twin brother, Harben. My uncle owns the bank and resides over things, but mainly has turned the reins over to my cousin Penelope."

"Interesting, isn't it?"

"What is?"

"That they decided to buy up all this pristine land and keep it a secret from the rest of the world."

Amsel rose long enough to poke at a log in the fireplace, "Secret?"

"What would you call it? Most towns fight to attract tourists for their survival, and yet Glenhaven seems to be competing for most obscure destination."

"I call it being good stewards. Why should it be suspicious to want to protect something?"

"Hidden things are always suspect, Dr. Richter."

He moved with surprising speed and pulled me gently from my chair. All doubts I'd had about witnessing this strangely fierce emotion vanished. Up close and personal, it sent goosebumps all along my body.

"Please don't call me that. I need to hear you say my name."

This moment hardly felt real, like I'd fallen through a wormhole and landed in some alternate place where only the two of us existed. I let his name escape in a whisper, "Amsel…"

Arms of steel closed around me and suddenly his lips were burning into mine.

My reaction betrayed me. I molded against the hard contours of him with a yearning that transcended everything I'd ever known, everything that had even been before.

My mouth opened to him, demanded more of him. And I was driven by an unsatiable hunger that left me trembling.

Somewhere in an interior quadrant of my mind, the voice of reason clawed its way through the haze of desire.

I was breathless, but I managed to push him roughly away.

Dark pools of violet stared back at me.

"What the fuck was that?" I asked.

"I simply wanted to be open about my feelings for you, Helene. I sense the same feelings within you," he said. "And since you seem to prefer things to be out in the open and mistrust hidden things…"

"No! Don't put this on me. You took liberties that you should not have."

It was all I could do not to punch him in the face for turning my own words against me.

"What was it in my body language that indicated I wanted you to do that?"

He shrugged indifferently, "I acted on a mutual attraction. Are you going to deny that you don't feel this too? That you haven't been watching me, wanting exactly what just happened?"

I felt the telling flush of color. He was right. I had wanted it. But it was dangerous to want it. It was dangerous for me to feel anything this intensely.

"You misunderstood."

"You are afraid of your emotions. You've shackled your true self and you know this. You don't have to water yourself down for me. We are melded of the same metals, Helene Parish."

The way he said my name was like a soft caress. His words stoked deep emotions. Everything he said was true. That he could see this, was unnerving.

"I should go. Thank you for the dinner. I would actually prefer to walk back."

If I'd been expecting an argument, I didn't get one.

"Go with her, Rogue. Make sure that she gets home safely."

Amsel turned his back and faced the roaring fire. Outlined against it, bathed in shadow and flame, he appeared otherworldly.

The idea tugged at me, nagged at me, that there was more to him than what could be seen with the naked eye, that inside of him, lived another world. One that I belonged to.

I belonged to Glenhaven. It was a deep knowing that I couldn't deny. And I still had absolutely no idea why.

I headed down the hill. Rogue trailed close behind as if he understood what his master wanted him to do.

On the way, in the horizon, a pale beam of greenish light rose above the trees and climbed into the clouds, light where there should have been none.

The moon was in the wrong place to be its source and according to Mark there weren't any houses in that area.

It was difficult to pinpoint the exact location, but it appeared to be coming from the clearing, the area Mark said the pit mining activity had been in.

He'd warned of the danger there, but I couldn't ignore what my intuition was telling me.

Whatever caused it, whatever it was down there, drew me, a siren's call from the blackness.

It whispered through the subtlest of vibrations, of ancient and dust covered things. It carried across the breeze, a sojourn of all that was hidden, all that was hidden and wished to be found.

As I contemplated this, I also fumed, cursing Amsel Richter with every breath.

I had wanted him to take me right there and then. He had seen everything I did not want him to. He had brushed up against the dormant thing inside of myself, the only thing I'd ever truly feared.

61

Damn him. Damn him to hell.

CHAPTER SIX

GHOST OF THE GREASY SPOON

Lightning flashed through the window.

With the first rumble of thunder, the lights flickered. Then came the torrential downpour that cast me into complete darkness.

It was 2:00 in the morning. I should have just closed my book and gone to sleep, but instead, stood peering out the window.

I had always been in awe of storms, the beauty of them, the way they barreled across the landscape without apology.

When I was young, I often stood outside and waited for them to come, my toes grabbing onto the grass while the wind twisted my hair into frenzied knots.

I'd almost been daring them to unleash their wrath upon me. But it had been a long time since I had been a temptress of storms.

Somewhere along, I began to hide within the gathers of the ordinary.

Only, I wasn't ordinary. This I had always known.

A blur of motion drew my attention toward the edge of the driveway.

Something lingered there. Something unnaturally tall, impossibly wide.

I strained to see through black sheets of rain, and when my brain could not classify what it was that I was staring at, a prickle of apprehension set in.

It seemed to be studying me, intelligently aware that I had noticed it.

But when another bolt of electricity spread like a crack in the troposphere, what I was sure had been solid form, became a fleeting outline. And there was nothing there at all.

In the time it took to trip over the boot that had been angrily kicked off in the middle of the floor, I'd convinced myself that it had been a combination of things.

A trick of shadow and light. The play of wind in the trees. Being too tired to trust my own eyes.

However, this didn't take away the feelings I'd been left with.

I was rattled.

I stumbled around blindly and found a battery powered lantern in the cabinet beneath the sink.

There was relief when the room swelled with cool white light. Eventually, I managed to fall asleep.

I awoke to lamplight shining in my face.

Thankfully, the power was back on. But it was a dreary day. More investigating the lights in the woods would have to wait until the weather cleared.

I was tired of the things I had to eat in the pantry and decided to brave the rain for one of Mary's delicacies.

I hated that I searched for Amsel's SUV. I also cringed at the way my body reacted to thoughts of what happened between us last night.

Mary waved from the back. "Be right with you."

I'd made it in time to mingle with the lunch crowd. I was happy when I saw Mark rushing up to greet me.

"Hey, you. Where did you go Wednesday night?"

"Yeah. Sorry about that. You were fabulous, by the way. I stopped by the store yesterday to tell you so, but you were away."

"You could sit with me. I haven't ordered yet."

"Sure. That sounds good." I slid across from him and decided on a pizza.

"So…it was obvious that the song was written for Sadie," he chuckled.

"Obvious to me, but not to Sadie."

This made Mark beam with absolute delight, "This is all rather good news."

When he reached across the table and gently caressed my cheek, I slapped his hand away. "Stop being a goofball."

He leaned on his elbows, laced his fingers together, and propped his chin on top, smiling like a love sick puppy. "Sadie came in to get her to-go lunch. She's watching us."

My jaw dropped. "Stop it, right now!"

Mark smiled wider and used his napkin to wipe an imaginary crumb from my face.

Under the table, I kicked him squarely in the shin. "Are you serious? How can you play with her emotions like that? Not to mention, making an enemy for me."

Mark groaned, "You may have crippled me for good."

"Serves you right, toying with someone's emotions like that! You deserve as much. Just tell her how you feel."

"Come on, Helene. She hasn't given me the time of day in all these years and now you tell me she might be jealous of you. Why not let her see that I'm desirable to another woman? Why not let her ponder that she may have let a good thing slip away?"

"First of all, you're terrible. BECAUSE…it's dishonest. AND….it could backfire. What would you do then?"

Mark stared outside to where Sadie dodged raindrops, her Styrofoam lunch container held high above her head to block them.

He was completely serious now. "Please, Helene. Engage in a little friendly flirting with me tonight. I need you! Help me get her to see me. I mean…really see me."

"Fine. I can't believe I'm agreeing to this. It's so wrong."

Mary brought out our food and he devoured his sandwich in record time.

"Did you swallow that sandwich whole? Honestly, I think I can make out the shape of a roast beef sandwich through your shirt."

"Sorry, I have to get back to the store," he said. "I'll see you tonight. Might I suggest wearing something low cut. Cleavage. Lots and lots of cleavage."

Mark only laughed at the stink eye I cast his way.

Left alone with my pizza, I took my time, savoring every bite of cheesy deliciousness.

I watched Mary as she hopped from table to table, taking orders, disappearing into the kitchen, and then exiting again with a tray full of mouth-watering entrees.

For the first time, I noticed that Mary was the only server, and the place was really busy.

She hadn't even broken out in a sweat. She wasn't even rushing. And yet the flow of service seemed effortless.

It also occurred to me that I had never seen a cook. Suddenly, I was very curious about this mysterious person who cranked out all of this food.

Mary stopped by to fill my water glass. "Mary, who's cooking back there?"

"I don't have a cook. Lord knows, I don't have the patience to deal with employees." Then she zipped off again before I could ask her anything more.

I chewed my pizza in a sort of bewildered reverence.

How was she doing it?

She hardly stayed in the back for more than a few seconds, yet everything came out perfectly hot and perfectly delicious.

As I watched Mary, I developed some theories.

She had acquired a time machine that she used for the unselfish purpose of providing the best possible service to her customers.

Mary's Diner was haunted by a ghost who was a master of the greasy spoon.

Mary Romano was really a cyborg, programmed with super speed and culinary expertise.

Now that I had noticed this oddity, it was all that I *could* notice.

But the mystery would have to remain for another day. I left the money on the table and headed toward city hall to see what records I could find on the town.

Officer Baron Fulton was around, sixty years old with a large Neanderthal brow which supported his sprawling grey eyebrows. But he was completely bald on top.

By default, he was the records keeper for the town. He was both amused and perplexed by my interest in Glenhaven history.

"Got some old records left behind by the mining company. Original surveys...stuff like that," He scratched his bald head and stared at the filing cabinets which lined the ten by fifteen-foot room.

After a half hour of rifling through them, he procured a stack of ledger books and papers, "Here you go."

I took over an empty table and carefully poured over everything.

There were many features on the survey that I recognized, including Misty Lake, the cliffs, and the hollow where the mining activity had been focused.

One of the ledger books came from a general store that the mining company had kept for its men and their families.

A few accident reports showed nothing too serious; broken bones, cuts requiring stitches, and respiratory illnesses, likely resulting from exposure to coal dust.

Then the accounts took on a different twist.

Wednesday, September 6th, 1948

The men presented with nausea and abdominal pain, all violently ill. A contagious factor cannot be ruled out. A few men are experiencing nose bleeds as well.

But the reports, dated in the following weeks, were truly bizarre.

Thursday, September 27th, 1948

Symptoms of the men are worsening. Severe headaches, high fever, diarrhea, rash, as well as shaking, dizziness, and disorientation. One man has died. There is hysteria in the town with people sealing doors and windows and avoiding contact with people outside of their immediate families.
The fear is great that this could be an epidemic. We've sent word that more doctors are needed to evaluate the situation. So far, the illness is restricted to the miners, no family members have shown signs of sickness.

And then there was a third, final, stunning report.

Friday, October 8th, 1948

Illness is still contained to the original group. Among the dead and dying, are men who have lost most of their hair, which falls out in clumps, fists full at a time. Their fingernails are blackened along the entire nailbed. A gruesome sight to behold. Quarantine has been put in place. I am sure the six who are still living will not survive the night.

I searched the folder for more documents, but there were none dated after October of 1948.

The mine stopped operations in Glenhaven in 1949, right before the Richter family purchased the land.

It was more than probable that the company abandoned the area because of the mysterious illness that struck down all of their workers in one wide sweep.

All the symptoms detailed in the reports were classic indicators of radiation sickness. But how could they have been exposed to levels capable of causing almost instant mass death?

Surely, Amsel's father had read these reports before he bought the land. As a doctor, he would have recognized the symptoms as well.

Why would he have wanted anything to do with this place after learning that?

Could the source of the radiation still remain?

I had been hoping to find something that would explain the lights I'd been seeing in the sky. It was the only reason I'd been interested in digging into town history.

And then to find something like this, something so disturbing, and out of the ordinary.

70

Why was everything about Glenhaven drenched in secrets?

I turned the material back over to Officer Fulton.

"Did you find what you were looking for?" he asked.

"Only more questions, unfortunately."

"How so?"

"I've been seeing these lights up in the hills at night."

"You must be talking about the swamp lights?"

"Aren't we a little too high up for swampland?"

"Nope. High-altitude wetland."

"But the reports here about what happened to the miners are strange. Have you read them?"

"I have. Those miners opened up the earth and let out a bunch of gases that made them sick. That's what happens when you tamper too much with mother nature. Now, the rain water don't flow the way it should, and we got little, stagnate ponds sittin' up there breeding mosquitoes like it's nobody's business."

He slung the documents onto his desk, tipping over his coffee mug, which missed the papers, but dripped all over the linoleum tile, "Aw…heck."

"Let me help you." I grabbed some napkins from a stack near the window and handed them over. "Forgive me, but it seemed like there was more going on with those men than just exposure to a vent in the earth."

Officer Fulton stared me down. "Curiosity can be a good thing, but it also, killed the cat. Now don't you go fooling around up there. It ain't no place you need to be, and it ain't safe. Understood?"

"Loud and clear."

I understood alright, but that didn't mean I still wasn't going to do my darndest to get to the bottom of it.

Glenhaven was not a normal town. And those lights had everything to do with it.

Around eight, I surveyed the closet for, *Operation Make Sadie Jealous.*

I ignored Mark's wardrobe suggestion of something a little more wanton whore, and purposefully opted on faded jeans and a shapeless v neck sweatshirt.

I pulled my hair into a ponytail and didn't even bother to touch up my makeup. Then I slid on an old pair of ballerina flats that I knew would be good for dancing.

He totally asked for this.

When I arrived at the diner, Mark did a double take and frowned. "Obviously, you look beautiful no matter what, but this is a deviation from the discussed wardrobe."

"I don't recall a discussion. If I remember correctly, you made recommendations that I have chosen to ignore."

Mark bought a couple of draft beers and took a booth next to the pool tables. Prime location since Sadie was a pool player.

A few minutes later, Sadie gravitated to the same spot she'd occupied on Wednesday night.

I had to give her credit for playing it cool. Other than a friendly nod, she hardly looked at us.

Mark stuffed about a million quarters in the jukebox and pulled me onto the dance floor. It had been a while since I'd cut a rug with someone, especially someone as good as Mark.

I wasn't so bad myself. The years of ballet and dance that my mother had forced upon me had its useful purposes, including making intended people jealous.

An hour later, Mark asked, "Are you ready for the Dirty Dancing lift?"

"No. But apparently you've already tried it and knocked all the sense out of your head."

He grinned at this and spun me around before whispering in my ear, "What's she doing now?"

"Ignoring you."

"I can't have that, now, can I?"

Before I could think to run away, to run, far, far, away. Mark pulled me close and planted a kiss on my lips.

I curled my fingers in his hair, making sure to tug hard enough to inflict a fair amount of pain.

Mark stepped away from me and rubbed the back of his head, but his smile never left his face.

He winked, "I'll get us some more beers."

I watched him make his way to the counter. He was movie-star handsome. And yet, I'd felt nothing when he'd kissed me.

The exact opposite of what I'd experienced with Amsel.

I avoided looking in Sadie's direction, afraid I'd see hurt on her face.

At that point, I'd have no choice but to march right over and tell her the truth.

In barely a blink of an eye, Amsel Richter made his way from the front of the restaurant. Sparks flew from his violet-colored eyes.

Sadie may not have seen the kiss, but he had.

"What are you doing, Helene?"

The alcohol had numbed my senses enough that I was completely unfazed by the angry brute towering over me. "I'm having a good time."

I cringed at the slight slurring of my words.

How many beers had Mark shoved in my hand?

I couldn't remember.

"You're drunk."

"No! I have a buzz that you are currently killing, so shoo. Go do your brooding tyrant thing someplace else." I poked my finger into his chest and wished I hadn't.

It just made me want to touch him more.

Where was Mark?

Anxious for him to return, I searched the crowd, and spotted him deeply entrenched in a face-to-face conversation with Sadie.

Amsel gripped my arm. "I'm taking you home."

"I beg your pardon. You'll do no such thing."

An attempt to wrestle my arm free proved fruitless. And before I could protest, I was being led out into light drizzling rain.

"What do you think you're doing?" I asked.

"I'm saving you from embarrassing yourself. Making out on the dance floor, Helene? I hadn't pegged you as an exhibitionist."

I wrenched my arm away and stumbled off balance when he simply let go.

"What I do, who I kiss, how much I drink, even if I streak naked through the streets, is none of your goddamn business."

"ANYTHING you do in *my* town is my business."

With the grace of a pickpocket, Amsel retrieved the keys from the pocket of my jeans.

"Give those back."

He ignored me, "I'm parked in front of my office."

Stupefied, I stared at his departing back. Then anger set in.

Did he just expect that he could manhandle me into doing whatever he wanted?

I was not going anywhere with him.

Before he could do anything about it, I turned around and stomped in the opposite direction, toward the cottage.

I tried to ignore that it was suddenly raining harder and that I was freezing.

Mark would wonder where I'd gone. Let him. His stunt had pushed the limits a bit too far.

Not only that, but it had provoked the wrath of the devil himself.

The Land Rover approached and slowed down beside me. Amsel rolled down the window on the passenger side, "Get in."

I offered him my middle finger in reply.

75

"You're being ridiculous. You don't even have a rain jacket."

I didn't bother to answer him.

My shoes were already coated in mud and it took a feat of focused concentration on the road ahead, as well as willpower, not to get in.

"Suit yourself."

Moments after his tail lights disappeared, I remembered he still had my keys.

How would I get inside?

I lamented not being a world class spy who could easily pick locks.

Stinging, blinding rain swept in sideways and lashed me in the face.

After I'd exhausted my repertoire of curse words, I was both shocked at myself and amused when I began plotting out implausible ways to kill off Amsel Richter.

I especially liked death by bowling ball, but death by feral cats was a close second.

How fortunate for him that Glenhaven had neither a bowling alley, nor an adequate supply of stray cats to make this feasible.

Also, he was too far away from me for him to really be in danger. At least, that's what I thought.

Rounding the bend, I was relieved to see the soft glow of light shining through the cottage windows.

I contemplated exactly which credit card I was willing to sacrifice to the break in but noticed that my keys hung in the door.

He'd been inside. I could smell him everywhere.

It was the oddest kind of torture, this yearning for contact with someone that I was pretty sure I despised.

After a hot shower to knock the cold from my bones, I was almost fully sober, but too riled up to go to sleep.

I remembered I hadn't gotten around to hanging Georgia's painting and found a vacant spot on the living room wall for it.

I felt comforted by this lady who stood strong in the face of adversity. If she could overcome the darkness that hunted her, it gave me hope that someday I might be able to do the same.

But maybe I could just start with figuring out why I felt the need to be in Glenhaven.

Tomorrow I would rise early, and get as close to the mining area as I safely could.

I would have pale light from the rising sun to guide me. With any luck, I would be in and out before Mark decided to go for one of his hikes.

I didn't want him worrying about me. And if I did happen to bump into him on my way back, he would be none the wiser about what I was really doing there.

For the first time since arriving in this town, I was plagued by images I couldn't shake from my mind.

I saw men with sunken eyes collapsing where they stood, dying on the hillside surrounded by weeping wives and children.

Their cries of despair filled the air, but there would be no savoir to rescue them from an invisible killer.

CHAPTER SEVEN

COMPLETELY RECKLESS

I shed my jacket to the warming temperature and contemplated the barren terrain that ran like a scar from the hillside into the valley below.

The cliff perched above was a good spot for surveying what stretched out below, but I still could not see far into the clearing.

The hawk circling the blue sky above had an enviable viewpoint.

The fact that vegetation had begun to tentatively creep back into the area, I took as a positive sign. Still, it was anorexic compared to the luscious growth surrounding it.

Remarkable really, the destructive nature of mankind and the tunnel vision that made this kind of exploitation possible.

The only way to fully view the pit area without ignoring all the posted signs and walking down into it, would require climbing gear and expertise I did not have.

I pulled a protein bar from my knapsack and nibbled at it absentmindedly as I scanned the hillside.

Then I saw it.

Almost completely hidden by the trees was the top portion of a slate chimney.

The home of Amsel Richter.

There was a thinning there with access to a ledge which overlooked the pit. From what I could see, the only way to get a clear view at a safe distance was from the doctor's property.

All morning I'd had a sense I could not shake of being watched.

I'd stopped and listened along the path but there was nothing, no crunch of leaves other than my own, just the eerie quiet.

Although the sense was pervasive, I eventually dismissed it as mere paranoia.

One only had to spend a short time out here to appreciate and understand why the Richters would want to preserve all of this.

But I knew there was more to it than that. There was an energy here, buzzing through the air, a feeling I couldn't shake, that things were not quite what they appeared to be.

I'd spent my entire life living with those intuitions, having visions, seeing things that would come to be.

It was both a blessing, and a curse.

People were afraid of this, and for that I was always set apart. But there were occasions when I had shared what I could see with others.

The instant I'd I met Sally Bellefonte, the new employee at the credit union, I'd known that she was not who she said she was.

I saw glimpses of her past, things that did not quite add up. And then there was the name itself. It didn't feel right.

The name was all wrong.

Our branch manager eyed me with disdain, "Everybody likes her Helene, except for you. I checked her references, and nothing is out of sorts here. Maybe you find her popularity threatening."

There had been no mistaking the dig.

I wasn't popular. I didn't socialize. I did my work and kept to myself.

And there was no way to convince her that there was anything to my feelings other than petty jealousy.

Before leaving her office, I'd paused in the doorway, "Ok. But when the Feds show up, just remember that I tried to warn you."

Two months later the Feds did show up.

Sally Bellefonte was really Paige Springer, a wanted felon who had somehow managed to steal the identity of someone who looked enough like her that nobody had batted an eye.

It wasn't as if I gloated about this. I never barged into our manager's office like a *gangsta*, got in her face, and said, "I told you so, *biatch*."

But I didn't have to say anything. My manager never looked at me the same after that.

Something had invaded her perception of me. I was other. I was connected to a force she didn't understand, a force that could unleash flying monkeys, a swarm of locusts, and demons from hell, all at the same time.

It was the same look I sometimes caught in my mother's eyes when she thought I wasn't looking.

It was as if she were trying to reconcile what had happened that day, trying to look through my skin to see the creature hiding inside of it.

My being in Glenhaven was no coincidence. It was a major piece in the jigsaw that made up my entire life.

Up until now, the important pieces were always just out of reach. But not this time. This time I would find what I'd been missing.

I tried to memorize as much of the trail as I could as I headed back.

If I ever came back here at night I didn't want to get turned around. I certainly did not want to spend the night in the woods because I'd gotten myself lost.

"Early hike? I'm glad to see you've fully recovered from last night."

Amsel's voice startled me.

He sat hunched over in the Adirondack chair that was entirely too small for him and scrutinized my running shoes.

"Go away." I brushed past him and through the door I'd left unlocked.

He was incredibly, quick, inside the instant I was.

I remembered last night's miserable walk home and reeled toward him. "Did you not hear me? I want you to leave."

"I'm sorry, Helene. I wasn't myself last night. I let emotion take over. I reacted to seeing you with Mark although I knew it was just a pretense."

"Excuse me? A pretense? You don't know anything. I happen to have strong feelings for Mark."

He smiled and shook his head. "When he kissed you, you didn't react. Your pulse never quickened. The hairs on your arms didn't stand on end. Not like they do with me."

"And you could see all this from across the room?"

"Yes."

"You're delusional. What you sense is repulsion."

He stepped closer. Deep oceans of violet penetrated my defenses causing my heart to race faster.

As if to prove his point he gently touched the throbbing pulse on my neck and I found myself allowing this sensuous gesture.

"You don't want to want me, Helene. But you do. And I don't want to want you. But I do."

And then he kissed me. This time his lips were supple, so faint and so soft, they left me aching.

Any thought of pushing him away dissolved as I kissed him back, fervently, digging my fingers into his shoulders and pulling him toward me until I could feel his arousal.

I was vaguely aware of his hands removing my t-shirt and bra. I felt the sheets against my naked back, his lips on my breast, and his hand between my legs.

Every nerve ending screamed out for his attention.

When his mouth found the most sensitive part of me, my body convulsed, and I cried out.

I pushed him back and explored the hard contours of his body, inebriated by the salty sweet taste of him.

He was the most beautiful man I'd ever seen. When I reached his member, the size of it drew an audible gasp.

He laughed then, flipped me onto my back, and straddled me, "It's too late to turn back now, Helene. You're mine now."

I didn't want to turn back. I'd never wanted anyone this way.

There was a morbid curiosity to find out what would happen if I just let go, to find out if this desire would burn us both to cinders.

He penetrated me slowly at first, letting the sensation ripple through me. Then he dove deeper into me, again and again, as my hips rose and fell in rhythm beneath him.

Waves of pleasure washed over me. I came again and again while Amsel held back, torturing me to the point of raw pain before I felt his body finally shake and release.

Amsel hadn't worn a condom. And I hadn't been on the pill in years.

But I wasn't concerned. I knew from years of trying to get pregnant with Brian, and the opinions of scores of doctors, that I was infertile.

Scarring from endometriosis, and numerous surgeries, had taken their toll on my reproductive system.

He propped his weight up on his elbows, but he made no effort to move off of me or out of me.

Instead, he stared down into my eyes and tenderly ran the tips of his fingers over my cheek.

"That wasn't so bad, was it?" he asked.

It wasn't bad at all. It was exceedingly, fantastically good. And my body still reeled from it.

"It was completely reckless," I said. "I must be out of my mind. I don't even like you."

He laughed, a deep hearty sound that vibrated against my naked flesh. "Oh, I think you do like me. I think you like me very much."

I blushed, thinking about the intimacy of what we had just shared.

Suddenly, it was too much, his gaze too direct.

I felt when he looked into my eyes, he could read every thought I had, but I could pick up nothing about him, and it left me feeling vulnerable.

"You're crushing me," I lied.

Again, he laughed, aware of this. But he rolled off of me anyway, watching me slip out of bed and into the bathroom.

With the door closed I tried to get my thoughts together.

You are a lonely woman who has not had sex in a long time. This is purely taking care of needs.

I washed off, and slipped on the robe I'd left hanging on the door before returning.

Amsel had slipped on his pants and I was slightly disappointed by this.

I gawked at his broad muscular shoulders as he searched for his shirt that had been discarded in a pile with my own clothes.

"I have to check in at the clinic." He kissed the top of my head. "I will come by later to pick you up."

"Pick me up?"

"Yes. I'm making dinner for you tonight."

He left me there, mouth agape, not really knowing how to respond to this.

Part of me wanted to say, *No way. I won't be going home with you. Who the hell do you think you are?*

But my body did this silent dance.

Excitement settled in the pit of my stomach at the prospect of making love with him again, so much so that I was shocked by my wanton behavior.

But I would be lying if I said, there wasn't another motive behind agreeing to go to Amsel's house.

There would be clear skies and enough moonlight tonight to see clearly. Being at Amsel's gave me the perfect opportunity to get a direct view down into the forbidden area.

I was finishing a bowl of cereal when Mark called. "Hey. Where did you go last night? I figured you were really mad about the kiss thing."

"I was a little angry but that's not why I left. I…I had a disagreement with Amsel Richter. I wanted to get away from him, so I left."

There was silence as he processed this. "So…Sadie was right. She said she thought she saw the two of you walk out together. I didn't know you even knew each other."

I didn't want to go into detail about things happening between me and Amsel and changed the subject.

"You and Sadie got to spend some time together, then?"

"We did. And the funny thing was she was really upset for me, and sympathetic because she thought you had deserted me for another guy. I hope you don't mind that I let her entertain that idea. In fact, I'm kind of milking it for all it was worth."

"I suppose it's OK. Although, I do mind that she dislikes me because of false pretenses."

"The real reason that I'm calling is because I have to drive out to the dairy farm. Lester Fields is having trouble with his truck and I told him I'd pick up ours and Mary's delivery. They have a new calf. They say she's as white as the snow. I thought you might like to see her."

"Sure. Why not?"

What was my alternative?

Driving myself crazy thinking about what had happened this morning?

An hour later we were at the farm.

The calf was a breed called Charolais, which I learned Lester was fondest of.

According to him she had the brightest, most ultra-white coat he had ever seen. He named her Carol Anne after his first ever girlfriend, who had hair the color of cotton.

She was precious with her big brown eyes. She was also, ecstatically happy, her every movement defined by erratic bursts of energy, which I jokingly referred to as cow skipping.

I rubbed the top of her head, the hair as luxuriously soft as you would expect a baby's to be and she rewarded me by nuzzling her nose into my jeans and leaving wet snot trails behind.

The dairy was spread out over 20 acres of land with several outbuildings surrounding a two-story house that was beginning to show its age.

A series of fenced areas were gridded out, and I learned that the cows were rotated around the farm into various areas depending where they were in their cycle of milk production.

Pregnant cows or those he suspected were pregnant, went into a special area, and were allowed to wallow in a state of leisure in this section, a sort of mini-vacation, until they had birthed their calves and were ready to go back to work.

Lester and I chatted while Mark loaded the milk crates. I learned he was a widower of four years and that he had a son that had broken his heart by moving to San Francisco to work for a tech company.

I also got the skinny on him and Mary Romano who apparently had been secretly dating off and on for several months.

I learned that she was hot headed and independent, and he didn't know quite what to do with her sometimes, kiss her or run away as fast as he could.

I guessed Lester was around 68 years old. He was in good shape. His hair had turned grey but he was still a ruggedly handsome man.

I could see him and Mary together. His Southern drawl alone could charm the devil himself.

There was also something else I sensed in Lester after watching him interact with the animals around him. I sensed it in the way I often did with people I observed who had special abilities.

He understood them in an intuitive way. Without words, they interacted in perfect synchronicity.

The strangest anomaly about Glenhaven, possibly more so than the strange lights, was how the people here had more of these types of abilities than would be found in an average sampling of the population.

Lester explained his coming to the town in this way, "When I was a young man running wild, a true Alabama redneck, I spent most of my time getting into trouble. I was maybe headed for some hard time. It wouldn't have really taken much to influence me into doing the wrong thing. I was drinking a lot and running with a troubled crowd. But then I had a dream. I saw my life laid out in two separate paths; each milestone marked off until the day I died. I saw if I didn't change, I was going to be butting against the grain my whole life. But on that other path, there was an abundance of love. It felt so good to me, I woke up in tears, wanting that so badly."

"Is that when you came here?" I asked.

He nodded. His expression was relaxed, but there was a careful surveillance of me, "It took coming here for me to be able to stop feeling like there was something broken inside of me. I feel like you can relate to this," he said.

Mark treaded up the porch steps and our conversation ended. "Think I've got everything loaded up. Are you ready?"

I stood and Lester held out his hand. "You know where to find me if you are in need of some decent conversation."

"I will try not to take that personally," Mark grumbled, oblivious to what Lester meant, that if I needed to talk about things that most people wouldn't understand, his door was always open.

Lester slapped him on the back. "Son, I can't help it that I've lived a lot longer than you and have far more worldly and interesting experiences to share."

"Oh, playing the age card, are we? I can't win that one."

Mark climbed into the truck, but I hung back, "Thank you, Lester. I may take you up on that offer some day."

He just smiled. "I'm certain you will."

CHAPTER EIGHT

SOMETHING IN MY DNA

The bells on Georgia's gallery door rang when I entered and I heard her call out, "Helene, I'm back here."

I found her chopping up vegetables in a small kitchenette.

"How did you know it was me?"

She shrugged. "I don't know. I just did."

"I was coming to see if you wanted to grab lunch. I still owe you. But it looks like I'm too late."

Georgia smiled, "Not at all. I have enough if you would like to join me for some salad and fresh hummus."

"I'd like that. Can I help?"

"You could set the table." She motioned to the open shelves behind me where the dishes were stored.

There was a tiny table against the wall and two pink vinyl vintage chairs from the 50's that were in excellent condition. "Should I grab another chair for Alexia?"

"Oh, no. She'll eat when her classes end in about an hour."

I set the table for the two of us and placed the basket of pita bread and bowl of hummus on the table.

Georgia poured ginger dressing over the salad and brought it over. Then she grabbed two wine glasses in one hand, and used her teeth to pull the cork out of a bottle of homebrewed mead and let it drop onto the counter.

I didn't stop her when she sat the glass in front of me and filled it all the way up to the top. After the morning I'd had, a little numbing of my senses was most welcome.

"What has Mary told you about me?" she asked.

The color rose to my cheeks remembering the bit of gossip Mary had shared.

She grinned at me. "You don't have to be embarrassed. I know you're not the gossipy type. I'm going to tell you the real reason I ended up in Glenhaven. But you can't tell Mary. I won't tell her a thing unless she asks me herself. It's a matter of principle."

"She thinks you fled from Alexia's father."

"I fled. But it was not her father I ran away from."

"Georgia, you really don't have to talk about this."

"I want to. It's been bottled up inside way too long. And I feel a connection with you. I know you will understand."

Georgia began her story in Quebec. She was an up-and-coming artist. The stars were aligned and her path to success was almost certain.

She met Alexia's father, a wealthy developer from Dubai, and they soon fell in love. They became engaged when she discovered she was pregnant with Alexia.

In a single day her life fractured into a million pieces, all because of a chance encounter.

"I was invited to a business dinner, a group of men from an obscure organization were looking to develop a private hotel in Dubai that would cater to their people, a members-only kind of thing.

She paused long enough to take a long swig of mead. "There was something odd about them. I can't explain it. It was like they were pasted into this reality, but they didn't belong in it. And I could feel the darkness in them. I was on edge the entire time, and relieved when it was over."

"Did you tell your fiancé about these feelings you were having?" I asked.

"No. He didn't know about this part of myself. We hadn't been together long, and I was afraid it would scare him away. So, I said nothing. But these men were really hyper focused on me that night, asking all kinds of personal questions. I had no idea that I was being targeted."

She shivered and rub her arms. The memory seemed to chill her from the inside out.

She closed her eyes for a moment and when she opened them again, stared past me as if she were seeing these phantoms of her past.

"My painting studio was in a run-down area, a huge warehouse that lots of artists rented cheap and divided up. Thinking back, it was a dangerous place for a woman to be alone at night. There was no light at all, until I got into my work space. After the dinner, I was wound up tight, and kissed Amir, told him I was going to work until late and not to wait up."

She looked at me then, and I could see the pain in her eyes.

"They were waiting for me in the shadows. They beat me and chained me to the leg of an old radiator. Then they went down the hall to make a phone call."

As Georgia spoke, I could see the scene unfold in real time. I could feel her emotions, her fear, and her sadness. "My God, Georgia." I didn't try to hold back the tears, letting them run unchecked down my cheeks. "Why, would they do such a thing?"

"I could hear every word they said to the person on the other line. I heard them say that Amir was dead, and that I had told him nothing, that he was ignorant. And that they would take care of me soon."

Georgia began to weep. "I was trembling. Why? I was nobody. I had done nothing wrong. I'd never hurt anyone. I was a simple artist. Had they mistaken me for someone else? I was heartbroken, terrified. Part of me just wanted them to kill me and be done with it. But then I thought about the baby growing inside of me. And it was as if a higher power took over, I lifted the radiator up and realized it was attached to nothing. The chain fell right off."

She gave a little chuckle between her tears. "You can imagine their surprise when they came back to finish the job and I was gone.

I escaped through a broken window and never looked back."

"I'm so sorry, Georgia. Did you go to the police?"

She wiped her tears away with her forearm. "No. I knew they would be waiting for me to do that. I never went back to my apartment. I cleaned out our bank account and fled to the states. There was a small mention in a Canadian newspaper, where they labeled Amir's death as a suicide. It said he had jumped from the balcony of his hotel room."

"And you have no idea why any of that happened?" I asked.

She looked at me as if deciding if she should say more. "They kept calling me, *amalgam*, spitting that word at me like I was something unclean, something that needed to be weeded out. As a person of Caribbean descent, at first, I thought the attack might have been racially motivated. But…"

"But what?"

"That wasn't the reason. They knew I had abilities. That I could see things with a sixth sense."

She released a shaky sigh. "Whoever those people are, they are connected to an extensive and powerful network that has existed for a very long time. They wield violence the same way the KKK does and for similar reasons. They hated me, Helene. Not for the color of my skin, but for something in my DNA that is different. I know that sounds incredibly farfetched, but it is the truth."

"Georgia, no…you don't have to validate your intuition to me. If you felt that, there was a reason. I'm sorry about Amir. You're very strong to have been able to carry on after what happened. And I'm honored that you trust me enough to confide in me."

Georgia looked at me, taking in my features, as if she were searching for something that was hidden there. "You're part of this too. I'm not sure how. But it's clear to me, and has been since the moment we met. Something binds us together."

"I was adopted. For all we know, you could be my long-lost sister."

She laughed, and I was happy to see light return to her eyes. "As much as I would love to gain a sister such as yourself, I do not think that is it. But we are sisters, through the misery of loss and the thing which makes us not fit in with other people. It's not an accident that we have been drawn together, Helene."

I grabbed her hand and squeezed. "Sisters, then."

Georgia's words touched upon the strange mix of belonging and apprehension that I had felt from the moment I'd stepped foot in Glenhaven.

There was also the sense of something sinister and dark lurking in the shadows, something with the capacity to change the fabric of everything I believed.

We finished our lunch, the topics turning toward lighter things, and were still chatting when Alexia took her break.

She bounded into the room, a whirlwind of energy, but stopped short, immediately disappearing back into her shell the instant she spied me sitting with her mother.

"That wild puma that just crashed through that door is the real Alexia, not the one hiding behind me."

Her daughter took offense at this and spoke up, "I'm not a puma! And I'm not hiding."

"Then you are pretending to be a meek little rabbit," her mother teased.

"I'm not a rabbit either. I'm just Alexia."

As if to prove herself, Alexia pulled up a chair close to me and dug into her salad.

To my surprise, the shy girl became quite animated and boisterous, letting me into her world. I learned she had two fantail goldfish, Nessie and Polly. She had a pair of unicorn rainboots. She loved peach cobbler, adventure books, and Dolly Parton.

I couldn't help but wonder as I listened to her, if the nose that was slightly thinner and longer than her mother's or her eyes which were lighter and more golden than her doppelganger mother, were like her father's.

It was all so grotesque and heart wrenching to have someone violently ripped out of your life. I felt an affinity with her and Georgia.

I wondered if they even had a photograph to remember him by?

On the way home, I pulled up the Dolly Parton song Alexia made me promise to listen to, *Little Sparrow*.

I had never heard this song before. It was beautiful and haunting, about heartbreak and sorrow, a strange choice for one so young.

Had all the pain and loss Georgia experienced passed on to Alexia in utero?

Was it embedded in the code that created her, casting its shadow over her life?

It certainly seemed so.

The afternoon passed by slowly and I grew more nervous the later it got. I sifted through the books I'd taken from the library.

I'd never been particularly interested in astrology, but I'd been drawn to one about astrological charts and had added it to my pile to take it home with me.

I opened up one of the romance novels by the same author I'd just read. But it was hard to concentrate.

I couldn't stop thinking about Amsel.

I knew nothing about him. What kind of man was he?

I guessed that he was older than my 35 years. Why hadn't he married?

Or perhaps he had married and divorced.

What if he was a terrible adulterer?

Somehow neither of those scenarios felt right.

Then there was the issue of my plan to get a better view of the lights from the ledge behind Amsel's house and how I would execute it without him knowing.

With this in mind, I slid the flashlight I'd found earlier in the day into the pocket of my jacket.

I read for a bit longer before deciding to take a nap.

When I opened my eyes, Amsel was sitting on the edge of the bed watching me.

Instantly awake and on guard, I sat up. "How long have you been there?"

"Maybe ten minutes."

This both excited me and unnerved me. "Why didn't you wake me up?"

He grinned, "You need all the rest you can get as I am not sure if we'll be doing much sleeping tonight."

I blushed at his insinuation.

"I see you didn't pack a bag. But you really won't need clothes," he winked. "And I have an extra toothbrush."

I wondered what to make of this strong and powerful force pulling me to him. But I also felt a sense of wariness, like there was far more to him than what met the eye.

I kept on the yoga pants I had been wearing, threw on a thin oversized sweater, and laced up my athletic shoes. Before leaving, I grabbed my jacket from the couch.

If he had been hoping for sexier attire, he did not let his disappointment show.

When we stepped over the threshold of his house, I half expected and half wanted him to tear my clothes off on the spot.

Instead, he walked straight to the refrigerator and perused its contents, "How do you feel about fettuccini alfredo with grilled chicken and zucchini?"

"That sounds delicious."

"Do you mind chopping these?" Without waiting for a reply, he pushed the zucchini and onion my way and soon a domestic scene unfolded as we quietly prepared dinner.

Occasionally, his hand would graze my back or he would stand over my shoulder so close and sensuously that even though he hadn't touched me, my pulse went wild.

I was almost jealous that the alfredo sauce he was focused on preparing was receiving way more attention than me.

We ate our meal in the dining room this time.

It was a formal room with a domed ceiling and antique molding done with such craftsmanship it was hard to ponder the cost of such a space.

On the ceiling above, scenes unfolded. A mural of gods and goddesses with long flowing hair who appeared as winged creatures, that looked like it had aged an eternity.

"This is a beautiful room. It feels very old and precious."

"That's because it is. This room was purchased from a castle in France. The new owners, dreadful people with no interest in preservation, were going to demolish the whole thing and start from scratch. My father got wind of it and convinced them to sell the room to him. He paid a fortune to have it painstakingly disassembled and reassembled here."

"I can't imagine a small country doctor would have the means to do such a thing."

"Let's just say that my father and mother both come from wealthy bloodlines, old money that got passed along generation after generation. They looked at their wealth as a way to do good in the world. And that has always been more important than anything, even me."

"And do you share that philosophy? Or do you resent it."

"How could I not share it? I lived most of my life being dragged from one third world country to the next. You can't see the suffering that goes on in these remote places and not develop a deep empathy and caring."

He opened a bottle of pinot grigio and poured it into the crystal wine glasses.

"But I used to resent it, when I was younger, the burden of it. I spent a good portion of my youth rebelling. I became quite a playboy. But then I settled down and realized how foolish I'd been. I had responsibilities I had to come into."

"And you came here?"

"Yes."

"And have you ever married or been serious enough to marry anyone?"

"No. Never. How is your dinner?"

Fine. Change the subject then.

"It's very delicious."

Quiet settled in as I focused on my food and pondered Amsel as a playboy. I supposed you didn't become that good in bed if you hadn't had a plethora of experiences.

Suddenly, the idea of being just a notch on his belt, did not sit well with me, even though I neither expected nor wanted anything from him.

It was silly of me to worry about that. What did it matter anyway?

But somehow it did matter.

I had to be careful to keep things in perspective. He was the first man I'd been with since Brian. I didn't need to turn this into something that it wasn't.

"What about you, Helene? You must have a life waiting for you back in Washington."

"Without family, there is really nothing to rush back to anymore. I took care of my mother when she was dying. And then Brian followed shortly after. That doesn't really lend itself to developing strong friendships."

"You've seen your fair share of death. That can't have been easy."

I wanted to say that I had an intimate relationship with death, that it tethered itself to me like a lost hungry child who demanded the souls of those I loved.

"I had people in my life who cared for me deeply. Some people never get that in a whole lifetime. I'm blessed to have had that for a while."

Looking back, my life always made sense for me. I was never going to live as normal people did. I paused and weighed whether or not to delve deeper into the nature of the latest reality I found myself in.

I knew that if I'd said what I was about to someone back home, I would have found myself in a home for psychopaths. But here, was different.

In this place, it was almost expected.

"I don't know how to put this. I have had this feeling lately, of being pulled toward something greater than myself. That I am supposed to do something important. I'm supposed to change an outcome. Only I don't know what that is exactly."

I could tell by the way Amsel stared at me that my words concerned him, as if he'd taken them as an alarm bell sounding a potential threat from the outside. "And do you think this important thing you're supposed to do has something to do with Glenhaven?"

"I do know it's no accident that I'm here. But that's all that I understand at the moment."

"You are not like anyone who has ever come here, Helene. You confuse me. Surprise me. You've cast a spell over me that I can't explain."

I took my last sip of wine, not knowing how to respond to this and realized that he had been waiting patiently for me to finish.

Amsel lifted me out of my chair as if I weighed nothing at all and carried me up the wide staircase.

He swung me gently onto his massive four poster bed as his hands skillfully tugged my sweater over my head.

When he leaned in and kissed me passionately, forcefully, there was none of the playful tenderness of this morning.

It was raw, unfiltered passion and I was completely lost to it.

The rest of my clothes were removed without it even registering, leaving me naked and at his mercy.

The intimate part of me throbbed, aching for contact with him as his lips took a tortured path down my neck and shoulder, across my stomach, and back to my breasts.

And then he lifted me to a standing position and entered me, sending ripples of pleasure coursing through.

I groaned in complaint as he drew away and swiftly maneuvered us toward the French doors. He swung them open and the room was instantly flooded with moonlight.

I wasn't sure if the shivers that tore through me were from the cool night air or the intensity of his stare as he drank in every inch of my naked body.

His eyes were deep violet seas of emotion, unbearably tender. But cutting through that was solid and unyielding steel.

When he lifted me up, I wound my legs around him tightly. This time he moved slowly, sensuously.

His lips trailed down my neck, stopping at my erect nipple.

I ceased to notice the cold. I was suspended where time stood still, only faintly aware of the hoarseness of my own voice crying out.

Climax sent me spiraling.

I released my hold on this earth to climb up toward starlight, to the place where pure light made ash of flesh and bone.

He clung to me, compressed me under the weight of his arms, and I succumbed to this, leaning into it until I was confident my legs could hold me up again.

I shuffled into the bathroom and turned on the shower.

He didn't follow and I was grateful for a moment to recover rational thought.

Every nerve in my body suffered from heightened sensitivity.

I didn't try to hold back the tears.

It wasn't sadness I felt, more that I'd brushed against something achingly beautiful and impossibly pure in form. It had penetrated through the protective layers shielding my heart.

This vulnerability was foreign to me. And I wasn't sure how to process it.

It was a dangerous thing to let go unchecked.

I let the hot water rain down on me, until I stopped feeling off kilter, until I'd managed to build up a soft shell of logic and reason to protect myself from these frightening sensations.

I wrapped myself up in a towel and ventured back into the bedroom where I found my clothes laid out neatly on the bed.

I slipped on my underpants, socks, and the sweater that fell a few inches above my knees, before following clanging sounds back to the kitchen.

Amsel stirred something on the stove.

He'd dressed in an old t-shirt and flannel pajama bottoms. His hair was wet, so I guessed he had showered in another bathroom.

"Hot cocoa?" he asked.

"Sounds decadent. Can I help?"

"You could get us a couple of mugs. Cabinet behind you, right door."

Inside, I found a ridiculous number of mugs for one person to own. I chose an elegant blue and white floral for myself, and for him, a red devil with a pitch fork.

He grinned, "I think I know which one is meant for me. I'll try not to take offense."

"None intended," I said, smiling through my lying teeth.

"You would be terrible at poker."

He poured the thick chocolate liquid into the mugs, and we settled onto the Italian leather sofa in the den.

Like the rest of the house, it was comfortable yet simply elegant.

He cued up a movie, a low budget sci-fi film. We laughed at the overacting and cheesy special effects, that were only eclipsed by the giant plot holes and unsatisfying ending.

"It was like a creeping runaway train that just rolled until it finally hit a rock," I said.

"Sorry about that. Maybe you will have better luck. Your turn," he handed over the remote.

I found a documentary film about haunted places in the South, which promptly caused us both to nod off.

At some point we turned off the lights and made it into his king-sized bed.

I lay in front of him with his body spooned around me. I waited for signs that his breathing had change. I waited for him to fall asleep and my chance to slip out before he even knew that I was gone.

That was the last thing I remembered.

CHAPTER NINE

THINGS YOU MUST DISCOVER

Sunlight poured in through a crack in the heavy drapes. For a second, I was disoriented, then I recognized that I was in Amsel's bedroom.

Images from a disturbing dream still lingered in my head.

At first, it eluded me, with blurry edges that I couldn't quite make out. But then the details opened to me and revealed themselves.

I'd fallen asleep, only to awake and realize that I was alone in Amsel's bed. I'd searched the house but he was nowhere to be found.

Then I'd put on the rest of my clothes and used my flashlight to navigate the property behind the house. The closer I came to the area overlooking the clearing, the brighter the sky became.

Lights danced, exploding into tentacles of brilliant greens, blues, and purples.

What I saw was impossible, really. Auroras didn't happen this far south.

I heard the flapping of wings before I saw what made the sound. It rustled leaves and splintered a thick branch with its powerful forward movements.

And then it was there. Another impossible thing, standing right in front of me.

It was enormously large silhouetted against the glowing horizon and it towered over me.

It had wings. Wide and expansive wings.

I ran, dropping the flashlight in my haste to get away.

I fled blindly into the darkness of the woods with my heartbeat rising into my throat.

And then the ground gave way. I found myself rolling down a steep hill, rolling over the damp cover of leaves, blankets of acorn shells, and brambles until my head struck something hard.

There was a sharp intense pain. Then everything went black.

I threw the covers back and tried to sit up.

I winced from the sudden pain that made me feel slightly nauseated.

"I would take that slowly. You had a nasty fall during the night," Amsel leaned against the door frame with a look of concern.

I could feel a massive bump on the side of my head.

"What happened?"

"You rolled off the bed and hit your head on the nightstand. Do you remember me helping you up, and waking you to check on you throughout the night?"

I shook my head to indicate that I hadn't, then regretted it. "I feel like I have a hangover."

"Just a slight concussion."

I slid my legs over the side of the bed and realized my whole body hurt. I'd really done a number on myself.

It was no wonder I'd had such a crazy dream.

"You should eat something."

"I should really get back to the cottage."

"I'll take you there. After breakfast." There was a stubborn set to his jaw which conveyed this was not up for debate.

He'd already prepared breakfast. Two plates with stainless steel cloches waited for us on the kitchen island, along with orange juice and coffee.

The sight of eggs, toast, and bacon made me realize that I was famished in spite of my headache.

I dug in, slathering on a gluttonous portion of apricot preserves.

"These are divine," I said.

"Irene makes them."

"Not surprising." Everything I'd purchased from their small store had that stamp of quality. "They are such a kind and considerate family."

"Yes. You and Mark especially, have become quite chummy."

I searched his face.

Was he being sarcastic? Was this jealousy, even though he had already figured out there was nothing romantic going on between the two of us?

The dull lingering pain in my head might have been responsible for my deliberately impish response.

"We have. What a personality. He's so funny, and talk about talent! Not to mention how handsome he is. What a catch."

I could tell by the way he pressed his lips together and the slight angry color that rose to his face that my words had hit the mark.

He was jealous. Then too quickly, his face was shielded again.

I almost felt bad. Almost. "Thank you for making all of this."

"Anything for you, Helene."

"I can't believe I fell. How embarrassing. What time did it happen?"

"Around 12:30 this morning."

He went to refill my coffee, but I placed my hand over the top. "I think I'm good. I'll just go and finish getting dressed."

I washed my face off in the bathroom and caught a glimpse of myself in the mirror.

There was a glazed over brightness to my eyes that was unusual. A result of the concussion, maybe?

The side of my head was still very sore and sudden movements triggered an intense throbbing pain.

Already bruises formed on my right shoulder. My neck was incredibly stiff. But along my left hip there was a two-inch scrape that had begun to scab over.

What could have caused that?

The dream penetrated into my thoughts again.

Rolling over and over, tumbling over damp earth. It had been so vivid, something tearing into my flesh and the sound of brush cracking and breaking.

Amsel approached from behind and kissed the back of my neck. I jumped, startled because I hadn't heard him come in.

"Are you ready?" he asked.

"Sure. I'll just grab my jacket."

We were quiet on the drive down. I was surprised by how cold it had gotten. The gage on the vehicle's dashboard indicated it was 48 degrees Fahrenheit.

"I'll stop by to check on you later," he said.

"That's really not necessary. I'm fine. I need some time to myself." I opened the car door and climbed out before he could lean in for a kiss.

He didn't press this, acknowledging my words with a simple nod.

I watched him pull away.

The strangest mix of emotions came over me; relief to be alone with my thoughts, longing for the clean earthy smell that always clung to him and the irresistible notes of citrus and sandalwood in his aftershave, and the feel of his body beneath my roving hands.

The morning sped by as I lounged on the couch nursing my wounds.

But there was also a growing uneasiness. Just thinking about the thing from my dream, caused my heart to pound, my pulse to race, and brought back the terror I'd felt.

It had all been so real. But it had only been a dream.

Why was I still so shaken by it?

By Late afternoon, I felt well enough to drive into town for a much-needed distraction and comfort food.

I found a booth directly across from the kitchen and waited for Mary to finish with another customer.

Through the window, Alexia stood on the edge of the sidewalk in front of her mother's gallery. She looked both ways before crossing the street and disappearing into the library.

I imagined books were her main source of entertainment with no other children her own age in the town to play with.

I searched the street parking for Amsel's Land Rover. There was a sinking feeling of disappointment when it was nowhere to be found.

Mary appeared, shielded her mouth from potential eavesdroppers, and whispered, "I have one serving left of meatloaf today. It's all yours if you would like it."

Meatloaf had never been my favorite, but I didn't want to spoil Mary's joy over the gift she offered, "I'll take it."

She returned with a plate of mashed potatoes and meatloaf, and slipped into the seat across from me while she waited anxiously for me to taste it.

Not surprisingly, it was delicious. "This is so good. It has a bit of a kick."

"I put chopped up jalapenos in it this time. Did I overdo it?"

"No, not at all. It's perfect."

She leaned closer, studying me like I was a strange curiosity floating in a glass jar of formaldehyde, "Oh, Lord. You've fallen like a ton of bricks."

"I beg your pardon."

"Don't try to hide anything from me, honey. I can sniff out love sick woes a mile away," Mary smiled and I knew it was pointless to try and lie.

I lowered my voice so that others wouldn't be privy to what I had to say, "Ok. So…first thing, I am not love sick. More like, disgusted with myself for letting my womanly needs get in the way of my better judgement."

Mary crossed her arms and raised her eyebrows in disbelief, "Uh huh."

"Don't uh-huh, me. It's the truth. Trust me. If I were going to fall in love with anyone, Amsel would be the last person on the planet I would let that happen with. He is the most arrogant, infuriating person I've ever met."

"You forgot to mention sexy," Mary winked.

"Mary! Stop! I am not having this conversation. In a few weeks, I'll probably be leaving, and this will all be moot."

"Leaving? I was just thinking how well you fit in here. I see people come and go." She motioned to a group of bikers in the corner. "Those fellows ride in from time to time, have a good meal and leave. I've gotten pretty good at figuring out who's going to stick around."

"Miss!" One of the bikers, a burly older man with a full, grey beard called for Mary. "Check, please."

112

Mary slid to her feet reluctantly. "Don't pay any attention to me. Minding my own business has never been one of my strengths. Oh, Mark was looking for you. Said to tell you that you had some mail at the post office."

Nobody knew I was in Glenhaven.

All of my mail was being held on Whidbey Island. I couldn't imagine what could have found me here.

I watched Mary cheerfully make her rounds, fueled by her limitless supply of energy.

When the door to the kitchen swung open, I struggled to catch a glimpse inside before it closed again.

I wasn't sure what I'd been expecting to see in there. Maybe, an elaborate and sophisticated system made up of conveyor belts and powerful heat lamps that radiated like the sun.

Or magical woodland animals sporting aprons, cheerily working behind the scenes.

So far, I had only caught a glimpse of a commercial vent hood, spotless and practically gleaming pots and pans that hung from the ceiling, shelves with rows and rows of spices, and containers filled with gorgeously vibrant vegetables from the Houston's store.

Nothing at all to explain the mystery of how Mary did it.

And then it happened, the break I had been waiting for.

The door flung to with just a little more momentum, causing it to swing wider, close, and then open again.

It was just enough of a gap to give me a full view of the top of the stove.

Huge stock pots rested over open gas flames. And in one of those pots, a spoon stood upright. It swirled around, slowly and deliberately stirring the contents inside.

What was unusual about this, wasn't the spoon or the stirring. It was that it was doing this, entirely on its own.

I was still staring at the closed door, absolutely slack jawed, when Mary waltzed out, carrying two bowls of soup.

Our eyes met and there was the slightest hesitation on her part.

It was as if she realized she'd been caught in something.

What that something was, wasn't entirely clear, but a guilty shadow crept across her face before it quickly fell away.

A spoon moving all by itself? How could that be?

It wasn't. It was utterly and completely impossible.

What I thought I had seen had to be an illusion. But as I considered this, I was positive it hadn't been.

I was sure I had seen exactly what I thought I saw.

And what did that mean exactly?

That Mary had some unworldly ability, like telekinesis.

What else could Mary do?

And if I asked her about what I had just witnessed, would she come clean and admit to it?

I wasn't even sure how to phrase the question.

I finished my meatloaf, left money on the table that included a big tip, and decided to disassociate myself from this conundrum for a while.

I arrived at the post office minutes before it closed.

The letter addressed to me had arrived via a courier service.

There was no return address and I did not recognize the handwriting on the envelope.

When I shoved it inside my pocket, I remembered the flashlight that I'd taken with me the night before. It wasn't there. It must have fallen out somewhere.

It was unseasonably chilly today. I turned on the heat in the car and was waiting for it to warm up when Alexia exited the library, appearing in my rearview mirror.

She smiled and waved to someone in the distance.

I looked in that direction. There was a man standing there that I'd never seen before.

He wore a white and blue seersucker suit which was completely out of season. His thick wavy hair was bright white in the sunlight. He looked to be the quintessential Southern gentleman.

The blur of Alexia's orange jacket drew my attention as she moved toward him. But then she stopped short, her smile faltering.

When I glanced back to where I'd seen the gentleman, he was gone.

It was as if he had simply vanished, leaving Alexia and I, befuddled, staring at the spot where he'd been only seconds before.

At that moment, Georgia emerged from the gallery, "Alexia, what are you doing? Come eat."

The young girl seemed reluctant to move at first, still transfixed, gazing at the same spot.

"Alexia! Come now!" Her mother put her hands on her hips, clearly annoyed.

A strong wind whipped one of her braided pigtails into her face and she brushed it away. Then whatever spell that held Alexia in place, was broken.

She looked both ways, before running to her mother.

I made a cup of tea and stared down at the elegant handwriting.

Dear Helene,

I hope this letter finds you well. My name is Demetria Courtenay and I am your mother.

There was a sick feeling in the pit of my stomach as the words sank in.

In all these years, I had never asked about the woman who had given me up.

She had wanted nothing to do with me, handing me over to Harold and Lela Parish to raise. And I had in turn, shunned the idea of her, refusing to entertain any notion of the woman she might have been.

I was angry.

How dare she seek me out now? I was tempted to rip the letter to shreds. But my outrage and curiosity prevented this and I read on.

I am assuming you think the worst of me. You think me a callous and selfish person without the capacity to love, a person who cared little for you, so little that she chose to give you up. The truth is much more convoluted, I'm afraid.

Harold and Lela risked so much in helping me, and agreeing to raise you. I am hoping you will honor this request to finally meet. This one time, please grant me the chance to explain how truly remarkable your parents were and what they gave up for me in order to protect you.

I have business in the states soon and will contact you when I arrive. At that time, it will be up to you whether or not you choose to grant me this. But there are things you must discover about who you really are.

Demetria

My head throbbed. I swallowed down two more ibuprofen and conceded that my day could not get any shittier.

With a blanket wrapped around my shoulders, I sought refuge in the shadows of the front porch.

It made no sense. Why contact me now?

And how had she known to have the letter sent to Glenhaven?

Decades worth of suppressed emotions surfaced all at once.

Mostly, these were feelings of guilt, that maybe there was something cursed about me that doomed everyone I

117

cared about to suffer unimaginable pain, that something within me drew in the darkness.

There are things you must discover about who you really are.

What had she meant by this?

That night so long ago, Harold's heart stopped in the ambulance. He'd lost too much blood, and they could not revive him.

My mother and I didn't speak on the way home from the hospital. Neither of us cried.

A heavy silence fell over us, a numbness that we had hid inside of as long as we could.

Maybe if we didn't speak about it, it never happened. If we didn't say it out loud, my father wasn't really dead.

The investigators questioned us.

"There was a neighbor who witnessed the attack on Mr. Parish from his window and called for help. Helene, he said you turned around to face the man. And that he simply caught on fire. Do you recall doing anything that could have started the fire?"

My mother interrupted, "This is ridiculous. She was standing ten feet away from him. We didn't touch the man. And frankly, I don't give a damn what happened to him. As far as I'm concerned, he got exactly what he deserved."

The man doing the questioning was young, newly promoted to his position.

His face flushed brilliant red. "I'm sorry. I know this is hard and nobody is accusing Helene of anything. We are simply trying to understand it."

"If you don't mind, we have nothing more to add, and I have a funeral to plan," Lela snapped.

When the two officers left, I couldn't contain it anymore. I had to tell her.

"But I did have something to do with it," I said.

Lela hugged me. "No. You can't blame yourself for that horrible man's death. How could you have possibly done that?"

"But I did. I wished that he would die. And then he began to burn. I thought it and it happened."

My mother pulled away, rested her hands on my shoulders, and searched my face.

Usually, it was so hard to read her. But this time, I had taken her by surprise. I could feel her emotions.

She believed me. And it absolutely terrified her.

We never talked about this again. Even after the cause of death came back from the coroner's office as spontaneous combustion.

Lela died from advanced breast cancer. It was as if her grief, and all the things she held inside, eventually consumed her from the inside out.

I missed my parents. I missed Brian. I missed being able to fool myself that the world made sense and that I somehow fit into it.

I knew how much my parents had loved me.

But I also knew and had always known that they held back, that they were not really living the life they wanted to live.

There was a pretense they kept up, and a secret they held to tightly.

I had always wondered why I never met any other family members, not even my grandparents, and why there were no pictures of them.

And in sensing there was more to the story, something dark, I never dredged up the past.

If they were protecting me, hiding me from something, wasn't it safer not to know what that something was?

I didn't want to meet my real mother. I didn't want to hear anything she had to say, even if her letter had been somewhat cryptic.

I didn't want to find out that everything I had ever known about my family and my life was fiction.

I was just fine with the lies.

I heard the familiar SUV approach, slowing as it passed.

Had Amsel seen me sitting in the dark? Where was he going at this time of night?

I was disappointed that he hadn't stopped.

A part of me knew being in his arms would make everything feel better. But then I'd pretty much told him today to leave me alone.

It was past midnight when I finally stumbled to bed, but sleep didn't come.

Details of the lucid dream last night kept playing out along with the words from the letter.

To my own disgust, I found myself imagining what this woman looked like. What kind of life had she led after giving me up?

I was infuriated that I couldn't just let go of all of these questions.

She said my parents had risked so much. What had they risked, exactly?

The last time I had looked at the clock before waking up at 9:00 am had been 3:45 am, so I must have slept a little.

I brewed a pot of coffee and threw on some jeans and a sweater, relieved my headache was gone.

A walk in the woods was just what I needed to clear my mind.

I wound through the path slowly. Again, I noticed how completely silent this portion of the woodland was. Where were the birds, the insects?

I discovered another overgrown, but distinct trail which I was certain would connect to Amsel's property.

Half an hour later, I was proven to have been correct.

Far up the ridge, I recognized the stone wall which enclosed his back garden.

It was so familiar, exactly as it had been in my dream. I knew if I kept going, I'd eventually reach the bluff overlooking the mining pit.

A few minutes later, I caught sight of a smeared partial footprint, peeking out from under a thick covering of leaves.

The tread was clearly defined and I recognized it instantly.

It was identical to that on my own shoes. Obviously, the world was full people who wore the same brand. Any day-hiker could have made their way here.

But then I saw it, black plastic strewn a little higher up the steep side of the hill. I made my way toward it carefully, holding onto nearby trees to prevent myself from slipping.

It was a flashlight.

I studied it. The compartment that once housed batteries was cracked and empty. It had a silver label and a deep scratch in the shape of a hook, exactly like the one that had gone missing from my jacket.

I had been here. It wasn't a dream.

If it hadn't been a dream—if I hadn't hit my head on the nightstand—if I *was* here two days ago, then Amsel Richter had lied to me.

With trembling hands, I slipped the broken flashlight into the back pocket of my jeans.

I felt a dizzying imbalance overtake me.

Had Amsel come looking for me and found me injured here? Had he carried me back?

Why had he not confronted me about sneaking out in the middle of the night? Why make up an elaborate story about hitting my head on the nightstand?

The being I'd seen had a wingspan of at least ten feet across. It had pursued me through the darkness.

Had that thing meant to harm me?

And then there was the nature of the otherworldly lights.

A realization struck me hard and I seethed from the sting of this elaborate deception. Whatever it was, whatever was going on, Amsel knew about it.

For so long, I'd diluted myself down to a version of me that it was safe to be and had become numb in my life. Then the nightmares woke me up and drew me to Glenhaven.

All the synchronicities could not be ignored. I had the uncomfortable feeling that I was drawing closer to truths that would finally lay waste to Helene Parish.

But where this would lead, I shivered to think.

CHAPTER TEN

SADNESS THAT SQUEEZED MY HEART

For two weeks, nobody knew where Amsel Richter had gone or when he would return.

He hadn't tried to call me. There was no note left behind.

He'd simply slipped away into the night.

With so much time on my hands, I'd done little other than think about Amsel and stew over the mixed bag of unanswered questions he'd left me holding.

My anger with him had me breaking things. It had led to a nice sized hole in the bathroom wall that I would gladly pay to fix.

It had been worth it, a moment of release that made me instantly feel better.

I had cried myself a river. The sense of loss was as palpable as the sadness that squeezed my heart in wrenching pain.

Had I been just another conquest for him?

Had he disappeared to avoid being confronted with questions he didn't want to answer?

I'd already made up my mind. I didn't care how long I had to wait.

I wouldn't leave town until I'd had a chance to confront Amsel.

He would tell me the truth.

Then afterwards, he never had to worry about seeing me again.

Since the incident in the woods, I had been tormented by my memories of the shadowy being. The sounds of flapping wings were branded into the neurons in my brain.

The dark circles underneath my eyes drew many stares. I knew people were confused and curious about what had happened between me and Amsel.

The only person who did not avoid the topic, was Mary.

"I don't know what happened, but I'll just say this. Amsel has never been interested in anyone before. And I know you aren't thinking this is true right now...but he is a good man, with honorable intentions."

I rolled my eyes at the absurdity of it. He was a liar and a coward.

But I had nothing to gain by telling her this and spoiling her naïve notions about him.

Mary pressed her lips together into a firm, tight line, "That's it. Go home. Take a shower. When was the last time you washed your hair, Helene? Take a nap too. You have bags under your eyes the size of Texas. Then you drive over to Lester's and we'll all have a nice dinner tonight. Say around 7:00?"

Mary stomped to the back, not waiting for an answer as it had been more of stern order.

I had a feeling if I didn't show up, Mary would find me and drag me out by my hair.

Who knew what she was truly capable of?

She meant business and I did not have it in me to fight that battle.

She was right, though. I was pathetic. And I didn't smell so great.

I drove back to the cottage under the cloak of gloomy mist that refused to clear and that perfectly reflected my mood.

But instead of stopping, I continued up the hill and parked at the closed iron gate.

I admired its scrolling detail of vines and what looked like cranes, one on each side. The stone wall extended on either side of it, surrounding the property in its entirety.

Beyond, the house sat in silent and stoic darkness. And Amsel's vehicle was not parked in the driveway.

Finally, satisfied that he was not hiding out here, I climbed back in my car.

When I noticed that the road extended on past the house, I decided to follow it to see where it ended up.

I wasn't expecting the tiny cemetery or the massive stone mausoleum with its thick columns of white quartz that virtually disappeared into the folds of the fog.

As I drew closer, I saw that it also had a gargoyle crouching over the entrance to the tomb.

It stared down menacingly at those who would enter. Its wings fanned open as if ready to swoop down the instant it perceived a threat.

But it was different from the carved figures that I had seen on other buildings in the past. Its face was distinctly reptilian, right down to its vertical pupils and the scaled talons that gripped the edge of the ledge.

But it wasn't grotesque. There was something regal and wise about it.

Was the body of Amsel's father entombed here?

Nothing on the outside indicated the Richter family name.

And like the Richter house that felt so primordial, this creature too felt that it had been sitting in this place watching the years turn over for centuries.

At this thought, a chill swept through and the unshakable, persistent dread would not let go of me.

After a long shower, I slipped naked between the sheets and slept for two hours.

When I awoke, I felt better, but the heavy feeling was still there.

I prayed I could hold it together long enough to get through an intimate dinner with friends without collapsing in on myself.

Once I turned onto the long dirt driveway to Lester's farm, I caught sight of Carol Anne.

She had grown quite a lot since my last visit.

Her coat had lost some of its ultra-whiteness. She looked excited to see me, walking the length of the fence until I drove out of sight and approached the house.

From out of nowhere, Rogue appeared. He wagged his tail excitedly and licked my fingers as he followed me up the porch steps.

Lester met me at the door with a hug. "Good to see you. I knew our paths would cross again."

"I was wondering who was looking after Rogue."

"Yes. Amsel asked me to feed him and take care of him until he returned."

"Where is he, Lester?"

"That, he did not tell me. Only that he had an urgent matter that he needed to take care of.

Like urgently avoiding me until I finally gave up and went away.

I stepped inside, but Rogue refused to follow, backing away like a rambunctious child, as if being in a confined space was where he drew the line with his affections.

"What does Mary have on the menu for dinner?"

"Coq au vin. But Mary isn't cooking tonight. I am."

"It smells wonderful. Can I give you a hand with anything?"

"Would you mind getting the table ready? Mary always makes it look so beautiful but she got held up. Seems plumbing decided to back up at the diner, but she should be here soon."

"I don't mind. Just point me in the right direction."

Once the table was ready, I helped Lester with the salad.

"There is something different about you."

"According to Mary, I look like hell regurgitated these days."

Lester walked closer and looked into my eyes, "Helene, you're pregnant."

My eyes grew wide at this and I began to laugh, thinking it was a strange joke. "Ok. Would you call that dry or dark humor?"

"It's not a joke. You're pregnant." He said this so matter of fact, without a shade of doubt.

"Come on, Lester. It's impossible to look into someone's eyes and know something like that."

"You, of all people, understand that it is very possible."

"Trust me. Brian and I tried for years. I am barren. All the doctors agreed that I can't get pregnant." I dismissed this and turned my attention back to chopping a tomato, but Lester stayed my hand.

"The doctors were wrong, my dear."

The front door slammed shut and Mary's voice floated from the other room, "It smells like heaven in this house."

Lester placed a finger over his lips, then said, "I won't tell a soul."

That was fine with me because there was nothing to tell.

Mary bustled in and tried to take over, but Lester promptly shut her down, "This is my kitchen, missy. Go sit down. I bet you haven't done that all day."

She smiled and kissed him, "Fine, Mr. Crabby Pants."

Mary grabbed my arm and pulled me with her to the living room where we chatted until Lester brought out the food.

Everything was delicious. Lester was equally as good of a cook as Mary.

During dinner, I turned over the best way to broach the subject of what I saw in the woods. How did I bring it up without sounding insane?

"Have either of you given much thought to the strange lights over the mining area? Baron Fulton thinks it's just swamp gas, but I know that's wrong. It's something else."

In unison, they lowered their forks, and I could see on their faces that I had struck a nerve.

"You think there is something weird going on there too, don't you?" I asked.

Lester glanced at Mary before answering. There was a subtle nod from Mary.

"We have discussed the matter," he said.

"What's in there?"

"Trust me we have tried to find answers. But it's too dangerous to go down there. There is a terrible history to that area," Mary said.

"I know about the illnesses and the miners that died. I found the documents at city hall."

"Then you understand why it's best to let this go. It's probably exactly what people say it is, some kind of natural phenomenon, a gas of some kind leaking from the earth," Lester said.

"What if it isn't? What if those documents have been left there to keep people from getting too close and discovering what's really there?" I asked.

"And let's say you're correct, that there is something supernatural going on? What would be the good in getting close to a force that doesn't want you there?" Lester took a long gulp from his wine glass.

"Because maybe it's the reason we have all been drawn here."

He shrugged. "What then? What if knowing will only make our lives more complicated?"

"I saw something out there, Lester. Something that shouldn't exist."

You could have heard a feather drop in the heavy silence that fell over them.

"It chased me through the woods."

"What was it?" Mary asked.

"It was dark. And I wasn't sticking around for a closer look. But whatever it was, could fly, and the wingspan was ten, maybe twelve feet across."

"It could have been an owl or something," she said.

"Really? An owl? The size of a giant man?" I asked.

Lester and Mary exchanged glances.

I understood exactly how this sounded. If I were in their position, I'd be wondering if I had a screw loose too.

That's why I was surprised when Lester said, "We believe you, Helene."

"You do?"

Mary placed her hand over mine. "Honey, I've got a built-in lie detector. I know you saw what you said you saw. I know it scared the hell out of you."

All of the stress of the past two weeks came spilling out.

Mary was suddenly by my side. She wrapped her arms around me and I let myself enjoy the comfort of this support before sitting back and wiping the tears away.

"Promise us you won't go back in the woods alone," she said.

But I had never been alone, Amsel Richter had been there too.

But I didn't say this. For reasons I couldn't explain, I left Amsel's involvement out of the conversation.

"Ok. I won't go back alone."

"Mary is right. It will be safer if someone goes into the woods with you. Tomorrow, the two of us are going to retrace your steps that night and see if we can get some clarity around this."

I nodded. "Thank you, Lester."

"Now, on a happier note, who wants apple pie and ice cream?" Mary smiled.

There was a sense of relief after I'd told them, relief to not be alone in this. I was grateful to have friends to confide in, people who accepted me the way that I was and what I said without question.

I'd never had this before. It was as if I'd found my tribe, in the back country of Tennessee.

What I couldn't bring myself to share with them were the nightmares, the prophetic visions of the possible destruction of life as we knew it.

I was angry that my encounter with that thing had turned everything upside down and shaken me so. I had this irrational urge to track it down, to shake it with my bare hands until it was as terrified of me as I had been of it.

CHAPTER ELEVEN

RAYS OF A BLUE STAR

The next day, Lester met me just after dawn. The sky was completely clear, but the air was cold, still carrying the bone penetrating dampness.

I zipped up my jacket, knowing I would eventually have to tear it off once I got moving and it warmed up.

Lester led the way, slowly, meticulously, searching the trail for signs of the creature I'd seen.

Once we reached the spot where I'd recovered the flashlight, he stopped suddenly, held a hand outward, and closed his eyes.

I watched him, holding still and quiet as a church mouse. I knew that he was sensing things about the environment.

When he finally opened his eyes again, I asked him, "What are you picking up?"

"Energy. It doesn't just vanish. It gets recorded and stored, in the trees, in the soil, in the very plane we exist on. There was something here…something powerful.

Something that exists in our world, but also, in between our world."

"Like a spirit?"

"No. Something else. But not dark…not malicious. It was almost like…," he trailed off and shook his head.

"Almost like what?"

He laughed nervously and rubbed sweat off of his forehead. "Almost like the thing was protective of you. But you were afraid because it was unlike anything you've ever come across in our natural world. This winged being, was similar to us, with light and dark…some might call it a fallen angel."

"An angel? Aren't fallen angels supposed to be bad news?"

"But there is another way of looking at them. They were cast out of heaven, because they didn't follow God's orders. They were punished because of a mutiny. Does that mean they are all evil?"

I shrugged, "It's a rhetorical question. There is no way to know this."

"Humans have light and dark within them, but are capable of redemption. It's not so outlandish to think that such a being would be designed by our creator in a similar way. Listen, I'm not saying that's what we're dealing with here. I'm just saying it's not made of the same earth stuff that we are. It came from someplace else."

"And for whatever reason, one of these supernatural beings is chilling out in Glenhaven?"

Lester stared me straight in the eye, "Yes. That is what I'm saying."

"Then what does it want?"

"I think we may be dealing with some sort of portal here."

"How sure are you about what you're sensing?"

"I trust my intuition completely. I only hope that one day, you will be able to do the same. Trust what is in your heart, Helene. Not what is in your head."

It should have seemed like utter madness, standing in the woods pondering whether or not I'd brushed paths with a supernatural entity.

But it didn't seem mad at all.

It felt like the truth. And the outside world, the one where these things did not exist, felt like the lie.

Ahead of us, we could hear footsteps approaching and all at once, an extremely tall and attractive woman came around the bend.

She wore stylish boots, a pair of dark skinny jeans, and a blanket scarf tied like a shawl around her shoulders.

Her blonde hair was pulled up in a perfectly messy bun.

The woman, who looked like she could have stepped off the cover of a Ralph Lauren catalog, said, "Oh…hello there. You must be the Helene I'm hearing so much about." She held out her hand.

I took it, noticing how smooth and soft it was, a person who likely had never washed a dish in her life. "And you are?"

"Penelope Richter. Nice to meet you." Her accent was as strange as Amsel's and she had the same deep violet eyes.

"Likewise."

This time she addressed Lester, "I never pegged you as a hiker."

Lester's spine stiffened and he became more guarded, "Oh yes, Helene has turned me onto the benefits of nature bathing. I could say the same about you. I didn't think you ever left your office."

She laughed, "Obviously, it's because I have to get up ridiculously early to have any time at all for myself now that father has turned everything over to me."

She pointed to a sign that was posted on a tree up the hill.

Danger. Restricted Area. Hiking Is Prohibited

"Tread cautiously. Be mindful of the signs. This is not a safe area to be exploring in," she said.

"We would never dream of venturing anywhere dangerous. Yet you seem to have come from there without suffering any harm." There was a glint of humor in Lester's eyes that softened the accusation.

"I was only taking the back trail from Amsel's house. Just keeping an eye on things while he's away." Penelope turned her attention back to me. "Amsel has always been such a naughty boy. Who knows what kind of adventure he's off on now? Ever the playboy. Of course, I am tolerant of all of this. He can't help what is in his nature."

She smiled, but there was something lurking beneath the surface friendliness, something in her face, a self-confident arrogance that solicited feelings within me of being entirely inadequate.

I felt that it was calculated and wielded to achieve that very reaction.

And her familiarity with Amsel, insinuated a deeper level of intimacy that made me cringe.

"I must be going. So glad to finally meet you. I'm sure we are bound to run into each other again," she said.

"Yes." *But not if I see you first.*

The second she was out of earshot Lester rolled his eyes. "Shines like a diamond on the outside, as hard as one on the inside. Don't let her get into your head. She and Amsel couldn't be more different. She's been shamelessly throwing herself at him for years and he's had the good sense to steer clear."

"But they're cousins. Isn't that a bit taboo?"

"Only in modern times, but common among families of old money."

"Anyway, it doesn't matter. We've made no promises to each other. Frankly, I don't give a shit about what Amsel does."

Lester looked at me in a way that said he clearly didn't believe me.

The impact of Penelope's words left me winded, like an aluminum bat swung directly into my chest.

They only reinforced what Amsel had gone out of his way to demonstrate with his ghosting act, that I'd been little more than a shiny new toy to him.

I didn't at all like how much that hurt.

Amsel and Penelope had clearly been cut out of the same cloth. They deserved one another.

We continued on the back trail until we'd nearly reached the stone wall.

"Whatever it was you saw, it's not here now. We should go back."

"Come on, Lester! I know you want to find out as much as I do about what's down there."

"You're not wrong, Helene. I would like some answers. But if I do this, not a word to Mary. She'll be fit to kill."

"My lips are sealed. I promise."

"This is a dead end. What do you suggest?"

"It looks like the vegetation thins here, like it was once a trail. And the elevation changes are more gradual and not as steep. I say we go in that way."

Lester took off his hat and wiped away the sweat collecting above his eyebrows. Then he took a moment to examine the overgrown vines and foliage. "Alright. Let's do it."

We took our time, pausing occasionally to look for any signs of toxicity before moving on. When we reached the edge of the restricted area, Lester stopped abruptly, closed his eyes, and lowered his head.

"I feel it too," I said.

The vibrations around us were so intense, they made me light headed.

It was as if the air itself were saturated with an energy that held a density that was almost malleable.

I stepped back and the feeling instantly went away. I stepped forward again and the same sensation returned.

"It has a clear edge," I said.

Lester did as I had done, stepping back and then stepping forward many times while he analyzed the difference. "You're right. It's like in science fiction movies, when they talk about a force field. I think we are on the edge of one."

Even what we were able to perceive with our eyes, changed based on whether we were outside of the edge or inside of it.

Outside, it was as if the edges were smeared, like a painting that someone had accidentally brushed against while it was wet.

Inside, things stopped being distorted. They were sharp and clear, the colors more vivid. Even the light surrounding us became brighter, taking on a hue that made me feel as if I were bathing in the rays of a blue star.

"I think I was right on the money," Lester said. "This is crazy. But there is definitely a doorway here that connects this world to another one."

"Lester, a little while ago you told me a giant fallen angel might have chased me through the woods. How is this any crazier than that?"

"Well...when you put it like that, I guess it isn't."

Almost immediately, I felt my energy rapidly being siphoned away.

Part of me just wanted to charge ahead quickly, to find out what was waiting there, what was hidden there. But I was suddenly so exhausted, I wasn't sure I could push through whatever was happening to me to do that.

I could tell Lester was grappling with the same issue that I was. The field around us was impacting our bodies, buzzing at an extremely high frequency that neither of us was accustomed to.

"We shouldn't go any farther. Not until we've slept on this," I said.

"I agree. And not a peep to Mary about it."

Back at the cottage and alone with my thoughts, it wasn't Lester's outrageous theories of fallen angels or some kind of super highway to another dimension that plagued my thoughts, it was Amsel.

It was the feel of his naked body against mine, the depth of emotion in his eyes whenever he'd looked at me.

How could I have been so wrong about him?

But Penelope had cleared it all up for me.

After all, it did make sense. If he had cared for me even a little bit, he would have never run away.

CHAPTER TWELVE

A RANDOM ACT OF VIOLENCE

My period was late.

For someone who could set their watch to its arrival down to the minute, this was concerning. I had no choice but to try and find a pregnancy test.

And then there was also the matter of waking up for the past two days, barfing my brains out.

Could Lester have been right? Was I pregnant with Amsel Richter's child?

A part of me was joyous about the possibility of a tiny life growing inside of me. I had wanted a child for so long. All of those agonizing months when Brian and I had tried and failed, took their toll, until we finally let go of this hope altogether.

Life without the burden of ovulation cycles and scheduled intercourse that had become almost mechanical, was peaceful.

We accepted that it was just going to be me and him together, passing through quiet ordinary days.

Amsel was right. I felt safe in my marriage. I hid inside the details that Brian planned out so carefully, letting life ebb and flow, but it was only a dream.

It was inevitable that someday I would have to wake up.

When I'd first had a knowing about Brian's illness, I'd clung to him drenched in tears as he slept. Afterwards, I hadn't told him. I had convinced myself that I had to be wrong.

When the official diagnosis came, our hours were spent at the cancer center around other people suffering and trying to cope with the disease that had infiltrated their lives.

That's where I came to understand that cancer had a smell, one that only I seemed to be aware of. The foul odor that had begun to cling to Brian, clung to all of the patients we passed in its hallways.

I held on to guilt and regret. I'd known something was wrong, yet I had ignored what I knew.

It was my fault the cancer spread so far before it was detected.

It was my fault my father had died. If I'd acted sooner, he would have survived.

If I had talked things out with my mother, forced her to let me in instead of shutting me out after his death, she wouldn't have let grief eat away at her until she'd made herself sick.

What good was having abilities, or glimpses into the future, if we did nothing to change it?

Never again. I would never hesitate to act if there was even just a remote chance that I could change a disastrous outcome.

Considering his disappearing act, I couldn't imagine that Amsel would be happy about this pregnancy. He obviously wanted nothing else to do with me. But he needn't ever know. I was perfectly capable of raising a child on my own.

The pharmacy in town was small, but I was relieved to find a small selection of tests hanging on a wall near the register.

I was also equally relieved that I didn't know the young girl named Olivia who was more interested in singing along to the lyrics of a Taylor Swift song than paying attention to the items she rang up.

It was bright out. I pulled on my sunglasses as I stepped off of the sidewalk. Irene Houston paused from planting orange mums outside their store to wave.

I waved back, looking both ways before crossing toward her. Halfway, I saw the black SUV with tinted windows.

It was already on top of me. I didn't have time to react. Then I felt arms around me and I was swept out of harm's way.

James Houston stared down at me with relief, his hands still holding me tightly, "Are you alright?"

I was dizzy. It had all happened too quickly to process, "I think so."

Irene was beside us now, "Oh, my God! Damn, crazy tourists. I wish I'd gotten their plate number. You're shaking like a leaf. Let's get you inside for some hot tea."

I didn't argue. Once my adrenaline returned to normal, I turned to James, "Thank you! You saved my life today. I didn't see them."

He shook his head. "I did. Whoever it was pulled away from the curb and sped up the minute you stepped into the street."

"You're saying they targeted me?"

"That's exactly what I'm saying. I'll call Baron and give him a description of the vehicle. We should all be on high alert in case this person is still around.

Fulton came immediately. He took statements from us and spread the word around town to be on the lookout for a black Escalade with illegally tinted windows.

"Can you think of anyone who would want to hurt you? Forgive me for asking, Ms. Parish. But we don't know very much about you," he said.

I began to laugh at how absurd this was. "Trust me. Nobody would have any reason to harm me. Probably, just a distracted driver. I was in the wrong place at the wrong time."

I could tell the Sheriff did not believe this. In his world, random acts of violence did not occur. They were so insulated from the craziness of the outside world; it was much easier to believe that there was an ulterior motive behind what had happened.

I was more afraid of the results awaiting me from the plastic stick I had in my shopping bag.

"I'm fine. Really. You're making a bigger deal of this than it needs to be."

The Sheriff excused himself, "I'm going to make the rounds. Find out if anyone else saw anything. I'm glad you are alright."

I was embarrassed that such a fuss was being made over my carelessness.

"I haven't seen Mark in a while. Does this mean that he and Sadie have been seeing more of each other?"

Irene smiled, "He has always had a soft spot for her. It seems she just needed to fear losing him to a very attractive older woman to realize her true feelings for him."

"Oh...there was nothing between me and your son."

She patted me on the hand. "I know that. And I know that you did not abandon him. He told me how you helped him out against your better judgement."

"I still feel terrible about deceiving Sadie like that."

"Don't be. I have a feeling she is more than happy about how things have turned out. And to answer your question, yes. They have been joined at the hip these past days. We hardly see him anymore."

I enjoyed hanging out with Irene, but I knew she had things to do and I was keeping her from them.

I purchased a carton of milk and headed back to the cottage where I peed on the pregnancy stick, replaced the cover, and sat it on the bathroom sink.

When the timer went off, I paced around from room to room for an extra five minutes, trying to psyche myself up to face the results.

The irony was I'd never done a test like this before. Brian and I had never had a false alarm. There was never a moment when we thought I might be pregnant.

I never in a million years ever thought I'd be sitting on a toilet seat staring at a little line in a tiny plastic window.

Pregnant.

My eyes welled with tears. For something I'd hoped for, to come in such an unexpected way, was surreal. I stared at it for a long time, wondering if at any moment the line would fade away indicating a false positive.

This changed things a lot. How long could I remain in Glenhaven before I eventually had to start thinking about what I needed to do to get ready to raise this child.

I felt extremely fortunate that money would not be an issue, thanks to my inheritance. And right now, I wasn't even sure that I wanted to raise this child in Washington, not with all the memories there.

If things had been different between me and Amsel, I might even have considered staying in Glenhaven.

A sudden sadness settled over me at the thought of leaving here. I had an image in my mind of Amsel, lovingly holding this child in his arms, of me by his side, happy.

I couldn't contain these emotions. They spilled over and didn't stop, even when my eyes were red and swollen.

For the first time, I allowed myself to admit an awful, terrible truth. It was the reason I had been so bothered by Penelope's inference that she and her cousin had an exclusive bond and understanding that I could never be a part of.

I was in love with Amsel Richter.

CHAPTER THIRTEEN

SOMETHING HORRIBLY WRONG

I spent hours trying to track down an OB/GYN within a day's drive who was taking new patients.

Dr. Kelli Kramer was a new doctor within a larger practice which included more established physicians. It was a two-hour drive, and I'd taken the first available appointment.

When I'd dressed early this morning, I had been surprised to find that already, my pants no longer fit me. I threw on a beige jersey style dress and a pair of brown leather boots.

I would pick up a few maternity clothes while in town for my appointment.

I parked in front of the traditional looking brick office complex and took the elevator up to the third floor. I'd written the suite number on a piece of paper, 356.

A receptionist handed me a clip board with paperwork to complete and I was surprised at how many questions involved family history.

I wrote, ADOPTED, in big letters, as I had done so many times in the past. But this time it created worry. Was there something in that history that I needed to know, something in my genetics that could potentially threaten the well-being of the child I carried?

I thought of the letter my birth mother had sent me. Was its arrival divine timing?

I hadn't planned on granting a meeting to her, but perhaps that was foolish. She could answer questions about my family history.

This was information my child might someday need. I had to put the possibility of a meeting back on the table for that reason alone.

The waiting room was full. An extremely pregnant woman across the room entertained her two-year old daughter.

When she went in for her appointment, an older woman with medium length brown hair took over care of the child and began to read to her.

They looked so much alike, the same heart shaped lips, the same bright blue eyes. It was obvious she was the child's grandmother.

What had I taken from my own family? Did I have someone's dimples? Their hazel eyes? Did they have the same darkness inside of them?

Could they make terrible things happen with just a thought?

"Helene?" A nurse called me back and collected a urine sample. Then led me to the examining room where I was handed a paper robe and left alone to undress.

The doctor entered and introduced herself. I guessed she was in her early thirties.

"I see that you are a widow. How are you feeling about this pregnancy? Would it be safe to assume that this took you by surprise?"

I gave a slight laugh. "That would be the understatement of the century, doctor. But I guess I'm just more confused than anything. I was told I couldn't have children. I mean, I tried, with my late partner. I was told by one specialist that, 'my cervix was a hostile place where sperm went to die', unquote."

"Ouch. That was a terribly insensitive thing that was said to you, and obviously, they were totally wrong."

The doctor began the examination and gave me a quizzical look. "You are three months along."

"That's impossible. Three months ago, I wasn't even sexually active."

"Hmmm…let's do an ultrasound and get a better look at things."

The ultrasound revealed a tiny fetus. The doctor pointed out fully formed arms, legs, fingers, and toes.

"See the little hand opening and closing. Everything is indicating that you are around 15 weeks along."

How could the doctor be so wrong about how far along the pregnancy was?

She moved the wand over my belly before pausing to linger over the same area for several seconds.

"That's strange," she said.

Concern flashed across her face, wrinkling her forehead up as she stared intently at the screen.

"What?" This hesitation made me anxious. "It looks like there's a …," she began, then abruptly smiled. "It's nothing. I think there was just shadowing on the image. The baby turned and I can see that everything looks fine. Would you like to know the baby's sex?"

Did I want to know? I wasn't sure. If something went wrong, it would make it that much harder to let go.

"I don't think I'm ready for that just yet."

"I understand. You can let us know if you change your mind."

"Could there be a reason for the baby to be so much more developed than what is normal, a birth defect perhaps?"

"I don't see any indication that there is a problem. But we can do a Genetic Amniocentesis. That will give us more information."

Sensing the doctor's thoughts, I realized she truly believed I was mistaken about the time of conception.

Dr. Kramer explained the minimal risks of the procedure, but it was the only way we could get detailed information about the baby's DNA. I saw no way around this.

She cleansed my abdomen and inserted a thin needle. There was a slight pain, and the entire procedure lasted less than a minute.

The doctor patted my arm, "All over. There may be some mild cramping today and tomorrow. We'll contact you as soon as we get the results back."

For the rest of the office visit, my thoughts drifted far away, busy trying to comprehend what this all meant.

Time slipped by, over 15 minutes, as I lingered in the parking lot with the car running.

Something was horribly wrong.

I wiped the tears away. It would do no good, worrying over things I could not control. Whatever it was, I would face this challenge the same way I'd faced everything else that had happened in my life.

Even if there was a serious problem, I knew that abortion was not something I would ever consider for myself.

Where could Amsel have gone? And how long could I wait for him to return and provide me with the truth about what was really happening in Glenhaven?

I was angry that I missed the sound of his voice. I hated this weakness that caused me to long for his hands moving across my naked body.

My world was out of balance.

I felt the anxiety creep in. For love to have surprised me so quickly, and for Amsel's feelings for me to have disappeared just as suddenly, it was hard to reconcile the pain this loss had triggered.

When I had composed myself enough, I pulled into traffic and used GPS to locate a shopping mall. The department store was essentially empty at 11:00 am on a Wednesday.

I was surprised at how flattering and fashionable most of the maternity clothes were. A couple of pairs of jeans, some slacks, and several tops would do for now.

There was no need to go overboard before the test results came back.

At the register, I searched for my wallet and felt someone staring at me.

I turned to find the man in the seersucker suit that I'd seen on the street with Alexia.

Today, he wore a pale blue linen suit that was equally out of season. He looked at ease with his white hair falling in perfectly formed waves as he leaned against the glass jewelry counter of an adjacent aisle.

He nodded and smiled. His movements were marked with grace, like a gentleman from some bygone time.

I returned this gesture and looked away before my staring could become rude.

What were the odds of running into such a character twice?

When I looked back toward where the man had been, just like the day on the street, he had simply vanished.

"Did you see where that man in the blue suit went?" I asked.

The older saleswoman glanced up from placing the last of my items in a bag, "What man, dear?"

"Never mind. Thanks for your help." I took my shopping bag and made a thorough sweep of the store that confirmed he was no longer anywhere.

But I couldn't shake the nagging feeling that he was there because of me, that he had sought me out on purpose.

That's ridiculous and paranoid, Helene.

I put it down to my emotions being so raw and not having my normal, clear thinking.

153

Also, I was starving. I had thrown up my breakfast before I'd left the cottage.

The grilled chicken salad from the food court tasted like cardboard, but I forced myself to eat a third of it.

The entire mall was deserted, and I wondered how any of the stores could afford to keep the doors open.

Empires rose and empires fell, I guessed.

New technology made the old ways obsolete, and now people preferred to do their shopping from behind computer screens while lounging in their pajamas.

I remained there for a long time as if anchored to that spot. There was nothing for me to rush back to. I knew if I needed to talk, I could turn to Lester.

We had not spoken since our discovery in the clearing. Lester was extremely gifted in what he could see. Perhaps, he had gained more insight around what we had discovered.

On my way back to town, I would stop by the farm to visit Rogue and Carol Anne.

If nothing else, it just might help take my mind off of Amsel Richter for a little while.

Back at my car, I scanned the parking lot carefully. The feeling of being observed was so strong that goosebumps formed along my arms and on the back of my neck.

But there was nobody else around, and no place for anyone to observe me without me seeing them.

A light drizzle began to fall as grey clouds seized the sky.

Back to Glenhaven. Home, for now.

PART TWO

CHAPTER FOURTEEN

BEHIND THE VEIL

Absalom stepped back behind the veil.

He'd let her see him, briefly. Mostly, because it amused him to play these mind games with his targets.

He watched the woman searching for him when he was only mere inches away.

Even though she could not possibly have known that he was there, she sensed his presence and understood on an intuitive level that his being there was no coincidence.

Up close, he appreciated her beauty, the aristocratic shape of her nose, the streak of silver that ran down the length of her hair.

It surprised him. He'd only ever seen that color on the heads of ancient djinn.

She was intelligent, as they all were. She also was aware of her abilities, at least the ones that had opened up.

They weren't always this tuned in. But then considering the bloodline that she'd come from, was it really all that surprising?

An amalgam from such a powerful line had never been born. And this was even more reason to handle this situation as delicately as possible.

He gave Demetria credit where it was deserved. She had done well in keeping her daughter a secret for so many years, but Absalom had never trusted her.

Unfortunately for her, she forgot how persistent he could be when he'd caught the scent of deceit.

He'd always been in it for the long game. He knew it was inevitable that as some point, she would make a costly mistake.

Presenting evidence that a member of the royal family had sired a child with a human, a thing that was strictly forbidden and dealt with harshly by their own Order, could go either way.

For some djinn, this slip-up might even evoke sympathy, or worse yet, a willingness to look the other way instead of a trial and the death sentence this act deserved.

That was why he had taken great pains to insure against this possible outcome.

With her own brother willing to turn evidence against her in return for the crown, it was a win-win.

Demetria would be held accountable.

And with the easily manipulated Prince Bertrand installed on the throne, he would not have to worry about anyone challenging his actions, actions that were necessary if he were to succeed in the total annihilation of all amalgam.

He intercepted the letter long enough to read it before it reached the girl. It was such a gift, so fortunate in its span, he'd at first believed it to be a ruse.

Upon arriving in Glenhaven, he realized the magnitude of what had been revealed to him.

An entire town of amalgam, concealed under a cloaking spell.

As great of a discovery as this was, the wind fall was so much more substantial, he was still reeling from it.

The cloaking spell was obviously ancient, put there in the beginning by the first djinn to cross over.

There were fine cracks in it and intricate patterns of patchwork resulting from hundreds of thousands of years of repairs.

All this time, the portal had been hidden in the town.

Had it not been for the letter which led him there, who knows when, or even if he would have discovered it.

To learn the girl was pregnant, was most disappointing but also advantageous. It could provide useful leverage to hold over Amsel.

Of course, he would eventually have to kill her and her baby. It wasn't personal.

He took no joy in this carnage, but it was his duty to carry out. He did not hate humans, not really.

In fact, there was much he admired in the way they struggled in the face of insurmountable odds to carve meaning into their short, insignificant lives.

Though there were things he admired about humans, he was repulsed by more.

Especially, the damage they inflicted on one another with their delusions of superiority, holding themselves above their fellow man.

They could never see beyond the shell that the human soul resided in, that they were nonetheless, all the same inside of it, mere humans.

Human kind simply didn't matter to him. And he brushed the half-breeds off the planet, the way he brushed an ant from the sleeve of his jacket.

Djinnis defiling themselves with them, was all the more reason to take drastic measures.

With the portal reopened, unfortunately, they would not be able to withstand the blast of that much energy. The age of the Anthropocene would officially come to an end.

For Absalom, that could not happen soon enough.

Djinn would no longer be cut off from the dimension from which they came. They would be fully powerful, free to go home to where they belonged or to rebuild here if that is what they chose.

It would be the way it was in the beginning, at its genesis.

This new development required stealth and speed. It was best to deal with things before politics could get in the way. Act first. Ask forgiveness later.

But there was no reason to believe Amsel was aware that he'd been found out.

He'd waited all this time. He would take his time to gather his own trusted circle near. They needed to plan this carefully while they still held the element of surprise.

The most pressing matter was how to handle Amsel?

He had always been exemplary in his devotion to the Order. The last time Absalom had seen him was during World War II.

Always with these tribal battles humans insisted on fighting, there was so much destruction. Much of his work had been done for him during that time.

Wars were always the great equalizer, reducing populations with large percentages of amalgam included in those death tolls.

Amsel intervened on behalf of humankind far more than he should have. But then he always did spend too much time living among them.

This should have given him away.

All this time, he'd known about the portal, and with his well-respected family, had carried out the ultimate deception right under his nose.

Absalom had never even suspected a thing.

He laughed out loud. "Well, well. You've certainly outdone yourselves."

Now it was just a matter of finding out which djinn could be trusted in the final phase of his plan and which would have to be systematically taken out.

The Richters hadn't pulled this off without help. He would track down those who had taken part in this.

Absalom thought of a remote, white country house in the region of Puglia, Italy, and was at once strolling through an olive grove which ran adjacent to it.

He waited patiently for Sergi to join him.

A maid from a nearby town worked inside. There was no reason to alarm her by materializing out of nowhere.

"My dear, Absalom. To what do I owe the pleasure?"

Sergi was six foot four and as wide as a linebacker. Flowing waves of blonde hair fell below his shoulders. He wore the red robe of a Tibetan monk.

The odd appearance Sergi took on amongst the humans, amused Absalom. "Still playing the part of the guru, I see."

"It is the only guise which allows me to be even remotely authentic. Have you not benefited from my work?"

Sergi had handed over unknown numbers of his amalgam students throughout the centuries. Absalom did not doubt his loyalty.

Even so, he needed to make sure.

The iron band closed around Sergi's neck instantly, exposing him to the gravity of Earth. The dense weight of him came crashing down to his knees.

The bones of djinn were nothing like those of humans. Their frames on average, neared a ton. Without their magic, they were completely helpless in this dimension.

Iron was the only substance on earth that could neutralize their power and render them prone to the same spells that humans were vulnerable to.

Sergi's dark eyes glazed over, suddenly cold and calculating. Absalom had seen that look before whenever his friend had been pushed too far.

"What is the meaning of this?"

"Please, forgive me for this transgression. I've discovered traitors, and until I'm sure of all involved, I must be careful."

"The offense must be very grave indeed for you to risk this! Get to the point. Ask me what you will, and be done with this violation."

Absalom glanced back toward the house to make sure the nosy housekeeper was not in range to hear the conversation.

As an extra precaution, he put up a screen between them so that they would not be visible to her either.

He curved the fingers on both of his hands until the forefingers and thumbs were touching. Then he held one on either side of Sergi's temples, left palm facing upward and right palm down.

An entity, resembling a pale blue flame, leapt out of the right hand and entered the ensnared djinni's ear.

The spell Absalom had cast made it impossible for his oldest friend to lie.

"I found the portal, Sergi. It is being hidden from us. Hidden by our own kind."

"You've really found it?"

"I have indeed," he replied. "Were you aware of its concealment?"

"I know that the portal was said to be closed over an eon ago. And that its location has been forgotten. I know

161

that we have sought it millennium after millennium. I know that most of us began to doubt the old stories, or that it even existed, and only a small number of us still seek it. But this is all that I know."

"I've discovered there are djinn among us, guarding the portal, maintaining a cloaking spell to conceal it from our view. Did you know about this?"

"I most certainly did not. I have always been loyal to you. It hurts me that you would even think this of me." His hurt pride spawned a rush of rage and Sergi attempted unsuccessfully, to stand.

"The Richters are among the guilty."

At the sound of Absalom's words, he became deathly still. His eyes widened and there was disbelief in his voice, "Amsel?"

"Amalgam are being drawn to Richter land, Sergi. He's protecting them there."

"I did not know. But this makes no sense. He has been a hunter, working along-side our ranks."

"Although it was convincing, I do not believe he was ever working toward the same goal as we were."

Absalom watched the conflict play across Sergi's face with a sympathetic expression.

The two of them had been like brothers. Sergi's own father, Lord Benowin, had treated Amsel like a son.

"I imagine this must feel like a dagger in the back. Please, forgive me for the pun. How tasteless considering what happened to Lord Benowin. But this does call into question the nature of your father's death…," Absalom let his voice trail off, his implication clear.

"No. That's not possible. Amsel would have never betrayed my father. His death was an accident."

"Just like he would never conceal amalgam or the portal? The events of that day always failed to make sense. How were two excellent djinn swordsmen overtaken by a band of half-breeds? How was it they killed your father, a hunter, but left Amsel alive but encased in iron shackles. Were they not afraid he would seek revenge and come looking for them?"

"If what you say is true, there will be a terrible reckoning for Amsel at my hands. I did not take part in this and I have only been a loyal servant, defending the purity of our race."

Absalom flicked his right hand and when he did, all that he had learned in Glenhaven passed from him into Sergi's consciousness.

He held the upturned left palm close to Sergi and drew the blue flame out of him. At once, the iron casing fell away and evaporated into the air.

Sergi was once again free but he made no move to get up. Instead, he settled onto the hard dirt beneath an olive branch.

Absalom, satisfied Sergi was not going to take a swing at him, sat close to him and waited patiently for his friend to process everything he'd just been shown.

"There were times I was envious of the two of them. He was my father, but Amsel was like the favorite son, the one who lived up to his expectations. Was Amsel deceiving us all that time? Did he take my father's love and use it against him?"

"It's more likely that your father discovered the truth, which forced Amsel to kill him.

Sergi stared out at the landscape which stretched on for miles before meeting the sea.

"I will reduce him to nothing. Everything he's fought to accomplish will come crashing down on top of him. Everything he loves will be taken from him. Starting with the amalgam Helene and his unborn mongrel."

Absalom was satisfied he could trust Sergi. There was much to do and they would cover more ground separately.

"As for Demetria, we must not interfere with her plans. Assign a sentinel to her, but tell them to give her a wide berth. She must not notice that anything is amiss."

"It will be done immediately. I'll also begin screening the ranks and put a task force together. Greater numbers will allow us to move faster. It's only a matter of time before someone figures out that we are onto them."

"Whatever you must do, Sergi, you have my consent."

The two men shook hands before parting ways, understanding fully well that this was an act of treason.

Sergi understood he'd been given permission to act in any way he deemed necessary.

Even if that meant acting against the Royal House of Courtenay.

CHAPTER FIFTEEN

VERY OLD MAGIC

Amsel could have simply wished himself onto Whidbey Island and materialized there in an instant.

Instead, he chose to drive the entire way, taking his time, stopping at places he felt Helene had also been.

He had hoped that by putting this physical distance between himself and Helene, his feelings for her would dull.

If anything, it had made him burn for her even more, feeling her in the fissures of tiny towns, in the silence of miles, and in traveler-worn hotel rooms.

The role of love sick fool had never suited him. In matters of the heart, his level head often solicited accusations that he had ice coursing through his veins.

He was known among women of his kind for playing the field and having a heart as fickle as damp flint.

And he had certainly never sought intimacy with an amalgam. It was forbidden.

But the first moment he laid eyes on Helene, his loins raged with desire.

A reckless and all-consuming need to possess her took hold of him. And he had not been able to stop himself from pursuing her.

Helene was so like a pure djinni, it was unnerving.

The smell of her was like an exotic flower containing lethally potent levels of aphrodisiac.

Her eyes were like opals made of fire. He was sure they had cast a gossamer spell of seduction over him.

And when she had cried out during their lovemaking, her voice so hoarse with passion, it had nearly done him in.

He was lost to her, a slave to whatever she demanded.

There was clearly something very different about Helene Parish. And he needed to find out what that something was.

He parked the Land Rover at the end of a private street that should have been her primary address and scratched his head in confusion.

It was only an empty lot on the Puget Sound.

After he'd confirmed that this was indeed the right location, he climbed down the rocky hillside to the pebbly beach below.

Amsel allowed his eyes adjust to the half-light, scanning the area as cold saltwater sprayed his skin. There was no house to found.

The area was secluded but there was a well-established path that he hadn't spotted before. Maybe the area was used by locals who came here to enjoy the beach when the weather was good.

Why had Helene deliberately given a bad address?

He pondered this while walking back along that pathway and nearly broke his nose on a sliding glass door.

The house was there alright, invisible to his naked eyes.

It was very old cloaking magic.

Its similarities to the elaborate and highly sophisticated system in Glenhaven could not be ignored.

The one there was older than he could fathom and so virtually flawless that it only required occasional repairs that could be done by any half-wit with a little magical knowledge.

This shield, on the other hand, had been constructed very recently. It was designed to be imperceptible to full blooded djinn.

There wasn't even the slightest hum of magic that could alert them that there was anything of interest lurking here.

Did djinn still exist with the knowledge needed to weave such a spell?

The priestess class was all but extinct with what remained of it contained in the lineage of the Courtenay family.

But the Royal family and its Order of the Blue Orchid were responsible for killing off amalgam, not protecting them.

He concentrated and summoned a pair of spy glasses from his study. They appeared in his hands, their lenses made of quartz, completely clear and free of any occlusions.

They had been given to him by Pythagoras when he was still a pubescent djinni under his tutelage.

He slid them on and a modern style of house with its mostly glass walls and black metal framing came fully into view.

The spell was not being maintained. Already the fabric of it was beginning to fray and unravel.

On his second time circling the house, he discovered a gap large enough for him to squeeze through without triggering an alarm. He removed the glasses he no longer needed and wished them back home.

Memories floated around him, bursts of energy that had imprinted within that space in different moments of time. He realized that Helen had grown up in this house.

Scenes played out for him, her first steps, her first heartbreak, the loneliness she'd felt growing up, realizing she was different from everyone around her.

She'd always had visions. She was born this way.

There were photographs throughout the different rooms, the only proof she had left that any of what she remembered of that life had really happened.

He picked up a family photo. Helene was maybe nine. People Amsel knew were not her real parents stood behind her.

Lela Parish's strawberry blonde hair was cropped short, any longer and her small attractive features might have been overwhelmed by it. Her yellow sundress seemed to glow against a backdrop of intensely green shrubbery.

Harold looked appropriately middle class and tanned in his khaki pants and white polo shirt, his salt and pepper hair slightly thinner on top. He looked like a person who worked too hard, a person who worried a bit too much.

They had a single hand placed on each of Helene's shoulders. Her hair was without its silver then. Every bit of her screamed insolent youth as she rested her left foot on a soccer ball with an expression that said she was done with taking staged after game photos in her sweaty uniform and cleats.

These people were chosen to care for and protect Helene, but chosen by whom?

Upon closer inspection and judging from the age of the cloaking spell, it was probably put in place from the moment Helene was born.

And if he had to guess, there were likely varying degrees of spells woven over the entire island, spells with the sole purpose of concealing Helene from view.

Amsel thought of the piece of jade Helene often wore. He wouldn't have been surprised at all if that same someone had embedded a spell within it too.

Why would they decide it was no longer crucial to maintain them?

He had a hunch that Helene's adoptive parents had played a key role in that. After they both passed away, there was no one left behind to do it.

It wasn't uncommon for the beacon that was placed over Glenhaven to draw amalgam later in life. Their gifts had to be open in order for them to perceive it at all, and for some, it happened late, sometimes never at all.

But Helene had always had this capacity.

When the firewall began to fail, all the protections that had carefully been built around her and that were integrally tied, no longer functioned properly. And she finally began to feel the tug toward the town.

Amsel took his time sifting through old papers and any items he thought might harbor a clue as to who her real parents could be.

There was a safe hidden behind a wall of shelves in the master bedroom closet.

The button mechanism was well concealed, designed to look like a part of the trim on the built-in feature. If a person didn't know it was there and if they were not a djinni, it would never have been discovered.

He sensed Helene had never touched it. This meant she was unaware of its existence.

Amsel pressed and the entire wall pivoted to reveal a safe.

With ease Amsel sifted through memories associated with it until he could see the combination being keyed in, 10-14-09-28-11-55.

The safe held a wooden box carved from acacia wood. On the lid, a blue orchid, its petals formed with inlaid lapis lazuli and its stem, polished malachite.

He lifted the lid and could hardly believe what was inside.

He'd only seen another in his lifetime, in a museum. Of course, it had only been the box, and the humans displayed it without realizing they had found a genuine djinn signet box.

In the center of its interior, there had been an attached moveable piece that hung lopsided and looked a lot like a spinning top that had fallen onto its side.

The description displayed beneath had amused him.

This box was found in the ruins of a Turkish archaeological site and is around 12,000 years old. We believe it once housed a child's toy.

They had not even nicked the edge of truth with their sloppy guesswork. At one time, the box had housed a finely crafted ring.

Only old noble houses of direct royal descent possessed signet boxes such as this one.

The way the ring and the box were created to balance in such a way, was a closely guarded secret that prevented forgery.

If it was perfectly balanced, the signet was authentic. The stamp was applied in the presence of a currier who could check the authenticity of the crest before the message was delivered.

But in the modern age of man, this practice had lost favor and become obsolete.

This box, however, was not empty. A ring sat perfectly balanced atop the mechanism.

It was made of 24 karat gold. Along its band, many superb, blue diamonds sparkled, while the face of the ring took the shape of a shield with a delicate ribbon of eight pointed stars bordering its edge.

The X in the center was made up of crossed swords. In the upper quadrant of the X, a crane took flight, and in the bottom quadrant, a field of blue orchids sprouted from the ground.

It was the crest of the House of Courtenay.

As direct descendants of a priestess class, the women of the Courtenay family had always been more powerful than the men.

This was the reason they still ruled the in-between worlds with an unbroken linage of Courtenay queens.

No other djinn possessed their extraordinary gifts and for this reason, none would dare challenge them.

Lore held that they were master manipulators of matter, time, and of space. They were shapeshifters. They possessed secret magic. And it was said that they could bend other djinn to their will with no effort at all.

From time to time, he came across a publicity piece in some prominent magazine, touting the generosity of this family.

They straddled the two worlds with ease. To humans, they were merely great philanthropists from old money. They had no idea of the bloody campaigns going on right under their noses.

The Order of the Blue Orchid was steeped mostly in mystery, but its main purpose was upholding a strict moral code among the djinn.

This included the sanctioned killings of millions of innocent amalgam.

But Amsel knew the order intimately.

He'd been recruited by them as all young male members of prominent families were. To turn down such an invitation would have only attracted unwanted attention.

He'd served his mandatory term of three hundred years, the blip of an eye to a djinn. And then he'd walked away, with nightmares of the screams of victims still haunting him.

He'd done what he could to sabotage their efforts. That too came at a terrible cost.

This explained the elaborate efforts someone made to keep Helene hidden. An illegitimate amalgam royal would be scandalous.

But then why keep her alive at all? Why leave a ring that could prove without a doubt her connection to the Courtenay line?

It would not be good for this place to be discovered.

Amsel did what he could to patch the frayed part in the cloaking spell. After many hours, the hole was finally repaired, but for how long, he could not be certain.

Without knowing what else to do with it, he removed the box with the ring and sent it to a vault in Glenhaven. There, it would be safe from discovery.

Helene was a royal. And she had no idea what she was.

On a hunch he spent many days at the library searching through archived newspaper articles for anything unusual connected to Helene.

Amsel sensed there was something about her father's death that still haunted Helene, a secret she kept close to her.

The molten silver in her hair was unmistakably djinn and extremely rare. Amsel had never seen this, but among the ancient ones, it was said they had possessed hair like shining silver.

But after hundreds of thousands of years on Earth, the trait had all but faded away.

173

For it to appear suddenly on an amalgam, made him wonder. Had something happened to trigger a powerful ability to open up for her, something that had activated dormant djinn DNA?

He found an obituary for a Harold Parish. Sparse with detail, it mentioned that he had passed away in Farmington Connecticut and that he was survived by a wife and daughter.

But it did not list their names or the cause of death. If this was her father, he would have only been 48 years old at the time, much too young for a natural death.

And the date he died, March 13th, would have been Helene's 16th birthday.

He knew it was common for amalgam abilities to emerge at around 16 or 17 years of age. It was often what got them discovered and eventually killed.

But her mother must have known this, and would have had the savvy to make sure things were spun whichever way they needed to be to best shield Helene from danger.

He felt there was more to this death and kept looking for an occurrence that happened on March 13th of that year.

In a Farmington newspaper, in the crime section, there was a list of robberies, arrests for public intoxication, and a murder by stabbing at a train station.

In the same newspaper a week later, he found what he was looking for. Not even on the front page of the paper, which would have been expected considering how utterly bizarre it was.

On page three, the headline appeared.

Local Criminal Dies by Spontaneous Combustion.

The article was brief and did not do the sensational title justice.

A local man, Mr. Henry Waller of #916 Roman Way,
who had a long history of committing violent crimes, died after
assaulting another individual with a knife on March 13th. The
cause of his death was recorded as fire from unknown or unnatural
causes.

When we asked the Farmington Office of the Chief Medical
Examiner for further elaboration on whether this would
qualify as an incident of spontaneous combustion, we received this
statement, "Since the nature of the fire which caused Mr. Waller's
death was in itself spontaneous, technically that term could be
applied. But in cases such as these, a natural cause is eventually,
always found."

We reached out to members of Harold Parish's family. Mr. Parish
was the victim of the attack who later died from his injuries. The
two family members who were witnesses to the crime and who were
still in mourning, refused to comment.

 However, a neighbor who had witnessed the incident from his
window said, "After Henry Waller stabbed that poor man in
front of his family, he pulled out a gun and pointed it at the man's
wife and daughter. Then suddenly, he was engulfed in flames. It
was the darndest thing I ever did see." The neighbor did not wish
to have his name used.

The Farmington Police department said there is still an ongoing
investigation into the incident.

Amsel searched months, even years out, and never found another reference to this incident.

He was relieved.

This meant there was nothing else that would have caught the attention of the Order.

He did another inquiry into Henry Waller. It was a pseudonym.

The instant he saw the old mugshot, he knew the man was djinn. And the lowest common denominator at that, a bounty hunter.

They scoured the human world for amalgam that could be turned over in exchange for money and favors. Unlike members of the Order, they were never held accountable for their actions when innocents got in the way.

Amsel wondered what the going rate was for an innocent life these days?

Unfortunately for this hunter, he'd tracked the wrong one.

Her parents had probably thought the short trip would be harmless enough, when all that it had done was put Helene on his radar.

Helene witnessed the murder of her father. The trauma of the moment triggered a latent power within her.

Her rage became the fuel. Her thoughts became the weapon.

This kind of power was unheard of, even for full blooded djinn. Sure, djinn had the very common ability to bend matter, to make things materialize, to alter their own appearance.

But the ability to act upon the DNA of another with simply a thought, this was a whole other level.

It also strongly supported a link to the royal family.

Although, the current elderly queen, Queen Eleanor, had been rumored to possess mediocre magical ability at best and deemed by many to be almost feeble-minded now.

This led to wide speculation that her children might also lack significant powers.

Her unmarried daughter, Demetria, was next in line to the throne and only rarely left the United Kingdom Between.

Then there was Prince Bertrand, also unmarried and an absolute scoundrel. He was notoriously promiscuous. Considering his undisguised hatred for humans, it was unlikely that he would have put himself in a position to father a child with human blood.

But one never really knew the secrets of the bedroom, especially a royal one.

Amsel had an inkling that this power of Helene's was only the tip of the iceberg. What else did she hold within herself, completely unaware?

He had unwittingly drawn an agent of doom to Glenhaven, someone with the potential to destroy everything he and others swore to protect.

There was also the matter of her seeing him in his true form.

He'd done his best to wipe her memory but it hadn't been complete. It was not an easy thing to do on someone so strong willed.

His actions were undeniably selfish and unforgivable. They had exposed everyone in Glenhaven to grave danger.

But it was the thought of Helene falling into the hands of the Order that plunged him into the icy depths of a dark and primal fear.

There was no way around it, he had to seek out Lilian.

CHAPTER SIXTEEN

LILIAN

The hotel lobby was open to the outside. It brought all the years of traveling around the world with his mother back to him. Amsel sat on a wooden bench between two potted banana trees and waited for Lilian to return.

Last time he'd spoken to her was shortly after his father passed away. They'd been somewhere on the continent of Africa in a village struck down by sleeping sickness.

He'd been angry upon being informed he was needed in Glenhaven. He felt it was a waste of his skills when his mother was much better suited to the task.

"Why will you not budge? There are other ways I can better serve our cause."

"Because I'm needed here. You know how superstitious people are in this place. It's taken me three years to get them to trust me. I am able to treat them now, and soon I'll be able to teach other local healers. We still have to get a system in place for clean water before I can even begin to consider moving to another location. And you know better than I, my sudden disappearance would draw unwanted attention," Lilian said.

Amsel had known that she was right. As much as he resented the forces of darkness that had thrust him into this life, as much as he hated the Order for shattering his faith in the world and for stealing his freedom to chart his own course, he could not turn a blind eye to the injustices occurring.

He knew nobody would miss him if he suddenly went away for long periods of time. He'd always done this and it would not raise suspicion.

Still, he'd been angry and this resentment had not been so easy to let go of. But now, it was all water under the bridge.

Lilian waved to him from the doorway. Her pure white hair fell perfectly down to her back. She held a large brimmed hat in her hand, and aside from the smears of dirt on her linen shirt and khaki pants, there were no signs in her appearance that she had been working non-stop providing medical care out in the field.

To humans she appeared to be in her late sixties. Her passport said she was seventy-one. She was in fact over twelve thousand years old. It was hard to say exactly how old since she did not know her birth year.

Djinnis were not immortal. They could live up to fifteen thousand years if they took care of themselves, but just like humans they were prone to genetic illnesses which could alter their lives tremendously.

Amsel senior died of what can best be compared to cancer at the age of thirteen thousand and seven hundred years. Lilian and Amsel were still mourning his death.

Djinn were simply not suited for the vibrations and density of Earth. It took a significant toll on them. But before they crossed over from the world of blue fire and came to this plane, it was said they lived for hundreds of thousands of years.

On Earth, djinnis held unequal power over humans. Their gifts were magnified and were as individual as the swirling lines in a fingerprint.

Some were blessed with a combination of gifts and there were other rarer abilities. Although all djinnis were capable of manipulating matter and influencing others through magic and spells, not all did so.

They could bear offspring even toward the end of their lifespan. Most djinnis partnered for life, choosing to live out their days in secret, in the hidden spaces they carved out for themselves, never even meeting a human.

Some flitted back and forth between two separate worlds for reasons of commerce or for seedier pursuits. And then there were those like his own family, who had perfected the art of living among humans.

Lilian was not surprised to see her son. She had dreamed of returning to find him waiting for her, in the exact same spot, in this exact same way, and had scheduled her day accordingly.

Amsel hugged her.

"I've missed you, my son. Can I assume this means we are on speaking terms again?"

Amsel smiled, "I was unaware we weren't speaking."

"When one doesn't hear a peep from someone in over five years, that is not too big of a leap to make."

181

"I hope you can forgive me for the way we parted last. My resentments should not have been directed at you," Amsel said.

"Of course, don't be silly. We are not so different. We both have fiery dispositions that neither of us can help. And we have obligations to a cause we both wish did not exist."

"Father swore we were both cursed with rotten stubbornness."

Lilian smiled, "And how I do miss getting under his skin. He could be such an old curmudgeon at times."

She motioned to a patio area set up with couches, chairs, and dining tables, "Shall we? The quail here is divine."

Lilian captured the attention of a waiter who secured a table for them with an unobscured view of the Pacific Ocean.

"Are you well, Amsel? You seem troubled."

"I'm afraid I might have gone and stepped in something."

Amsel's steady gaze and solemn expression immediately, put Lilian on edge. She knew whatever it was that had brought her son to her, was indeed serious in nature.

"There's a woman who has been drawn to Glenhaven. She's—"

Lilian held up her hand to stop him. She glanced around before throwing up a shield that would give them complete privacy.

To anyone observing, they were simply engaged in pleasant conversation, but anything said could not be heard by either human or djinn.

She stared into him. Always, when his mother chose to, she saw far more than he liked for her to. "Please tell me you haven't gotten involved romantically with one of them."

"I've behaved recklessly, placing not only myself but everyone tied to us in danger. But she is different from the others, powerful, maybe even more than most pure djinn, and she is…" Amsel paused, wondering if there was a way to cushion the information, but he knew there was not. "She is a Courteney."

An incredulous gasp escaped from Lilian. "A royal. The offspring of our enemy. And you have become intimate with her. How do you know that she is not a spy?"

"She knows nothing of what she is. Someone has gone to great lengths to hide her."

"How do you know this, Amsel?"

"It will be easier if I show you." Amsel clasped Lilian's hand giving her access to everything he knew about Helene. He hoped he'd been successful in concealing the most intimate moments and the extent of his feelings.

"It was smart to keep the ring safe, it might be the only leverage we have if the shit hits the fan. Someone wants her alive, and they kept the ring as proof of who she is. Why?"

"Maybe they were using Helene against someone, as blackmail," Amsel said.

"Or maybe they truly do want to protect her and for her to take her place in the family at some point, when the circumstances are more favorable."

"Either scenario seems plausible. This could mean that certain sentiments have shifted, that a change is in the wind."

"Perhaps. But there is more," she said.

The tender sadness in his mother's face meant she'd seen something else, something that he hadn't.

"Amsel, my dear boy, you have no idea, do you? This is so much worse."

"What do you know?"

"Helene is pregnant. She's carrying your child."

CHAPTER SEVENTEEN

SWEET REVENGE

On the corner of Corrington St. and Liberty, sat a tiny little Craftsman house that had been converted into a business. The house, painted in midnight blue with white columns and trim, was the epitome of Southern charm.

Even the tasteful wooden sign hanging gave no indication there was anything remotely unusual going on inside.

Marie Luttrell
Intuitive Counselor

Thousands of people drove by each day without even noticing it was there. And if they did notice, they were likely in need of the services she provided.

Of course, they would have to wait quite a long time for that appointment to happen as her waiting list was backed up, last time she checked, over three years.

Every week, Monday-Friday from 9:00am-5:00pm, she sat in the cozy little office and listened to the problems of clients. Her only employee was an assistant named Courtney, who was naturally intuitive in her own right and was convinced Marie Luttrell was super-human, or more accurately, not human at all.

The job paid well and Courtney was content to go about pretending everything was perfectly normal and that she worked for a mere mortal of exceptional psychic ability.

Marie was willing to ignore what this employee knew as she was hands down the best assistant she had ever had. Also, she made damned near perfect, macadamia nut cookies.

Why risk a good thing?

Marie Luttrell was a djinni operating in plain sight at that same location since 1999. She knew when the clients began commenting on how young she looked and asking what her secret was, that it was time for her to move on.

She figured she had a good fifteen years left before that happened. Next time, maybe she'd settle in a colder climate, a place with some mountains. As much as she enjoyed being on the gulf coast, she hated the hurricane season and the tedious business of boarding up and waiting out storms, season after season.

At 5:25, her session with Mr. Delaney had gone over.

"Hold that thought, please excuse me just a moment," Marie said.

She stepped out to find Courtney re-straightening the pillows on the sofa and tidying up the magazines. Her short, bleached-blonde pixie hair and propensity to drop F bombs gave the impression of stubborn feistiness, but she was really a marshmallow of gooey empathy inside.

"You go on. No reason for you to stay late too."

Courtney grabbed her purse from underneath the antique Tudor desk she loved so much. She had numerous fantasies while sitting behind it.

Some days, she fancied herself as refined lady with ass length hair coiffed high atop her head, almost the exact same color as a scarlet ibis.

She knew this was not a color a lady's hair would be, but hey, it was her daydream.

She almost never was without a regal dress made from some excitingly dazzling color of embroidered French fabric. But on her feet, hidden beneath the fancy silks and for reasons she hadn't explored, she always wore steel toed combat boots.

She was a lady of many surprises and a constantly evolving wardrobe.

Some days that same lady lounged in her chemise undergarment while a sexy maid, with bosoms bursting from the low neckline of her black and white peasant dress, fed her sea salt caramels that were in the shape of the Venus de Milo.

Courtney would have been shocked if she'd known the desk had once belonged to Anne Boleyn, Queen of England. Or that Marie had just decided, the day after the poor woman was taken to the tower to await her execution, to take it.

Marie despised Jane Seymour. As far as she was concerned, that woman did not deserve such a beautiful piece of furniture.

Anne had not been perfect but Marie had liked her.

She justified the theft by telling herself that Jane was hardly going to have any time at all to write letters with that demon of a man trying to sire a male child with her.

Tonight, for reasons she could not explain, Courtney was reluctant to leave. Marie had to practically push her out the door and lock up behind her.

Courtney hesitated outside the closed door. She had the sudden urge to use her key to let herself back in.

Was the coffee maker still on? Had she forgotten to do something important?

Moments later, she decided everything was fine and shrugged. Marie always double checked these things anyway.

But once in her car, she found herself still loitering, unable to force herself to leave.

Mr. Delaney had been a client of Marie's for years. He was sweet as pecan pie with vanilla bean ice cream on top. No, that wasn't what was bothering her.

It was just a feeling, and if she'd learned anything in all these years of listening to Marie counsel people and give advice, it was to always listen to your gut.

So, Courtney honored this feeling and sat quietly in the alleyway behind her place of employment, choosing to do nothing until she felt all was right in the world again.

She leaned her head back against the headrest, closed her eyes, and took in deep breaths. In and out, in and out, deeper and deeper. Just a few minutes later, Courtney Lazar was sound asleep.

Inside, Wyatt Delaney wiped away tears. It was a good session. He had made so much progress from the suicidal wreck he'd been the first time he'd stepped through her door.

Marie smiled and handed him a Kleenex, "You did great. This was good today. You released a lot of traumas you've been holding onto."

Mr. Delaney was sexually and mentally abused as a child. The hardest case she'd ever worked on. Since he began with her, he'd met his soul mate, opened the business of his dreams, become the father of an adorably precocious little girl, and was able to be the good nurturing person his family needed him to be.

He was happy. Mostly.

Over the past year, she'd come close many times to releasing him from therapy. Today, his breakthrough left her without a doubt. He could manage his own emotions on his own. He really didn't need her anymore.

"Wyatt, you know what that means? You've won the bonus round."

He grinned, "Wow...and it only took me eight years."

"You can't tell anybody this, but you are by far my favorite client."

He laughed out loud. "Of course, I am."

"Are you ready for your prize?"

"I'm ready. Let's do this," he said.

"Close your eyes."

The man closed his eyes and Marie Luttrell transformed. She was no longer the attractive, five foot three, raven haired woman, he'd known.

Her glasses were gone. She didn't actually need them to see but they completed the look of the studious professional. She grew two feet in height. Her skin became as smooth and as dark as obsidian. Her wings unfolded, forcing her to tuck them ever so slightly just to fit inside the tiny room.

But in this form, she could truly give him the gift he deserved. Sweet revenge.

When she clasped his arms, they traveled in the astral realm. They were invisible to all but were nonetheless, present.

They arrived at their destination and he was prompted to open his eyes, but he did not notice the jarring transformation his therapist had taken. His attention was focused on the building in front of him.

Beads of sweat broke out on his forehead, and his pulse quickened until every heartbeat rang in his ears like a tribal drum.

"Do you recognize this place?" Marie asked.

"It's...the apartment...he used to...how did you...," Wyatt turned for the first time and calmly took in the djinni's true form without flinching. "Are we really here?"

"Yes and no. Our real bodies are back in my office. But we are here in the astral plane. He still lives here, you know. Released from prison seven years ago."

Wyatt covered his face with his hands, throwing everything into darkness, blocking out the outline of the

190

building that had filled him with absolute terror and dread as a child.

All those feelings came rushing in. He was surprised by how raw they still were. Maybe Marie was wrong and he hadn't healed at all. Maybe these things were just buried very deeply, hiding inside of him.

It felt like a dream. He realized he was holding his breath and forced himself to take several deep breaths. Once his brain was oxygenated again, his heartbeat slowed.

He remembered all of the techniques his therapist had taught him. He remembered that he had to face the pain, feel this pain, in order to heal it, once and for all.

Finally, he uncovered his face. He was still back in his home town in Minnesota, and the enormous djinni was still by his side. "Why did you bring me here?"

"I thought I would offer you a choice. You see, you can do anything in this form that you choose to do. I will not judge you for it. And you will not remember anything of what you have done."

Wyatt stared up at a second-floor window and clasped his hands together, mostly to stop them from trembling.

"Are you ready to go inside?"

He nodded and they were inside a shabby apartment. The curtains and walls had yellowed from tobacco smoke. There were rips in the sofa where the foam, covered in brown ripples of water-stains, bulged out.

An elderly gentleman sat on it. The man was extremely thin and frail. He held a cigarette to his mouth, sucking in nicotine and all the other toxic ingredients in between his coughing fits.

191

With an empty expression, Wyatt moved closer to him. As a child, he had feared him. This man had been his little league coach, a position of trust that he used to gain access to young boys.

Wyatt's already abusive home life just made it that much easier for him to swoop in like a savior. But he wasn't that at all. He was the worst kind of evil.

"I can't believe this pathetic person has been the source of so much pain and fear for me."

"Hurt people hurt others. This man suffered abuse from a family friend. His family knew and did nothing. He's had the worst kind of life, and there is no one who loves this man."

"Does he regret what he's done?" Wyatt asked.

"I wish I could tell you that he does, but it would be a lie."

The djinni tapped the old man's head, which caused him to look up from the television and rub the place in confusion. "It's a cesspool in there. If he were physically able to do it again, he would. Fortunately, things have stopped working down there."

"If I killed him, I wouldn't remember anything?"

"Nope, and there would be no consequence for you. They'll find his body, the old stash of child pornography in the back of the closet, and they will secretly be relieved he's dead."

The tears began to roll down Wyatt Delaney's face.

His voice rose an octave or two. It was laced with a breathy frustration and anger that spilled out, as if he were vomiting up the last of these vile memories and the power they held over him, "You said I can do anything. Can I transfer my memories, everything he ever did to me, all my pain, all my terror, to him? Can I make it play in his mind like a repeating loop until the day that he dies?"

"I know that's what it's been like for you all these years. You can do that if you choose. Is that what you would like to do?"

Wyatt didn't answer right away and instead walked through all the rooms in the tiny apartment. He took in the rips in the carpet, the deeply ingrained stains in the porcelain tub, the overall filth, that he realized was merely an outward reflection of this man's inner world.

"Yes. That is what I would like to do," he said.

"Then it is done."

The djinni smiled and took his hand, surprised when he did not flinch or draw away in fear, "You're a strange one, Wyatt Delaney. I will miss our talks."

She placed his hand on the top of the pedophile's head with her much larger hand on top. The pain spilled out of Wyatt and into the old man, a never-ending stream that would flow through him, until the last beat of his wicked old heart.

All that would be left behind for Wyatt was a tiny seed. He would never lose another night's sleep or wake up from a nightmare with that man's face in it. He would never shed another tear about it.

His world would go on richer and fuller, and he would harbor no guilt for the actions he'd taken.

It was done.

Back in the office, Wyatt opened his eyes and stared up at Marie Luttrell, expectantly. He had no memory of Marie in her true form or of anything that had happened.

"Here you go. Your prize."

Wyatt took the card and studied it. The front was stamped with a pair of golden wings. On the back, it read,

It has been an honor to work with you. Your tenacious spirit will guide you in all that you do. You have earned your wings, so fly with grace. But should you ever need me, this card will show you exactly what to do.

"This is both sweet and cryptic. You're cutting me loose?"

"Yes. Not everyone gets one of those, you know. You should feel proud to make it into such an exclusive group."

This was not just lip service. In the fifty years she'd been a practicing therapist, she'd only given away nine of those. The card could never be lost. It was as good as a contract, and should he ever need her, it would appear, and he would understand what he needed to do.

The man stood up. He was short, stalky, and slightly pudgy, but he had the kindest brown eyes, older and wiser than his thirty something years. His skin reminded her of caramelized honey.

He wore his dark hair a little longer than what was normal, mostly because of his deep aboriginal roots on his mother's side.

His family had done financially well in the States, but they would always have that ancestral connection which tied them to a greater wisdom. Marie knew this was part of the reason he was so unique.

Instead of shaking her hand, he wrapped his arms around her, squeezing tightly, "Thank you, Marie, for saving my life."

It was bitter sweet for her, and she only wished she could lose more clients in this exact same way.

With Wyatt gone, she did her usual last-minute check of things before commanding her car to come and pick her up. Then she drummed her fingers impatiently against her thighs.

She would never get used to waiting for things to happen in human time, especially, when there was a porterhouse at Finnegan's with her name on it and maybe a glass of 35year-old scotch to drink in celebration.

If she hadn't been floating on cloud nine, she might have noticed that a member of the Order had been stationed a block away for the last hour, biding time until she was alone.

And she might have made a discreet exit while time remained to do so. By the time she sensed the agent of the court, it was too late.

The djinni stepped through the wall, blindsiding Marie. She immediately recognized the blue orchid lapel pin. He wreaked of old money and entitlement. It was hard to find two things that disgusted her more.

Something somewhere must have gone terribly wrong for them to be standing in her client waiting room.

The shackle locked around her instantly, and she fell to her knees.

"Is this about the speeding ticket?" she asked.

He laughed heartily. "That's good. It's nice when people have a sense of humor about things. Makes my job much easier."

Knights these days were hardly distinguishable from your run-of-the-mill high-powered attorney. This one was of a higher rank, but part of the goon squad. They did whatever someone at the top told them to do without question.

He unbuttoned the top button of his silk shirt and sat down on the sofa.

Soon another suit joined him, of an even lower rank, and younger. Marie knew this one had fought his way into the organization through pure grit. He lacked the self-importance that the noble class always possessed.

The first knight checked his watch. He was purposefully unremarkable. The kind of face you instantly, forgot, "Glad you could make it. Is that a mocha latte? You stopped for coffee? Really?"

"I was thirsty."

"Thirsty? What are you, a fucking baby? Put the coffee down. Did you get a pedicure too?"

The second knight was embarrassed and sat the coffee on Courtney's desk before closing all the plantation shutters in the front lobby.

He was equally unremarkable in appearance, but looked friendlier, the kind of a person who would give you a lift if you were stranded in the middle of nowhere. This was entirely deceptive, of course. He was a vicious killer, just like his cohort.

The older djinni leaned forward and cast a spell sending the blue flame into Marie's head without her so much as flinching.

"You're very calm. Are you not concerned about why we are here?" he asked."

"Should I be?" Marie sounded extremely bored.

He started laughing again, and the younger djinni, an obvious, yes man out of necessity, followed suit.

"She's funny, right?" he asked, looking over as his partner snuck a sip from his paper coffee cup. "If you touch that again, I'm going to take your fucking hand off."

This time the younger djinni snapped his fingers making it completely disappear.

"We must seem unprofessional. I apologize for my colleague. And to answer your question, yes. You should be extremely worried. Recent routine questioning has brought up some interesting information about you, Marie."

Marie was worried. Extremely. The cogs in her brain spun at hyper speed. What did they know? Had she been compromised? Had others been too?

He reached into the breast pocket of his suit jacket and produced a polaroid photograph which he held at eye level, six inches from Marie's face.

An involuntary gasp escaped from her.

She recognized the bloodied body of the djinni. His body split wide, his organs spilling out of the open wound.

In death, the victim of this grotesque act of violence stared back at her, eyes still wide open. "Mabis…," she whispered.

"He told us you two had a long history."

Marie felt nauseated. A dark and vicious anger boiled under the surface, but none of this was apparent to the two djinnis who'd been sent to question her.

"We were married. I haven't seen my ex-husband in nine hundred years. He was a scholar, more interested in his research than me, I'm afraid. I would not think anything he could have done worthy of this kind of treatment."

"Can't you, though?"

He leaned in close to Marie and stared into her eyes with cold calculation. She imagined he could hear her thoughts. It was all she could do to think clearly.

She stared back at him, trying to discern if he truly knew anything, or if he was simply fishing. That's when she realized that he knew everything.

Marie controlled the shaking as best she could and kept her voice calm, "I cannot. Certainly, not anything the person I knew back then could have done."

"You didn't know he was hiding amalgam?"

"What? No, of course not. That is very disappointing news."

"I guess I don't understand what you get out of this, working with them?"

"Them?"

"Humans. You don't think this is beneath you?" He made a sweeping motion with his hand as he glanced around the room.

"This is the way I give back. Some of us weren't born into noble causes. Some of us have to find our own. Have I not handed over enough of them to the Order to prove my allegiance?" she asked.

He held open his right hand and the other knight placed a folder in it, "See. That's just it. Something didn't feel right. And I went through your file over and over again. Then…I saw it."

"Saw what, exactly?"

"Well, they were all seriously flawed in some way. A lot of serial killers and the terminally diseased," he said.

"Are you really complaining because my contributions weren't healthy enough?"

His expression changed and the easygoing façade slipped away. His eyes became like orbs of liquid steel.

He unsheathed a sword. Marie recognized it as being forged of a meteor, the only type of blade that could butterfly a djinni in a second flat.

"Now, that's the kind of arrogant tone, I will not abide. You will tell me the truth, Marie Luttrell, and I had better like your answer. Have you conspired with others to hide amalgam and defy the Order of the Blue Orchid?"

"I have not."

The younger djinni stepped forward reluctantly. "I think she's lying."

"She can't lie. She's neutralized with iron and under a spell."

He persisted, "I know she's not supposed to be able to lie, but I'm telling you that she is."

Mere seconds passed as the two djinni pondered this possibility. If the spells weren't working, Marie Luttrell had not been neutralized at all.

Realization cast its shadow upon their faces as both men understood the predicament that they were in. But then the iron maidens closed around them. They were trapped. Completely immobile.

The men cried out when sharp spikes penetrated the layers of fat and muscle in their thighs.

She'd removed most of the spikes. That way they would not penetrate vital organs. She'd adapted them to allow for the slowest and most agonizing suffering.

Also, she didn't want anyone dying on her before she could get what information she needed from them.

Marie stood up, cast off the shackles, and stretched. "Finally, I get to use these things. You don't know how many years I've been lugging them around. Bought them at an estate sale for a song."

She changed form, towering over the men.

"You look a little stunned. Let me explain," she said. "You see, I came from the wrong side of the tracks, entirely insignificant within the caste system of the djinn world. Back then I was a slave. My master was a vicious djinni. Bastard kept me shackled for a thousand years."

Marie picked up the sword from where it had fallen on the hardwood floor. "Then one day, he left me for dead in the street. A beautiful golden light brought me back to life. It moved through me and I became part of it. It was a miracle that I can't explain. Luckily for me, ever since that day in Sumer, I've been immune to iron."

She paused long enough to consider the way the light glistened and bounced off of the hilt she held in her hand.

"You asked why it is that I help them. Because I love them. Because I have no desire to interfere in the freewill of humankind. I am not the higher power on this earth. And neither are you."

The younger djinni did not see the blade until it was impaled into his forehead.

He contemplated the elaborate scroll work forged on its surface. He'd never really looked at it before, normally, only handling it long enough to wash off the blood. What a splendid thing! This was his last thought before he died.

The older djinni screamed out in horror. Never would he have guessed when he kissed his wife goodbye yesterday that it would be the last time.

Marie's stomach growled, "Excuse me. I didn't eat lunch."

She pulled the sword out, unconcerned with the blood she'd splattered all over the ceiling. "You killed my ex-husband. Now, I'm going to find your wife and I'm going to kill her too. And I'm going to make sure she knows it's all your fault."

The older djinni closed his eyes, but not fast enough. Marie watched the teardrop escape and roll down his cheek. Of course, Marie would never hunt down and harm an innocent person, but he did not know this.

"What did Mabis tell you?"

"He told us he'd been working behind the scenes for years, monitoring them from afar, crafting spell work to cover their scents, and when necessary, hiding them with the help of a small well-organized network."

"What other names did Mabis give up?"

The djinni's voice shook and Marie almost felt sorry for him. "Alton Harringford, Conway Spizzeri, The Richters. Those were the only ones he said he knew."

"Who else knows this?" Marie asked.

"I don't know."

The room was smaller than average, and it was difficult remaining in this space for very long in this form. It was even more difficult to contain her anger and to not immediately, hack him into tiny little pieces.

She needed information, and she needed it fast.

Marie frowned and sliced off an ear. "What do you mean, you don't know? Who did you give that information to?"

Through his shrill screams, he managed, "I don't know…I don't know…I was told to seal everything and send it by messenger to a drop box in the United Kingdom Between. It was to be left at the palace guard house."

"Have you told me everything you know about this mission?"

"I have," he said.

"Is there anything you would like me to tell your wife?"

He gazed at her with horrible, desperate pleading in his eyes. It was heartbreaking, really. "Please! Don't!"

Marie opened the iron maiden releasing a tsunami of blood as the spikes exited his body, but he was still bound with thick iron bands around his ankles and wrists. Ever so slowly she slid the sword from groin to neck. The djinni was dead by the time she had reached his rib cage.

"I really am sorry I had to do that," she said. "You just picked the wrong side."

Marie quickly shifted back into her human form and turned her attention to the crisis at hand. She had to try to intersect those messages. She had to warn all the djinn whose names had been given up.

She had to disappear.

Marie Luttrell climbed into the sleek red sports car that was still idling outside, waiting for her, and drove to the back alley where Courtney snored loudly. She tapped on the driver's side window.

Her assistant wiped sleep drool from her mouth and looked at the clock on her dashboard. She felt a little foolish to have fallen asleep, but the feeling of impending doom was gone. She rolled down the glass that reflected the image of a lonely streetlamp.

"Something unexpected has happened. I'm afraid we're going to have to relocate." It was not up for debate. There was no way she was leaving the best assistant she'd ever had behind.

"What?" Courtney was barely awake and this made absolutely no sense to her.

"I don't have time to explain any of this. I need you to get in the car, and I need you to trust me."

Courtney did trust her. Unconditionally. With a shrug, she grabbed her sweater and purse, and slid into the passenger seat.

With a flick of Marie's wrist, the house crumpled up like a piece of paper and went poof. Courtney watched this happen with a wry expression on her face. It was not even remotely, shocking to her.

She looked back at Marie and in the flattest, most dead pan voice, said, "I'm fucking starving."

Marie shook her head. "You're always starving."

They drove into the night, and as they did, not a trace of them remained. Nobody would remember that they'd ever been there at all.

CHAPTER EIGHTEEN

THE WHEELS OF BETRAYAL

Demetria was surprised to hear the knock on her chamber door at a quarter past midnight.

She was still up. Royal business was never ending, and with ironing out the finishing details of her upcoming trip to the human world, much was left to do.

It was a tour the Queen normally did, every ten years like clockwork. But her mother was far too fragile for that now. For all intents and purposes, Demetria was now in charge.

She signed the last document in her pile, "Come in."

Sir Langdon, head of the Queen's guard and her trusted advisor, entered and bowed before her.

Like the royals and those who moved back and forth between dealings with mortals and djinn, he had grown most comfortable in his human form.

Demetria had no idea how old he was, having served many generations of queens in their lineage. She didn't even know what color his hair was since he kept his head shaved off. This only made his prominent, fleshy nose even more so. But this was a common feature among djinn men.

His forgettable face allowed him to blend into the ranks of his men all too well, many times lingering unknown amongst them just so that he could absorb juicy, tabloid worthy gossip.

Unfortunately, he did not always aim this talent in the right direction. He had missed lot.

Demetria did not fault him, exactly. Things had become lax under her mother's reign. A false sense of security had edged its way in and allowed the Order to have far too much freedom for her liking.

She knew things that Sir Langdon did not. She knew things that others would be concerned to know that she knew. There was a strong advantage in being underestimated.

Demetria stared into his most outstanding features, his eyes, eyes that appeared almost lilac when he stood in the sun. There was a hardness in them which hinted at the plethora of misfortunes he would gladly deal out to anyone who chose to cross him.

Tonight, there was also a heavy sadness in them that alarmed her, "Your Highness, It's Queen Eleanor…I'm afraid she has died suddenly. The physician was called in, but it was too late."

"Died. Mother is dead? What happened?" Demetria felt a gnawing in her gut, the feeling she always got when things were off.

"It is believed that her heart gave out. I'm so sorry. This saddens me. I did love her greatly."

According to all the healers that they had brought in as of late and all of the elaborate tests they had conducted, Eleanor's heart had been the healthiest thing about her.

Demetria felt her features turn to stone, a stoic mask she had trained since birth to perfect. She turned off her emotions to deal with the task at hand. This was the way it had always been.

Family and personal needs were secondary to managing a kingdom.

"I would like to see her," she said.

"Of course."

Demetria charged down the massive palace halls with Sir Langdon trailing behind, until she'd reached her mother's bedside.

Someone had brushed the elderly djinni's hair in a way that it cascaded over her pillow, shimmering like a shiny copper coin as it bounced off candlelight.

She touched her mother's cheek, cold beneath her fingers and serene as if she'd simply died in a state of deep, peaceful sleep.

Her mask instantly fell away and the tears came.

Demetria did not bother to conceal them. She did not care that Sir Langdon observed this from a corner of the room.

This was her mother. She had been deeply flawed. Her heart had been as unmovable as a Mesolithic stone cemented into place by layers of time. But Demetria had loved her.

From her, Demetria had inherited her impressive height, green eyes, her striking aristocratic features, and her full figured, stunning beauty.

The only things she had gained from her father, King Phillip, were the deep auburn hair that she usually wore secured in an elaborate chignon, a strong intellect that she never flaunted, and her kindness.

Demetria allowed herself a few minutes of stillness to grieve for Eleanor. Then she wiped away the wetness and composed herself. Carefully and stealthily, she perused her mother's body for any signs of a struggle.

On both wrists, there were ever faint bruises, in the exact location a thumb would have made contact if another had held them down.

She was positive she had caught the whiff of the slightest lingering residue of magic.

"Did my mother have any visitors last evening?"

Sir Langdon retrieved the log book and slid his finger down the list of names, "Prince Bertrand dined with her in her room. Also, Lord Sergi of House of Benowin stopped by to pay his respects."

Demetria felt a shudder pass through her. Sergi, was more a butcher than he was a Lord. In league with Absalom, they were together, hazards she had been maneuvering around for a very long time.

And Bertrand. He just wanted the throne.

Demetria perceived each of them to be her enemies, enemies that had grown bolder in the shadow of Queen Eleanor's ruthlessness and petty cruelty.

It was no wonder that Bertrand turned out the way he had. And who knows, if her father, the late King Phillip, had not spent so much time showering her with his kindness and attention, if she had not been such a daddy's girl, she might have turned out equally deplorable.

But were they so emboldened that they would commit an outright act of treason against the crown? Or did they know something, something that could be used against her?

The letter had been risky. But she had been so careful.

Demetria inserted herself in front of the window that faced out toward her mother's favorite garden. In the darkness it was backlit with lightbulbs that emitted a warm magical glow that reminded her of fireflies trapped inside mason jars.

"Could you please tell the gardeners to prune the roses? I'm afraid they have been greatly neglected since my mother fell ill. She did love them so. 'Red as blood, my favorite color,' she would say."

"Of course. Right away."

"And, Sir Langdon, schedule my coronation at first dawn. Notify my brother of this, but keep him under surveillance and restrict him to his quarters. Should he not comply, place him discreetly under palace guard."

Sir Langdon moved to be by her side, "As you wish. May I ask why the sudden break in protocol and the reason for rushing the coronation ceremony?"

"I'm afraid I can take no chances. Prince Bertrand has not hidden his criticisms of me. And I am afraid my mother's death was not of natural causes."

"Are you implying that your brother could have murdered his own mother?"

"I cannot say that he is as ruthless as that. But I also cannot be certain that he would not turn a blind eye to it, if something was promised to him. It is her other visitor that I am most concerned about."

Demetria turned to observe him.

He was clearly taken aback, understanding his new queen had knowledge she wasn't yet willing to share, but only said, "Very well. It will be difficult on such short notice, but not impossible. I will make the necessary arrangements. Also, I will quietly order an autopsy to be conducted within the hour."

"Be discreet about that. Let us bring someone from the outside to perform it, someone with no links to the Order of the Blue Orchid."

He turned to leave, but Demetria stopped him, "Could you also make sure that a car is ready for after tomorrow's festivities. I am going to take some time away to properly grieve."

"Yes, your Highness."

Sir Langford slipped out quietly and Demetria turned back to stare out at the garden.

Demetria knew it had been her brother who had informed Absalom of her pregnancy. That betrayal marked the moment Demetria realized the measures he would sink to in his bid for power.

Bertrand had always resented the matriarchal line of succession, and actively sought to undermine her at every chance. But he had no idea how transparent his ambitions were to her.

Demetria had lied to him. She told him the infant had died when in fact the infant had been hidden away, concealed until the time was right.

Her newborn's father, William Haim, had been prominent lawyer with close ties to a powerful family of djinn just as sympathetic to the plight of amalgam as Demetria was.

When William was ambushed and murdered miles from his home in London, the authorities only saw an accident. And as far as the Order was concerned, the loose end was dealt with.

It was too risky to allow that information to leak out, even if it would destroy Demetria. Prince Bertrand knew it could also threaten the House of Courtenay.

No, he and Absalom had patiently bided their time. They had formed a vast network of allies and people willing to back them. And she knew exactly who these people were that were willing to turn on her at his command.

The old magic, secrets that had been handed down to her, secrets only known to next in line for the throne, kept Helene safe.

The agents who became Helene's parents were trusted friends of William's. They had been loyal to him, and after his death, to her. They had sworn an oath to keep their child safe in the human world.

But with their deaths, she knew the matter was most delicate. Helene leaving the safety of Whidbey Island to disappear to a remote town, had forced Demetria do something she would not have normally done.

She knew Absalom watched her closely. What he didn't know is how long she had been building a case against him, plotting her revenge, and that she had laid a trap for him to step in.

Unsanctioned murder against a human was strictly forbidden. And Demetria had proof that her brother and the Order were responsible for William's murder and those of countless others who got in the way.

Helene was a bridge to the human world. Demetria could finally bring her back into the fold. She could take her rightful place in the family and the violence and genocide Demetria so abhorred, could at last be ended.

And now, with a possible murderous, treasonous act, it felt as if the wheels of betrayal had already been set into motion.

CHAPTER NINETEEN

THE BEST COURSE OF ACTION

Lilian woke up with the most suffocating dread.

She'd had a horrific vision of Mabis. She saw Knights of the Order appearing in his kitchen just as he'd sat down to enjoy the ceviche he'd made for his lunch.

Hours of relentlessly torture followed. She knew with certainty that he was dead.

If they had killed her long-time associate, it meant he'd told them everything they wanted to know. But what exactly was that?

Lilian clasped her hands together, twirling her thumbs nervously as her thoughts raced.

Amsel had not told her where he was going, saying only that he was going to take a few days to come to terms with the shame of what he'd done before returning to Glenhaven.

He had not been in a good place when he'd left the previous day.

Lilian knew this time alone was really her son trying to reconcile his feelings around Helene, more than anything.

He had tried unsuccessfully to shield his emotions from Lilian. She could have saved him some time and told him exactly what was behind them.

But what good would it have done to point out the nature of those feelings before he'd realized them for himself?

He had not responded to the messages she'd sent to his phone and she had no idea how to reach him.

What was the best course of action? Had Mabis given up her name?

They could be on her doorstep at any moment. Or worse, they could be headed to Glenhaven. As much as she hated picking up and running away in the middle of the night, abandoning all the people who depended on her, she would not be helping anyone if she ended up dead.

She dialed Alton Harringford's number. He did not pick up and at the tone said, "Alton, darling, I have been planning a soiree. It will be October 25th. Mark your calendar. We'll talk soon."

This was his distress signal. The code word *soiree,* meant they had been compromised. The date October 25th was irrelevant, however, it led to the next code phrase, *we'll talk soon.*

This meant the first safe meeting place may already be known and mark your calendar meant they must meet at the second agreed upon location to await further instructions.

It was a complicated system designed to give each person separate and completely different information. Even if Mabis's codes were known, they had no way of knowing codes for the others since each person had different exclusive codes known only between the two parties.

This ensured during the questioning process, if they had to give up information, they could only give up information pertinent to themselves.

Also, there were a whole other set of safety protocols beyond that point, a series of tests and signals to alert the others that meeting would not be advisable and to abort. She repeated this same process for the others. She only hoped it was not too late.

Someone had been loitering in the hallway outside for the past 10 minutes. Someone, very human.

Coincidence? Could it be a lost tourist? Hotel staff?

Whoever it was, they had not budged from their post outside. She sent her consciousness out so that she could perceive who was there.

It was a woman dressed in business casual, looking slightly bored as she simultaneously pilfered through her purse. She took out Chapstick and rubbed it over pouted lips while she contemplated Lilian's door.

Lilian was sure the woman was alone. But who was she and why was she casing her hotel room?

Next, the woman took out a piece of gum and stuffed it inside her mouth, smacking it rather loudly. Lilian was amused when the woman caught the edge of a fingernail on the zipper and cursed.

American, Lilian mused.

The woman rifled through her bag again and came up with a nail file. But as exciting as it was to discover the contents of the woman's seemingly, bottomless purse, Lilian didn't have this luxury of time.

Lilian grabbed her with astral arms. Suddenly, their surroundings disappeared and the two were standing alone on a remote spot at the edge of a jungle, many miles away.

The human woman, realizing she was now standing on a sandy beach, began to scream and ran as fast as she could toward the ocean. It was quite comical watching her trying to make headway in the sand in her high heels.

Lilian laughed, "I can turn this whole beach into quicksand if you like."

"Fuck! Fuck! Fuck!" She stopped and turned around, "Okay, no need to get nasty, Lilian."

Lilian threw up her hands, "Who on earth are you?"

"That's a fair question. I'm Courtney Lazar. I'm Marie Luttrell's assistant."

Lilian shook her head to indicate this was not ringing a bell for her, "Quick sand it is, then."

"Wait! Wait…great…that's not her real name, is it? I don't know. She's a djinni! I just learned this tonight. Alright, I knew way before tonight, but I didn't officially KNOW until tonight. Okay? She's a counselor. She lives…lived in Louisiana."

"Marie Sol?"

"Yes! I think. Maybe? Look. I'm supposed to tell you that the shit has hit the fan. Mabis is dead. They know. Marie has gone to head off the communication to the

Order. If she can stop that, they won't have the list of names."

"Where were the names sent?"

"Something about a Kingdom Between and a palace guardhouse."

"And for Pete's sake. When were you going to knock on the door to give me this urgent bit of information?"

"I was nervous. I didn't want to get zapped to oblivion or something. I was trying to work out what I would say."

"I have to go," Lilian began to walk away.

"Wait. Can you put me back? Please."

Lilian rolled her eyes, "Fine!"

Courtney found herself alone in the hallway again. It dawned on her that she was in a foreign country where few people spoke English, without a passport.

What if Marie never returned? What if she left that spot to go to the bathroom and Marie came back, didn't see her, and left without her? How long should she wait?

An endless stream of scenarios played out in Courtney's mind.

Her stomach growled. If only she had a tuna melt in her purse. *That would hit the spot about now*, she thought.

But alas, she did not, and all that she could do, was wait.

CHAPTER TWENTY

HARBERLINOM CLOVE, DRIED ARBILINE, TWIRLING MOGENDA VINE

On a backroad, just south of Cleveland, Ohio, Marie pulled her car to the side of the road. She had not visited the United Kingdom Between in over a century and the terrain was unrecognizable.

She glanced up at the enormous billboard. A shady looking man in a tan suit and orange neck tie stared back. It read:

Real Estate Done Right, Every Time.

Marie highly doubted its claim.

Across the street, she noticed a dirt road to nowhere running into a thick clump of trees. She cloaked her conspicuous red vehicle with an invisibility spell and began to make her way down the road on foot.

She thought she'd made a wrong guess and was about to turn back when she caught the unmistakable static charge of magic in the air.

She moved a branch and stuck her foot out, delighted when it completely disappeared, "There you are," she said.

The sharp stinging pain was a complete surprise. Her arm began to swell to twice its size causing Marie to instantly transform into her true djinn form.

She spun around and glared at the tiny sprite suspended at nose level by tiny little wings. They were no bigger than a hummingbird but their little stingers packed a punch.

"Have you lost your mind?"

The sprite was unfazed by her anger and spoke in a level and authoritatively, bureaucratic tone, "State your business."

"The nerve. My business is definitely none of your business," Marie began to walk through the portal that connected the Kingdom to the Earth plane only to once again feel a stinging pain, this time in her right butt cheek.

"For fuck's sake!" Marie reached up and grabbed the sprite by its wings, "Can you not see with your little beady eyes that I am a djinni? I have the right to enter the United Kingdom whenever I damn well like."

The sprite stared back at Marie with emotionless eyes, "State your business, please."

Marie blew out an exasperated sigh that ruffled the delicate downy feathers on the sprite's wings, "Fine. If you must know, I was planning on…on…. On doing some sightseeing today."

The sprite smiled, "Lovely, that's just lovely. We are always happy to have visitors. Do you mind?"

Marie reluctantly let go only to have him shove a clipboard into her face. "I will just need for you to fill out these forms first."

Marie's irritation grew as she thumbed through a thick pile of immigration documents.

"There are twenty pages of ridiculous questions here. How did I hear about the United Kingdom? Am I currently up to date with my vaccinations? Do I have a criminal record? Is this a joke?"

"Oh, no, madame. We can never be too careful. Need to keep out the riff-raff."

"You do realize if I were the wrong kind of djinni, I could just lie on these forms."

The sprite moved closer and stared into Marie's eyes, "Are you planning on lying?"

Marie rolled her eyes, "Of course not!" Deciding she had no choice other than to comply, she rapidly filled in every line, "This is bullshit. Here! Happy?"

"Yes, yes. Everything appears to be in order. I just need to collect the processing fee."

"How much is that?"

"Fifty dollars."

Marie pressed the money into the sprite's hands and mumbled under her breath, "This is literally highway robbery."

He produced a document that resembled a passport, stamped it, and handed it over to her, indicating she was free to proceed, "Enjoy your stay."

She resisted thumping the little bugger into a nearby ant hill, and gave him a stiff, overly polite smile before crossing the barrier.

Marie's expectations of a nostalgic trip down memory lane, were immediately dashed. Gone was the faint blue haze and the delightfully putrid stench of old magic wafting through the streets. This place had become a sterilized version of itself, a version that mimicked the human world.

In fact, if a human had managed somehow to slip past the bureaucrat at the gate, they might think they had somehow ended up at Disney Land, or some urban development with cobblestone streets and an outdoor mall.

That is until they caught sight of the legion of light orbs whizzing by, or came across a seven-foot-tall winged being.

At this hour, she expected most of her kind to be fast asleep. She stopped outside a closed herbal shop and breathed in. There it was, finally, smells of the djinn world—harberlinom clove, dried arbiline, twirling mogenda vine.

Thousands of very powerful spells could be cooked up using only those 3 ingredients.

The castle was quite a distance to the east. As much as she had enjoyed the leisurely stroll, she had to pick up the pace.

She had not used her wings to fly in ages. At first, she was a little wobbly but soon had her bearings. She missed this freedom of zipping around without fear of discovery or accidentally crashing into an airplane at 35,000 feet.

Living exclusively in the human world, it was almost possible to forget the things which set them apart. Almost.

She landed with a tumble a safe distance from the building she remembered to house the palace guard.

But it was also different. Gone were the legions of wallymackers, pale blue poultry that used to roam the grounds, bellies fat with griley worms.

Gone were the lanoshia trees with their fan shaped leaves and fuchsia blooms the size of dinner plates, blooms that fell to ground, seeping into it until it too was stained that very same color.

Time had cleared them away and replaced them with tidy, boringly bland and too perfect trees and shrubberies.

The mail slot was easy enough to spot. She was surprised to find that it did not possess even the most basic of security spells. It was almost too easy.

Or rather, it would have been easy, had a burly guard not emerged with a mail sack at that very moment and emptied out the box.

Marie slapped her forehead in frustration. She had no choice. She had to find out where he was taking it.

Instantly, Marie decided to take on the form of a bird. She hoped she looked inconspicuous in the night, shiny black with the slightest hint of indigo on the head feathers, a common grackle, abundant in this realm.

In fact, the djinn introduced them to the human world as well as cranes when they first crossed over.

The burly guard moved swiftly, albeit clumsily, disappearing around the corner before she could catch up to him.

Where had he gone to?

There was a maze of corridors, each with many doors he could have taken. She lit on the side of a fluted stone pillar and listened.

Marie wondered why the guard house was so extremely quiet and virtually empty. But then a thud inundated the silence and she flew toward that direction.

She spied the guard as he dropped the sack in the corner of the room, sat at a desk, and began eating what looked like fermented octopus.

It smelled heavenly, probably prepared in the royal kitchen. She couldn't remember the last time she'd eaten this delicacy and at once, her mouth watered terribly.

She landed on the floor, waddling quietly on tiny bird feet toward the mailbag and climbed up the side of it that faced the wall.

Inside, she sniffed through, trying to pick up the scent of the same thugs who had ended up in her iron maidens.

Marie began working her way to the bottom of the bag and when the familiar scent of cologne was detected on an envelope, wondered how she would retrieve it.

The weight of three hundred pieces of mail on top of it, was not an easy obstacle for a tiny bird to overcome.

A voice from the direction of the doorway forced her to freeze, "Sir Langford wants all the palace mail to be brought to him immediately."

"Can't do. I have strict orders from Lord Absalom to hold the mail here until he returns."

There were footsteps as the figure from the door moved into the interior of the room. Marie found herself being crushed underneath the weight of envelopes as the bag was hoisted onto the newcomer's back.

"Hey. You can't take that." The chair scraped loudly as the burly guard abruptly stood up.

"And by whose authority do you propose to stop me. It would do well for you to remember that you operate under the command of Queen Demetria and the head of her guard, Sir Langford. The Order does not have jurisdiction here. Tell Lord Absalom he can take this up with Sir Langdon if he so wishes."

Queen Demetria? Queen Eleanor was dead? Marie had heard nothing of this news. It must have happened recently.

"She's not queen yet."

"I don't like your tone. Do you know something that I do not? If so, please share what information inspires such blatant insubordination."

Several moments of silence fell while Marie imagined the two djinni in a good old-fashioned stare down.

"In a matter of hours, the coronation will be held for Queen Demetria. After which time, we may very well need to revisit your post here."

"Please forgive me. I did not mean any disrespect to the future queen. But I've had my orders and you are not taking that bag anywhere."

Marie heard a sound she understood to be a dagger ripping through flesh. The scent of blood rushed the air.

The mailbag fell to the floor and Marie fell hard onto one of her wings. Pain shot through her.

It was all she could do to hold this shifted form intact. Where in the human world, their powers were fueled by an almost limitless energy field, in this between place, it was more like the dimension they originated from.

Here, their powers had limitations and spell work with potions was a necessity for the average djinni to conjure magic.

Since Marie had been in the human world recently, she brought with her enormous energy stores, but how long they would last, she did not know. And shapeshifting required a great deal of power. She understood that the clock was quickly running out.

She regretted not simply overtaking the guard and using her magic to zip out of there. Now, she would not be able to merely wish herself back to the earth plane, she would have to travel out, the same way she came in.

And what to do about this new development. A guard murdering another guard—a new queen being challenged by the Order—this had all the signs of a coup. Marie realized she had stumbled into a situation that posed a broader scope of unwanted consequences for all.

The Order of the Blue Orchid was a bloodthirsty institution. Absalom was notoriously cruel and anti-human. Was this simply a power grab? Did he feel the new queen would not continue to support his sadistic agenda?

The fact that this guard was willing to kill for Absalom in order to prevent information inside this bag from landing in the queen's hands, supported this reasoning.

Could this mean the new queen was sympathetic toward amalgam?

This would change everything.

Marie couldn't just take the letter and leave. She had to alert the queen. It was a risk, but she didn't see that she had another choice.

If she hoped to get away undetected, she knew the best time was now, while the guard was distracted cleaning up the gruesome crime scene. Also, at some point he would have to dispose of the body somewhere.

But would she have enough strength to carry the letter? That was the question.

Marie used her beak to work the letter free and managed to drag it up to the top of the pile. She was attempted to hop with the letter, testing her ability to become airborne, when the bag unexpectedly tipped on its side.

This caused Marie to almost spill out into full view of the guard. Her delicate bird feet clung to the canvas fabric for dear life.

Marie hung upside down for a moment before realizing if she let go and hopped down, she could simply walk out with the letter in her mouth.

She stopped at the opening, eye to eye with the dead djinni from the queen's guard who lay in a pool of his own fluids.

She would have to be careful not to dip her feet in the blood. The last thing she needed was a trail leading them directly to her.

A large boot landed on the bag, mere inches from Marie. She realized in horror that she had nearly been squashed flat. The foulest stench of stinky feet wafted into her tiny bird nostrils. It was all she could do not to bolt out of there that very instant.

But she waited. One minute more, and regardless, she would have to make a go of it.

The burly guard removed his repulsive foot and began to roll the body of the dead guard into shiny fabric. Likely, it was his own cloak now being used for his burial shroud. Abruptly, the corpse was lifted out of sight. Feet shuffled away, echoing down the hall.

This was the opening Marie had been hoping for. She hopped out of the bag with the letter firmly clasped in her beak and made her way to the hallway. A glance in both directions confirmed the path was clear.

It was difficult balancing the weight of the letter using such a tiny body. A tip too far to the right, or too far to the left, had her wobbling in that direction.

She had not been expecting to see another guard turn down the corridor.

Marie had been so busy fighting with the letter that she hadn't even heard him coming. He was smaller in stature than the other guard, with kind eyes. His skin was like polished ebony, but his wings were an ashy, greenish grey. She was sure she had seen that very same color on a block of moldy cheese once.

Marie thought he was the most beautiful djinni she had even seen. She attempted to smile at him, but remembered that she was a bird.

"Hey little one, what have you got there?" He reached toward her and Marie hopped rapidly past him and toward the door.

This only caused him to laugh. "Oh, you want to play like that, do you?"

227

He chased after her, but Marie had already made it outside. She frantically, flapped her wings, lifted about two feet into the air, and then came crashing back down.

For fucks sake. This was not going to work.

The guard was bent over from laughing so hard and he held his gut suggesting the force of it caused him great physical pain.

Marie became angry. The heat rising into her shiny head feathers was beginning to turn the tips of them a fiery orange.

She knew she was going to have to change back into her djinni body if she hoped to escape and waited until the handsome guard kneeled down close to her before transforming.

When she did so, Marie's left wing knocked him off balance and onto his back.

He stared at her in a sort of stunned reverie, "Who the hell are you?"

"I would love to tell you that. I really would. You are beautiful, by the way. Maybe we could get a drink sometime. I'm really sorry," she said.

"What are you sorry for, attacking me or getting caught?" The guard stood and reached for his sword.

"Neither. I'm really sorry for this." Marie socked him in the head with the jagged rock she'd stealthily picked up from the ground only moments ago.

He was out cold. Marie regretted that he would have a terrible headache when he eventually came to, but he was nonetheless, fine.

She grabbed his feet, dragged him toward the tree line, and left him there, covered in branches.

When she approached the west side of the castle, she realized why the guard house had been so empty.

The coronation.

Most of the soldiers had been stationed along the main road leading through the palace gate. Beefed up security was necessary to handle the huge crowds of djinnis already showing up.

How in the heck am I going to get through that and have a chance at getting close to the queen?

She hoped she had enough energy left to orchestrate a plan. From her observations, this was apparently thrown together rather quickly and this was creating a lot of confusion. Confusion, she would use to her advantage.

The lack of official credentials had led to some people being turned away in outrage, while others were let inside.

Think, Marie, think. What was the one thing every queen needed for her coronation?

Why, a fabulous dress, of course. And what would be more catastrophic for a new queen than a wardrobe malfunction?

Marie produced a spool of the finest pure silver thread she'd ever laid eyes on and an elegant, yet simple, business card. *Marie's Precious Spools, Rare Yarns and Threads* was written in gold lettering, and surrounded by a delicate floral swirl border.

She used the last of her magical stores to don clothes worthy of nobility and a handsome leather bag to conceal the items inside.

Now, all that she had to do was sell it.

Marie got into line and stepped into character, ringing her hands nervously. When it was taking far too long with the couple in front of her, apparently the butter sculptors, she simply parted them with one of her wings and moved between them.

"Listen, I'm sure that it's REALLY important that the butter pats be shaped like cranes in time for the coronation. But I do have a true emergency here, if you could just let me through," Marie made sure to look completely unapologetic and annoyingly entitled.

"Well…I never," The butter artist glared at Marie and attempted to shove her out of the way, but Marie was having none of it.

"Do that one more time and I'll make sure you never carve again."

The guard looked completely overwhelmed. He scratched his head and decided due diligence required that he find out who this important looking djinni in the very finest of clothing, was. He certainly didn't want to be responsible for dropping the ball.

"What is the emergency?" he asked.

Marie allowed her voice to elevate a half octave. "The emergency is that the dress for Queen Demetria's coronation cannot be altered without the special thread that the dressmaker forgot to bring. Thank heavens I'm here to save the day." She attempted to push through, but the guard stopped her.

"Show this thread to me," he said.

"Why not? Let's just open it up right here and expose it to the horse shit and the grimy fingered peasants. I'm sure the queen will be very happy when I tell her all about it."

The guard pulled Marie to the side away from earshot of the others, and squeezed her arm rather forcefully. Through gritted teeth, he said, "If you don't show me, you don't get in."

Marie sighed, feigning great reluctance as she slowly opened the bag enough for him to peer inside. There was a sharp intake of breath the instant the light struck the spool of silver. It gleamed and sparkled with a blinding brilliance that even impressed Marie, who could not have hoped for things to unravel any better.

Marie closed the bag, smiled, and handed him her card.

The next thing she knew, that same guard was personally escorting her through the castle. Marie tried to appear unimpressed by the grandness of the main hall. He touched the wall and a doorway appeared, revealing a hidden staircase.

How clever. She wondered how many of these secret doors lurked unseen in plain sight inside this enormous place.

Marie joked with her escort, "Has anyone ever gone missing in here, never to be heard from again,"

Without a hint of humor he said, "Yes, many times."

Marie's smile faded. She wished she had paid more attention to all the turns and doorways they had taken.

On the inside, the castle appeared to have been carved out of a single massive island of marble, the floors, walls, and ceiling, all merging together seamlessly.

Occasionally, they passed by things you would expect to find in an old castle, a coat of armor, an old tapestry embroidered with pastoral djinn scenes, a bust of a long dead royal or two.

It was quite cool and damp and she shivered, regretting that she had not also conjured up a cape to wear. At last, they stopped at a doorway carved out of red carnelian.

"This is the queen's private sitting room. I will leave you now to make haste."

Marie had almost forgotten her ruse. "Oh…yes…yes! Thank you, good sir. You are too kind. I will make sure the queen hears of your good deed."

She waited until he had gone, took a deep breath, and knocked on the door.

From inside a voice called, "Come in."

She stepped inside the room and was at once an arms-length away from Demetria Courtenay, new Queen of the United Kingdom Between.

The queen did not look up, as she was busy smoothing down a section of her dress, a dress composed of thousands of tiny diamonds which sparkled with her every movement.

"That must weigh a ton," Marie said.

Demetria startled and turned. "You're not palace staff! How did you get in here?"

"No, Your Majesty. I have come here to warn you. I'm afraid there's a coup, happening as we speak."

The queen was about to hit the alarm button, but stopped in her tracks, "Explain yourself."

Marie told her about the Order showing up on her doorstep, about the murder of Mabis, and the events leading her here.

"I came to the guard house to stop Absalom from getting his hands on this list." Marie held up the letter. "But I could not just run away without trying to warn you. I have spent a large portion of my life trying to protect innocent people from being killed by your family's Order. So many have been killed without justice or mercy, simply for having been born. But a world with Absalom having more control, will be a dark one indeed for both humans and djinn alike."

The Queen's expression appeared unmovable like the stone walls of the castle she dwelled within. She held out her hand, "Let me see this list."

Marie handed it over with the seal still intact. The Queen saw that it had been created by a member of the Order, before she cracked it open and read. She remained silent for some time before she finally spoke.

"Marie, at this moment, you may be the only person in this entire kingdom that I can trust completely. If you help me, I promise no harm will come to you, or to your friends."

The Queen circled Marie, "Now, we must make sure no one sees you."

The Courtenay were powerful. This was the main reason they remained in power, unchallenged, millennium after millennium. Their secret magic was closely guarded and intermarrying with cousins had intensified this power in the blood line.

But without open demonstrations, had at times, seemed like myth woven with the purpose of keeping Courtenay hands on the reins of power.

Queen Demetria waved her hand, "That should do."

From Marie's perspective, it was completely anti-climactic and it didn't appear as if anything at all had happened. She moved to a mirror to see the damage.

Only the queen's reflection was visible although Marie stood directly in front of her. Marie was completely invisible.

"I have to say I'm impressed," Marie said.

"Stay very close to me and don't say a word." The Queen pressed a button concealed underneath a vase and almost immediately, her advisor appeared, "Yes, Your Highness."

"Sir Langford, I have it on the utmost authority that there is a coup underway this very minute."

"I can assure you. There have been no signs of unrest beyond the palace walls. I do not mean to challenge what you say, but if you refer to your brother, he is currently in his quarters under the watchful eye of my men, and has been since we last spoke. I hope you do not question my loyalty to this family or to you."

The queen touched his arm. "I trust you completely, Sir Langford. My brother does not act alone. Guards loyal to him have infiltrated the ranks. Absalom has authorized unsanctioned killing of djinn and humans. I'm afraid it is not the first time."

"But Absalom is far away from the palace, and your brother has spoken to no one. I can understand the level of anxiety about the responsibility you are about to undertake. Do you think it's possible you have blown this out of proportion?" he asked.

Queen Demetria whirled around to face him, "There is a level of unchecked misogyny my mother tolerated that I will not. Are you questioning my ability to make sound decisions? Has my mother caused you to forget the power that passes through my blood? I assure you. My judgement is quite sound."

Sir Langford blushed and dropped to his knees, "Please forgive me. I humbly serve you. I have years of military experience, but I have seen no evidence of what you suggest. That is all."

"Earlier, you sent a guard to collect the mail from the guard house. He is dead. My spy was able to escape with this letter. It came to me with an unbroken seal. The Order seeks to kill these djinnis without trial."

Sir Langford took the letter and rose to his feet before studying it, "If this is true, we've been blindsided. I do not know where to begin. I've failed you."

The queen unlocked a drawer in her desk, and handed him a piece of paper, "Sir Langford, do not feel bad. You did as my mother commanded. She tinted the lens through which you viewed the world. She was always far too trusting. This is a list of all those within your rank still loyal to me. Gather them secretly and do not deviate from the plans we've made for the coronation. Everything should appear as if we are still blissfully ignorant of what is happening beneath our noses."

"We should have a determination from the coroner within the hour," he said.

When Marie and Queen Demetria were alone again, Marie said, "You think Queen Eleanor was assassinated, don't you?"

Demetria did not see the point in lying to her new ally, "I do."

"What do we do now?"

"We carry on as if nothing is wrong. I have a coronation in two hours."

Marie found herself being impressed with this new queen, who was a bad ass in the true sense of the word. Enough so that she allowed herself to be hopeful that there might actually be real change, that those living in fear might finally be safe.

And for this reason, Marie was bound to do everything within her power to protect her.

CHAPTER TWENTY-ONE

PRINCE BERTRAND

Sergi fumed. The letter was not there and he was unable to reach his agents. He poured over the visitor's log which tracked all traffic in and out of the United Kingdom. The courier had made it back with intel. Intel that had somehow gone missing.

Then he saw it, *Marie Luttrell.* The name would have flown under the radar had he not recognized the scent still clinging to the paperwork, a scent that was unmistakable.

He gazed in disbelief.

Marie Sol

All these years, he'd thought her dead. He'd left her for dead. She was behind this. He knew it.

They were so close to the prize. If ever there was a time for bold actions, it was now. They could not allow the coronation to occur and for Demetria to be seen as the legitimate ruler, even for a second.

Demetria in power, would be the end of the Order and everything they had fought for. It was never going to happen.

No, they would install Bertrand instead. That was the agreement. It was all it had taken for the prince to turn a blind eye, leaving Sergi alone at his mother's bedside.

Prince Bertrand had known good and well what would happen the instant he was gone, staying true to his nature as a conniving sociopath. His morals had always been questionable, his narcissistic need for the spotlight always more important, and his primary loyalty, always to himself.

Sergi had expected an autopsy. The royal physician was loyal to the Order and was willing to say the Queen's death was from natural causes. But then there was a kink in their plans. The autopsy was being conducted by an outside source.

So, Demetria already suspected something. But how much did she know?

Sir Langdon had to be stopped before he could give her those results. Sergi gave the word, and almost invisibly, control of the palace switched hands.

"Where is Prince Bertrand?" he asked

The guard shuffled uneasily, "He is being held in his quarters at Sir Langdon's request. Restricted visitation for his own protection."

"And you did not think this break in protocol needed to be brought to my attention?" Sergi fixed his steely coal black eyes on him and it was all the young djinni could do not to run for cover. His face flushed red as he waited for whatever retribution was to come.

"For your sake, I hope there is still time to gain control of this situation. Alert Absalom about the sudden death of Queen Eleanor. Let him know that the Order is taking over security of the palace to stay the coronation of Demetria Courtenay. He will understand what needs to be done."

The Order had not dared expose the extent of their power. This transfer had happened little by little, every time Queen Eleanor allowed others to make decisions on her behalf, until she had lost all real power. This was made possible by her aging, feeble, and trusting mind.

The plan had always been to place Prince Bertrand on the throne. Not because he was stronger, but because he was weaker. Like his mother, he would be the puppet which kept up appearances and the illusion that kept everything copacetic.

The Order would lay out the case for the execution of Demetria. It would be too easy to spin the facts in order to present her as a traitor to her people.

With haste, Sergi made his way to the prince's quarters. He expected to find him there, basking in the approaching realization of his lifelong dream, to be the first King ever to rule.

But when Sergi entered without knocking, it was obvious Prince Bertrand had been nervously pacing around inside his gilded cage. His mane of sandy brown hair was disheveled from hours of running his fingers through it.

The dark circles, a stark contrast to his light amber eyes, were the only indication on his handsome face that anxiety had been brewing, "Oh, thank the stars! I've been trapped in here for hours. I thought maybe we'd been found out."

"Found out? I am sure that I have no idea what you are talking about."

Sergi did not particularly care for the prince. He was merely a means to an end.

Soon, the influence of humans would be erased and the djinn would rise up in their true forms, free from hiding and restraints, free to once again rule over the earth.

Once the portal was opened, things would be different, and there was nothing anyone could do to stop it.

Prince Bertrand smiled, "Right. Of course. I was worried you might have had second thoughts about our *agreement*."

Sergi could not let this slight roll off without commenting, respectfully, of course, "I am wounded by your lack of faith in us. Haven't we always had your back?"

In fact, the Order had concealed so many of his salacious acts, one could hardly keep track. With his taste for having those who crossed him murdered, the bodies alone could fill the Mariana Trench.

"Of course. Of course, I apologize. Being cooped up in here for so many hours had begun to play tricks on my mind."

"I came to offer my sympathies on the loss of Queen Eleanor." Sergi had no idea if the room had been bugged or not. It was best to keep up pretenses.

Pure elation fell over Bertrand as he began to sniff what was finally so very close, but then he shielded it long enough to look appropriately, mournful. "Thank you. It is a great loss. And does my sister understand her place, what is expected of her now?"

"I do not believe so. I thought we could go together and that you could have the honor of explaining things to her," Sergi said.

"Yes. I would very much like that."

"But first we must clean you up. We can't have our future King looking all frazzled and desperate, can we?" *And guilty*, Sergi thought.

The prince caught sight of himself in the mirror, glimpsing what Sergi had seen earlier, a scared and desperate man.

That would not do. His destiny had never been to take a back seat to the women in his life. He was meant for so much more. This he had known since he was a child.

Now, everyone else would finally see it too.

CHAPTER TWENTY-TWO

GETTING THE HELL OUT OF DODGE

Queen Demetria stared at the clock with concern. They should have been there already to fetch her and escort her to the throne room to retrieve the scepter.

She pursed her lips, the only sign she was feeling apprehensive, one that was not meant for other eyes. In fact, with her companion being invisible, she had momentarily forgotten she was not alone.

"What is it?" Marie asked.

The Queen quickly regained her composure and the emotionless expression fell back into place, "Something is wrong. Sir Langdon should have been here already with guards and my ladies in waiting to fetch me."

She flicked her wrist as though turning a page in a book and the wall that separated her sitting room from the hallway outside became translucent.

Marie watched this show of power with admiration. The queen hadn't been to the human world in years, but it did not matter. The royals had no need to draw magic stores from the human world. They were genetically different from others of their kind.

In the olden days, when the djinn first crossed over, all the higher and secret knowledge was protected and kept by a ruling female priestess class. The Courteney family were what remained of it.

There was a guard stationed a considerable distance from the door, discreet, but it was apparent he was guarding it. "He is not palace staff. He has the Order emblem concealed underneath his belt. Marie, I need you to find Sir Langdon for me."

"But how? This place is terribly confusing. I will lose my way the minute I step outside."

"Nonsense, you will take this," Demetria held out her open palm.

"There's nothing there."

"It wouldn't very well do any good for you to be running around invisible with a pendant hanging around your neck that wasn't, now would it?"

Marie took the smooth heavy stone that was attached to a chain. When she slipped it on, she could see the entire layout of the castle in relation to where she was.

"My mother gave this to me when I was very small to help me navigate the grounds. It did not take long for me to realize that my mother could track my every move and every bit of mischief I'd been up to as well. Simply think of where you want to go or the person you are looking for, and it will direct you there."

The instant Queen Demetria opened the door. The guard was right there blocking it. He was also stopping Marie from slipping out.

"What are you doing, lurking about here?" she asked.

The djinni's face turned the deepest shade of ebony Marie had ever seen, "There is a security threat that is being assessed. I was told to keep you here until it is resolved."

Both Demetria and Marie knew this was a lie.

"Under whose command?"

"The Order has taken over palace security until the threat can be mitigated."

"Hmmm…very well then. Go about your business."

When the guard did not budge, the queen had to use a different tactic. She fixed her eyes on the painting behind the guard, raised her hand to her mouth, and cried out in horror, "What have you done?"

The guard glanced behind him and seeing nothing amiss, asked, "What is wrong?"

"The bloody painting. It's ruined. You must have leaned against it and scratched it."

The guard straddled a thin line between defending himself and not challenging the accusation which came flying at him from a royal mouth. "I am sure I did not lean. Perhaps it was already there," he suggested.

Feigning anger, the queen pushed by him and approached the landscape that hung on the wall. This forced the guard to follow her helplessly, and also left a clear opening for Marie to slip through, "Just look at it. You're lucky I'm kind, otherwise I'd have you hanged for this."

He gulped out of a growing concern, "Quite honestly, I do not see anything wrong with it."

"Right there! There," she pointed.

He shook his head in bemusement, "I'm sorry. I still do not see a scratch."

He watched as the new Queen leaned in closer. She lifted a non-existent thing off of the painting with her thumb and forefinger before pretending to flick it into the air.

She turned back and smiled. "Seems it was just a bit of dust. Carry on."

There was a subtle exhale as the soldier let go of the breath he'd been holding. He kept a wide girth between himself and the wall as he watched Queen Demetria slip back into her quarters.

Marie thought this was all hilarious and threatened to give herself away because she was laughing so hard.

She was amazed at all the little secret doors and tunnels she was being led through. Clearly, most of these passages were only used by the royal family themselves.

She had thought very clearly, *take me to Sir Langdon.* Soon she found herself descending lower and lower into the bowels of the castle. She had the most uneasy feeling that she was being led straight to the dungeon.

A few minutes later, a wall of iron bars confirmed this.

But where was Sir Langdon? The guidance had stopped, so he must be here somewhere, Marie thought. She leaned closer to the bars and peered inside one of the cells.

There was a crumpled-up blanket on the floor but nothing else. Marie moved on.

"No, go back!"

Marie jumped at the sound of the Queen's voice. "You scared the wits out of me."

"Sorry, I thought you understood that I could watch you. I suppose I failed to mention that I can speak to you as well. There was something in the corner."

"It's just an old blanket."

"I'm not so sure. The bars are iron. And I have no idea where they keep the keys."

Marie took hold of the latch, breaking it with no problem at all.

"Aren't you full of surprises? How did you do that?"

"Someday, I will be happy to tell you the whole story if you'd like." Marie was alarmed to find that the blanket was soaked in blood before she lifted it, "But now, we have a problem."

Sir Langdon lay unconscious beneath it, bleeding from a wound on the back of his head where he had been struck with something hard. But his pulse was strong. "Thank your lucky stars. He's alive."

"Check his pockets."

Marie searched the same pocket she'd seen him slip the list of names into earlier. "He still has it." There was also something else folded up with it, "There is an autopsy report here."

The Queen exhaled in relief. "Can you tell me what it says?"

Marie felt a sick feeling in the pit of her stomach. "I'm so sorry. It says that Queen Eleanor died by asphyxiation."

"Bastards. Can you lift him?"

"I believe so."

"There should be a car ready for me. Take him there, and wait for me. The coronation will have to wait. We're getting the hell out of Dodge."

Marie snorted at this, "Did you just use a cowboy reference? I will never be able to look at you the same way again. I will always see John Wayne and gunslingers. It's a bell we cannot un-ring."

"If we get out of here, I will be forever in your debt and will not mind that at all."

Marie tore off a section from the blanket and tied it around the unconscious djinni's head to stop the bleeding. Although he was tall and large in stature by human standards, not so much for a djinni.

Marie had no trouble hoisting him over her shoulder. She took her foot and arranged the blanket so that it appeared someone was still underneath. She also repaired the door with the last weak fizzle of magic she had left.

If anyone came to look in, they would not know the door had been disturbed.

She wound her way through the ancient looking tunnel before stopping at section of wall where there was supposed to be a door. Marie saw no evidence of one.

"How do I get through?" She waited but there was no reply from Queen Demetria, "Great!"

She heard voices approaching, becoming louder, but refused to panic. She thought back to every hidden door she'd been led through, searching her memory of the different methods employed. Many times, the opening appeared when both palms were pressed flat against the wall.

Please, please, please, let this work.

Instantly, the door handle appeared and Marie was able to slip through, closing it as quietly as possible. Once on the other side, she waited for the guards to pass. Sir Langdon began to stir and let out a pain filled moan.

"Shut up. I'm trying to save you," Marie whispered.

But he was once again, out cold.

The footsteps stopped and a deep voice said, "Did you hear that?"

"This place is full of naked mole rats," the other djinni said.

"It didn't sound like a mole rat."

"And you're an expert, are you? Ugly little fuckers. I once saw one drag a guard into the forest. It had nibbled off half his leg when we found him and beat the thing off."

"Now you're just making shit up!"

"It happened. Why would I lie about something like that?"

"Because you're a liar."

There was a thud, the distinct sound of someone's ass hitting the ground squarely as the guards began to struggle.

Marie held her breath and cupped a hand over Sir Langdon's mouth, just in case, as she waited for this childish argument to break up.

Eventually, the guards grew tired of fighting for dominance, completely forgot the reason the argument had started in the first place, and moved on.

Marie slid her hand around in the darkness until she felt a light switch and the room became flooded with light.

"I can certainly work with this."

It was an enormous airplane hangar. There were rows upon rows of cars, sleek sports sedans, SUVs, and several military style armored vehicles.

In the center of the room sat a helicopter. The ceiling above it was a large metal dome and when Marie pulled a lever on the wall, it began to spin open to the sky, looking like a wide-mouth monster with sharp metal teeth.

"Change of plans," she said and fastened the unconscious djinni into one of its seats.

Then she moved all of the luggage that had been packed inside the car, into the helicopter.

All those years of flying lessons would finally pay off. They had everything they needed to make an epic getaway.

Marie only prayed Queen Demetria would make it to them before they were discovered.

CHAPTER TWENTY-THREE

THE WINGED SERPENT

Amsel looked out beyond the towering cliffs.

This was the place he was always drawn to when his soul was in turmoil. The way the sea lapped against its jagged rocks, the way its crashing waves echoed up to great heights, soothed him.

Here, birds flew close to him, his wings convincing them that he was like them instead of an entirely different being. Here, he was nearly in the clouds, watching the first stars appear in the breaks between them.

There was so much more going on than what the human mind conceived, worlds within worlds, stacked together. If he focused in, he could almost make out the subtle imprints they left on the fabric of time and space.

In the fading light, this remote section of an archipelago resembled an alien landscape on some interstellar planet. It was difficult for man to access and Amsel felt safe being himself here.

The pressing matter was what to do about his feelings for Helene. Since the very first day, they had not been easy to manage, rushing in and overwhelmingly, stripping him of logic and common sense. He burned for her in a way he never had for anyone.

Like a coward, he'd run away in the night hoping to find what he needed to fight against this. But it had only made him long for her with a painful rawness that made his soul ache.

Their relationship was based on deceit. What would Helene do when she was presented with the truth? Would she forgive him? Could she ever love what he truly was?

Love? He felt breathless. His heart pumped with angry aggression.

He was in love with her. How had he let this happen?

He recalled the look of knowing in his mother's eyes. She'd been too kind to point out what was so blatantly obvious.

And when Helene realized what she was, and what his kind did to her kind, would she hate him for his part in it? Would she hate him for the child who, like her, would never be completely accepted in either of their worlds, a child who would be hunted down and targeted for extermination?

Finding love in this way, felt like being on the receiving end of the cruelest kind of joke. Even if he had earned this karma, Helene and the child had not.

If amalgam were only safe in the bubble of Glenhaven, kept ignorant of the true nature of who they were, it wasn't much better than living shackled in a glorified prison.

For far too long he'd endured the systemic genocide that was accepted by mainstream djinn. He'd often wondered how so many could turn a blind eye to what was happening.

No, keeping silent about this wrong, had only allowed the Order to grow stronger. Everything was different now. He was done with letting this fester in darkness.

It was time for things to change. And if it meant sacrificing his own life to save Helene and his unborn child, it would be the easiest thing he'd ever done.

Amsel had this feeling that all events in his life had been leading up to this moment, that he'd been sleepwalking through centuries, and that suddenly, some dormant thing inside had been activated.

There was a force greater than djinn. He'd felt its fingerprint on his entire life, guiding him even when he was closed off from it and reluctant to accept it.

What this force was, he did not know. The humans had believed in a multitude of gods. But they were all the same, just different perspectives of the same force that created all life. But time had almost completely erased the true memory of this genesis.

Amsel had never prayed before, but he found himself on his knees, forehead planted on the coolness of the abrasive rock beneath him.

"Please watch over us and grant protection to our resistance. If this is time for action, please show us how. Guide us so that we may escape the darkness that has befallen us. I offer myself in service to you and surrender my life if that is what is required of me. May all of us atone for our actions and be brought back into the light. May your power unite us all."

There was a noticeable shift in the direction of the wind. He glanced down at his hands studying the pale white thickness of scales. His eyes were still violet in this form, but the pupils transformed into vertical slivers of onyx.

He was in appearance, much like the winged serpent god of ancient Mesopotamia, or the Aztec god, Quetzalcoatl.

He remembered Helene's terror at the sight of him, his eight-foot height, causing him to tower over her in the darkness.

It pained him that once she knew the truth of what he was, she might never be able to accept him, that she might forever be frightened by the sight of him, that she might always cringe away from his touch.

But she deserved to know the truth. And whatever the outcome, he needed to consign himself to it.

In his years, he had been called many things from the humans he'd crossed paths with looking as he did now; The spawn of the devil, demon, you name it.

At times, he'd found it humorous. He'd heard these names so often, he'd begun to wonder if maybe they were right, that there was something inside of him which was as inherently evil as what they saw.

The last light of the sun had dipped below the horizon. He abruptly took flight, rapidly sailing through the air for several hundred miles before wishing himself into the Land Rover parked on the street outside of Helene's childhood home.

He welcomed the long drive back to Glenhaven. For just a little while longer, he could hang onto his hope for a future with Helene. He could dare to dream of a world where they could be together.

CHAPTER TWENTY-FOUR

A DIZZYING TAILSPIN

Demetria took her time weaving the fabric of matter around her. The spell had been discovered, she was sure, not by accident. It was as though she had been led directly to it, just so that it could reveal its dusty mysteries to her.

For many years, the spell had remained stored in the recesses of her mind. She had always known what it was, a spell of last resort.

What she didn't know was whether she was powerful enough to pull it off, or how long it would last. She wasn't even sure if she possessed what it took to undo it once it was cast.

Over and over, she chanted the incantations which were in the ancient language of the priesthood, *Faravle jeanut pre causerey. Holti renumbrum beno sey. Alleway me portudum.*

She felt a tug, tension in the subatomic particles themselves as the spell took over and began to work on its own.

She knew her part was done. The spell would continue to weave its way around the entirety of the United Kingdom Between until every last crevice, every crooked wall, every water-stained ceiling, was enveloped inside of it.

With luck, it would be their saving grace.

The Queen waved her hand, making her work undetectable.

She went about securing the last important documents related to royal genealogy, kingdom business, land deeds, and its entire history from the beginning of its inception, placing them into a time cube that was small enough to fit on a ring.

Once the spell was complete, it would eventually fold the entire kingdom within it as well.

Without warning, the door flew open and Bertrand stood before her, followed by Sir Sergi. Queen Demetria stared back at them without the slightest bit of alarm showing on her face.

She could tell this disappointed her bully of a brother, who felt most powerful when those around him could be made to feel small. "Dear sister, are you not surprised to see me?"

"I knew you would come."

"Always such a know-it-all." Bertrand pouted like a child and plopped down on the blue velvet settee. He pulled a grape from a bowl on the table and tossed it into his mouth.

"And you have always undervalued what I do know."

Bertrand began to laugh and motioned toward the silent yet towering, Sergi, who looked entirely too massive for the saffron dyed Kasaya he wore.

"Sir Sergi has readied a comfortable cell where you can await your trial, but first, I thought we could clear the air and be civil. After all, the more agreeable you are, the better it will be for you."

"A trial. For what? You are the ones committing treason. Shouldn't that cell house the two of you? Murderers!"

For a split second, Bertrand appeared dumbfounded by this accusation. She wasn't supposed to know this. And it had him feeling all too exposed. There was also the tiny flicker of shame, but it faded almost as quicky as it fell over him.

Demetria held her hand at her side, twirling the ring with its strange black cube around her finger. The djinnis gave no indication that they had noticed anything strange about it.

"Who will believe you? When they learn of the child you've been hiding, a certain, Helene Parish," Bertrand said.

Demetria felt a deep, visceral fear pooling in the pit of her stomach. For a brief instant, she thought she might vomit. But she managed to hold herself steady, not even flinching at the words that ripped at her composure.

She refused to give her brother the satisfaction of showing her distress.

Bertrand continued, "As we speak, Sir Absalom and his men are on the way to Glenhaven. And I bet you will never guess what else they found there?"

"You're boring me, really. Can we speed this up?" she asked.

It was all she could do to keep herself from going to pieces on the spot, when all she could think about was Helene and the evils the Order might at this very moment be subjecting her to.

"It seems Glenhaven is a haven all right, for amalgam, and also for the portal."

"You're mad. It's pure fantasy. It doesn't exist and if it ever did, was destroyed long ago."

"It exists, and I assure you, is very much intact," Sergi added. "I know you are not indifferent to the fate of the daughter you protected all these years. If you cooperate, we can assure her suffering will be minimal. I have always admired your iron clad stoicism. I would hate to find myself in a game of poker with you as I would almost assuredly lose."

"You're wise to see me as a worthy opponent, Sergi. My brother never has. But there is a certain power in being underestimated, don't you think?"

"And who has won this battle, Demetria? Who holds the power now?" Bertrand asked.

"That is yet to be determined," she said

Bertrand laughed heartily at this.

Demetria was not injured by his mockery. She had compassion for him. Her entire life she had shielded her gifts from Bertrand, more to protect his fragile ego than for any other reason.

"Look around. Your reign is over before it has even begun. Will your stubborn pride not allow you to admit that you are backed into a corner?" Bertrand asked.

"You perceive me to be helpless, outwitted, and outnumbered. But the interesting thing about perception is that it is limited to what you know. And there are things, my dear brother, that *you* do not know."

Sergi's intuition told him that not binding Demetria with the irons had been a mistake, one that needed to be rectified immediately.

But when he attempted to raise his wrist to cast the iron chains that would bind her, he realized he could not move.

Demetria smiled, "I am most certainly not backed into a corner."

Without understanding what had happened, both Sergi and Bertrand found themselves immobilized, staring back at Demetria in wide-eyed disbelief.

She had not moved a muscle, and yet they were powerless to do anything against her.

Demetria knew she could not control their minds for long, but they did not.

She gathered a shawl from a nearby table and wrapped it about her shoulders. Before leaving, she kissed Bertrand gently on the forehead, "I am not sure what made you so evil, brother. Yet in spite of all of your flaws and the horrible things you've done, I still love you. You will always be my brother."

Betrand, who had always managed to get in the last word in every argument he had ever had with his sister, found that his vocal cords were frozen in place.

259

The effects would wear off soon enough. And the Order would be in hot pursuit.

Without knowing exactly how long she had before the spell was completed, the Queen made haste, but not before stopping by the vault.

She wiped the shelves clean of each and every jewel, including the crown and scepter. As far as the other kingdom assets, they had long ago been transferred into human banks throughout the world.

Should Bertrand try to access any of it, he would find to his surprise that he had, many months prior, been abruptly and completely cut off.

Demetria found Marie and a still unconscious Langdon waiting for her in the helicopter.

"How did the coronation go?"

For the first time, Demetria let the strain of what she had discovered show on her face. "I'm afraid that will have to wait. Absalom is headed to the town of Glenhaven. He knows everything. And he claims there is a—,"

"Portal there," Marie finished.

Demetria glanced at Marie, "You've known all along, haven't you?"

Marie nodded and smiled sadly, "Absalom thinks the portal is something he can work his will upon, that he can open it and reconnect the bridge to the place all djinn came from. He can't. Our creator gave us what we wanted, to be bound to the material plane, and then he closed the door. He never intended for us to reopen it."

"And all that we have become is a calamity of wings, ushering in the darkness," Demetria sighed. "I have a daughter in Glenhaven. She's amalgam. You deserve to know. It is my greatest weakness; one Absalom will surely try and use against me."

"Then you understand what is at stake and why we can't go there. Not yet. We need time to come up with some sort of strategy. Do you trust me?"

Demetria realized that she did. "Completely."

At that very moment, the hanger door came crashing from its hinges. Sergi, whose face was distorted into an angry grimace, raised his hand to do a spell.

Knights of the Order of the Blue Orchid surrounded the helicopter as the ceiling began to reclose.

But Marie had already begun ascending. They cleared the opening moments before there was a blinding pulse of light, as bright as a thousand hydrogen bombs.

The explosion of energy propelled the helicopter out and into a dizzying tailspin.

Marie struggled to gain control as the gyroscopic leftward motion seemed impossible to stop. After minutes of adding right rudder, the craft stabilized.

All of the commotion jolted the Queen's advisor from his slumber, and they all glanced back in stunned silence as the kingdom began to collapse, folding in on itself, again and again, until finally, nothing of it remained.

There was a loud, almost animal like outcry from Sir Langdon, who had a wife and a large extended family there.

"What the fuck just happened?" Marie asked.

"I had no choice," Demetria said.

After what seemed like an eternity of awe-struck silence, Sir Langdon regained his ability to speak. "Your Highness? What have you done?"

"I ejected everyone from the kingdom and contained it."

"Are they…. dead?" he asked, his voice cracking with emotion.

Queen Demetria stared back at him in horrified disbelief, "How could you think me capable of something like that? Do you think I would just kill everyone off and call it a day?"

"My apologies. Forgive me. I'm simply grappling with this. What has happened to everyone, exactly?"

"They've been pushed out into the human world. I assure you the most harm that has been done is that they are completely dumbfounded and displaced," Demetria said.

"I see." Sir Langdon prayed his loved ones were safe and sound, but he had sworn to protect Queen Demetria. His loyalty and duty to her would always take priority above all else.

Neither Marie or Langdon had ever seen such a display of power before. This would quickly dispel any talk that the Courtenay royals had grown weak. If anything, the opposite was true.

"Sir Langdon, I will understand if you no longer wish to serve me. I'll release you from your duty, effective immediately, and will not think poorly of you." The new queen hung her head as she wrestled with doubt.

"I would never dream of that! It is my honor to serve you. You did what you had to do to prevent our home from falling into the wrong hands. You've shown those puss sacks just who it is they are dealing with."

The Queen allowed the hint of a smile to briefly replace the worry there.

Sir Langdon noticed then that Marie was there and stared at her in utter confusion, "Who the hell are you?"

"I'll fill you in on everything you need to know, but first, we have to make a quick pit stop."

At once, the helicopter hovered above the parking lot of a small hotel, just outside the hallway of the floor where she'd left her assistant.

Marie grabbed the mouth piece for the radio and turned on the outside speaker. "Paging Courtney Lazar. Courtney Lazar, your chariot has arrived."

Courtney stared back with pure contempt. Without a second's hesitation, she swung her leg over the balcony, took Sir Langdon's hand, and leapt through the open door into the helicopter.

Once she buckled herself into one of the seats, she held up a hand to stop Marie from saying a word, "I haven't eaten anything in 15 hours. I had to fight off a drunken German tourist who thought I was a prostitute and tried to hump my leg. I have welts, the size of lemons all over my body from the mosquito bites. I probably have malaria and crabs. And if I do not have a cheeseburger the size of my head in my hands, pronto, I will not be responsible for what I do."

Courtney remembered her manners and smiled at Sir Langford who sat across from her before extending her hand to him and then to Queen Demitria, "I'm Courtney. Nice to meet you." To Marie, she raised her middle finger.

"Will Wonder Burger do?" Marie asked.

"Fine. Yeah. They have good shakes."

Later, with her belly full, Courtney closed her eyes and dozed off, letting the day dissolve as if it never happened. That was one of the things Marie appreciated about her, she never held onto a grudge for long.

The sun was just beginning to creep up when they reached the house on the coast of Maine, in the town of Kittery. Warm light escaped from its large glass windows.

There were several cars already in the driveway so Marie decided it best to simply land on the front lawn.

She stepped out and approached the house alone for the benefit of anyone who might have glimpsed the royal crest on the side of the aircraft. She keyed in the correct code and entered the house.

She was relieved to see Alton Harringford and Conway Spizzeri, hugging them straight away. She was so happy to see them that she broke down in tears.

"Where is Lilian?" she asked.

"She went ahead to Glenhaven. We couldn't stop her. She couldn't reach Amsel and feared the worst. How did you get your hands on that?" Conway asked, motioning toward the royal helicopter.

Conway wore a black terry cloth bathrobe and his matching curly hair stood up straight from hours of nervously tugging on it.

Marie noticed he'd put on quite a bit of weight, over 60 pounds since she'd seen him last. She thought the numerous empty wrappers from his favorite prepackaged snack cakes that were scattered everywhere might be to blame.

"Aww...Conway, still stress eating I see," Marie said.

But he was too busy staring out at the state-of-the-art helicopter. "Yes, well about that...," Marie waved and the other passengers stumbled out, taking a second to get their land legs.

"Heavens to Betsy! Is that who I think it is?" Alton could hardly contain himself, his hand landing automatically on the handle of the gun he had strapped around his waist.

Marie always thought his Texas cowboy persona was hilarious. Over time, he'd taken it on like a second skin.

"Alton! What are you going to do? Shoot them? You do remember you're a djinni and that you don't really need a gun? Anyway, they are my guests."

Demetria stopped in the doorway, where Conway and Alton immediately bowed.

"Please, don't. I would prefer it if you didn't bow. Right now, I don't even have a kingdom."

Both men looked completely baffled.

"I'm sorry, did you say that you no longer have a kingdom?" Conway asked. "I don't understand. Were you overthrown?"

"No. I just stored everything inside this ring for safe keeping."

He grinned at her thinking someone at any moment was going to let him in on the joke, but moments later, when the somber look on her face remained, said, "But...but...that's impossible. Isn't it?"

Everyone stared at the ring, trying to fathom how such a thing could be done.

"If I hadn't seen it for myself, I would have thought the same thing," Marie admitted.

Alton and Conrad stared at Demetria with mouths agape.

"Sorry, don't mean to break the shock and awe and everything but where's the bathroom?" Courtney asked.

Marie pointed to a hallway and Courtney disappeared.

"A human?" Alton asked.

"She's with me," Marie said.

"Sure. Why the hell not? Something tells me this is all gonna' go down better after I've had a stiff drink and a strong cup of coffee," Alton said with a pronounced Southern twang, throwing up his hands in surrender as he went off to grind some coffee beans.

They all knew that none of the scenarios they'd planned for in the past, were going to be sufficient to deal with the scale of what they faced now.

But then they had never had the Queen of the United Kingdom Between or her top advisor on their side before.

Whatever they must do, they must do it quickly. If Absalom figured out how to open the portal, it would be too late for all of them, djinn and human kind alike.

CHAPTER TWENTY-FIVE

GLENHAVEN

Lilian materialized at the edge of Harben's estate and thoroughly scanned the perimeter of the property.

When she was positive there were no spies to see her, she used the spell key to open the hidden gate. It was two in the morning, but the large manor was lit up in its entirety.

He was expecting her.

Harben chose to live at the farthest edge of Glenhaven, hardly ever venturing into town anymore. At this point near the end of his life cycle, he left matters of business in the capable hands of his daughter, Penelope.

Lilian made her way through oversized hallways until she reached the study where she knew he would be waiting.

From his wheelchair, Harben leaned forward, one hand planted on the white marble surround of the fireplace as he poked at the blue flames dancing inside.

Untamable tufts of white hair stuck out in all directions. He was still handsome, his impressive height evident even as he sat with a spine hunched over with age.

Once he had been much taller than his twin brother, Amsel senior. It was hard for her to look at this nearly mirror image of her deceased husband without a pang of sadness and loss.

But that was where the likeness ended. Harben was hard edged with none of the warmth she had loved about his brother.

He sensed her presence but didn't immediately turn around, "I told my brother this would not end well. Our backs are against the wall and we are outnumbered."

"I see that you haven't lost your delightful optimism," Lilian smiled.

"Ahhh…the reason that I was not able to capture your heart for myself all those years ago. You never once put up with any of my antics."

He turned, opening his arms to embrace her.

"Any word from Amsel?" she asked.

"Unfortunately, no. It's strange for him to disappear in this way. There have been rumors floating around town. Are they true? Has Amsel become involved with one of them?"

Lilian nodded and Harben became enraged, waving his hand around until the glass of Tennessee whiskey he'd picked up from a nearby table and that sloshed onto the expensive Persian carpet, was nearly empty.

"Utterly Reckless," he ranted.

269

"It was reckless. I agree. But this girl is no ordinary girl. She's a royal, Harben."

His free hand flew to his chest as if he had been shot. For an instant, Lilian thought his ancient djinni heart might have finally decided to give up the ghost.

"Then he has brought ruin upon this family and the world. We are all doomed."

"I'm not so sure about that. Someone has been protecting her since she was born, with very old and very powerful magic. Having a royal sympathizer could be game changing."

Harben considered this for many minutes in silence, "And have you considered that she could be a weaponized arm of the House of Courtenay?"

"Of course, I have. But the woman doesn't know what she is. She doesn't know who she is. And there is one more thing."

"By all means, Lilian, lay it on me. I doubt that anything else could shock me."

"The woman is pregnant with Amsel's child."

"And there you go again, proving me wrong."

A long chain of curse words followed that Lilian hadn't heard in years. Unable to control his rage, he threw his glass against the fireplace. Lilian ducked to avoid the shard of crystal that would have otherwise punctured her eye.

Once he had calmed down, he asked, "You're sure that she is a Courtenay?"

"We are certain we have proof of this."

"Then let's hope that you are right for all our sakes. Any word from the others?"

"They are at a safe house in Kittery, awaiting word from Marie. And where is Penelope?"

"In town. She should be arriving shortly."

Penelope had in fact arrived long before Lilian and perched in her usual corner. It had the best acoustics, an area which perfectly captured any sound coming from the study.

She had learned at a young age how to navigate the manor unseen. It was a special gift she kept hidden, for this particular gift would be no good at all if others were aware of it and could mount defenses against it.

It had been most useful in studying Helene Parish, secretly trailing her, observing her habits, learning what others had to say about her, and most importantly, trying to discover exactly what it was Amsel saw in the woman.

It had always been assumed that she and Amsel would end up together. After all, it was not uncommon for djinn to marry their cousins. And in truth, she was in love with Amsel.

All these years, she had waited patiently for him to come to her. She had always believed in the inevitability of their union. Until now.

That day in the street she had merely meant to scare Helene away, but the feeling of rage that had taken hold of her was beyond her control. Had it not been for James

271

Houston, Helene would have been permanently removed from the equation.

Afterwards, Penelope had been more than a little shocked by her actions. She was not a killer. She protected amalgam and her family's secrets.

But if this woman was pregnant with Amsel's child, that was a threat to everything she had ever wanted. And she was not about to let her life and those of the ones she loved, be destroyed by a halfling.

Penelope also had the scoop on something that her father and Aunt did not yet know. The United Kingdom Between had suffered a major catastrophe, vanishing into thin air, and displacing all of its citizens.

It was all over djinn channels of social media.

Demetria Courtenay was missing, and there were rumors that she had escaped, destroying everything in order to evade arrest for undisclosed crimes against the Kingdom.

It seemed highly likely that Demetria was somehow linked to Helene.

Now, she only needed to figure out how to use this bargaining chip to her advantage.

CHAPTER TWENTY-SIX

SOMEWHERE IN BUTT-FUCK LOUISIANA

Black spots still floated in Sergi's field of vision, long after the flash of light consumed the whole of everything that had once been the Between.

To say Demetria had blindsided them all, was the understatement of a Millenia.

He was in a state of shock. He was reeling, unhinged, ready to pummel the next living thing he saw into an unrecognizable and bloody pulp.

Absalom could not have known that Demetria Courtenay was so dangerous. But then none of them had realized the power hiding underneath coiffed hair and epic stoicism.

The djinni didn't know what time it was or where he was. It was very early morning judging from the position of the nearly full moon in the sky. Thankfully, it provided adequate light to assess his surroundings.

He drew air into his nostrils. Cypress trees, miles and miles of salt marshes. He was pretty sure he was close to the Gulf Coast.

If he had to guess, he would say he was somewhere in rural, butt-fuck Louisiana. He hated Louisiana, for petty reasons he scarcely recalled, other than it had something to do with jazz funerals.

He marveled at just how quickly he'd been cast, quite literally, into an existential crisis.

The sudden collapse of an entire kingdom, finding out about Amsel and that he might have murdered his father, and the fact that Marie Sol was somehow alive, served to move the gage into the dangerous red zone.

Sergi did something he had not done in a very long time. He screamed out from the enormous chambers of his djinni lungs, from the deepest and most gnarly, twisted parts of his being. The vibration rattled the ground like the discharge of several pounds of dynamite.

Fortunately, the area was relatively isolated. Other than an alligator that rightfully feared for his life and disappeared beneath into the murky swamp, the event went unnoticed.

Marie Sol, he fumed. How could she have evaded him when there was a psychic cord that connected them? The cord was only ever severed in death.

It was a common practice in the olden days, back when djinnis were allowed to keep slaves, to ensure that this valuable commodity, even if they escaped their bonds, could quickly and easily be found.

Sergi realized she must have died, if only for an instant, and then been revived. But why would anyone save a life so

274

obviously undeserving of it? Remove her irons? Heal her wounds? The audacity of them. How rude.

But how could any djinni have recovered from those injuries? That was the question. How was it that she was still alive?

He remembered that day clearly.

He'd caught her at the kitchen door, handing scraps to a human child, an orphan, of around six years of age.

The boy had been covered in a thick layer of dirt that had accumulated on his sweaty body becoming a shiny spectral grime by candlelight. And he stank to the high heavens, dirt being the least offensive of the odors that had soaked into him and included what Sergi was sure to be Eau de dead rat.

It was not the first time he'd caught Marie in one of these random acts of kindness. Sergi did not understand it. Marie was hardly treated any better by him than the child had been treated by his human world.

Why was she not more concerned with her own survival?

To him the act showed a pathetic weakness.

He'd paid a pretty penny for her, and the meager rations he provided were meant for her to sustain herself, not some street urchin.

She had been warned. Many times.

"You dared to disobey my orders."

Marie turned slowly, gazing at him without any fear. There was a far more dangerous emotion inside of them this time. Indifference. She lowered her head but said nothing.

Sergi walked briskly toward the child, striking him soundly across the face. The force of it shattered the tiny jaw and sent many rotten, blood-soaked teeth flying into the alleyway.

His sickening screams as he made a spectacle of himself were almost enough to prompt Sergi to hit him again. But before he could do this, the child shrank back into the shadows from which he had come.

"It was your actions that sealed the fate of that child. He will not survive his injury and his death is your fault, not mine," Sergi said.

There was no emotion on Marie's face. There were no tears. She'd become as a mute, turning her head toward the tower of dirty dishes she had yet to wash, refusing to acknowledge that she understood that he was even speaking to her.

At first, Sergi thought that centuries of cruelty toward his servant had finally broken her. She had always been far more head strong than he was comfortable with.

But when she looked at him again, head held high, her chin thrust forward, he realized this was not the case. There was a look in her eyes, something serene and peaceful that disturbed him more than anything he'd ever seen there.

It was that look that had provoked Sergi to drive the iron spike into her heart.

And when she refused to give him what he desired, her terror and cries of agonizing pain as proof of his power over her, his fury over being bested by a slave, brought him to remove the spike and to try one more time.

This time he twisted the sharp iron spike, intent on mincing her stomach into thin strips of organ.

Sergi had been certain then that she was already dead. He had been certain that in the end, she had managed to deny him what he wanted most, to see that she at last understood his superiority over her.

This time, he would not make the same mistake. It would not be a quick death. He would take his time. When she grew near to death, he would bring her back. And then he would do it again and again, until she begged him to end her suffering.

And then it would be Amsel's turn.

Since hearing of Amsel's betrayal, he'd done little but replay moments from the past.

Sergi had always resented Amsel's relationship with his father. Where his own actions at times had been criticized by Lord Benowin, as excessive or cruel, Amsel had been more aligned with his father's values, the golden child who could do no wrong.

As far as Sergi was concerned, it was exactly that outdated chivalry that had gotten his father killed.

Absalom would be waiting for him. He dreaded having to face him. He had failed to secure the throne or the Kingdom. And he had absolutely no idea where Prince Bertrand was.

Luckily, there was an emergency protocol put in place by the Order of the Blue Orchid at its inception, for just such a chaotic event.

Every member worth their salt would remember exactly what to do, and they would fall back on Absalom's absolute authority, an authority which in crisis, completely usurped that of the Royal House.

Did Demetria have any idea at all that this clause even existed? Were her actions taken strictly out of panic, or did she have a grand plan that would bite them all in the ass?

All that mattered now was opening the portal. It would be the end of life as they knew it. A grand new beginning that would give djinn dominance upon the earth.

In good time, things would be the way they should have always been. The way the ancestors had intended it to be, before humankind began to brainwash his kind into believing the way that they did.

A day of reckoning was at hand.

Sergi took a deep breath. He began to feel like himself again. A calmness fell over him and he actually smiled as he took in the strange beauty of the land around him.

He looked almost serene as he unfurled his wings and took to the sky.

Somewhere in New Orleans, Mr. Wyatt Delaney had woken up early with the most wonderful feeling of peace he'd ever known.

He was sitting out on the screened porch, wrapped up in one of his wife's scarves that he'd grabbed from the coat rack, when a huge black shadow crossed the sky.

It was the most splendid sight. The enormity of the being stunned him into an awe filled silence. But he wasn't scared. For reasons he didn't understand, he felt comforted by the sight.

He felt grateful to have beheld it and at peace with the possibility that his world might be shared with things beyond human understanding.

The next morning over breakfast, he would make no mention of what he had seen to his wife and daughter.

PART THREE

CHAPTER TWENTY-SEVEN

A DESTROYER OF WORLDS

I looked out upon the ruined landscape. Everything, as far as I could see, was charred and blackened. Were it not for traces of color here and there, the corpses would have been indistinguishable from the scorched earth.

Remnants of a wide leather strap, the heel that had once been attached to someone's boot, links of heavy chain, were the only things that had survived complete annihilation.

The ground still glowed with blue white embers. I zeroed in on a speck of bright green ahead and made my way toward it, unhurried. My feet were bare and covered with smut, yet they effortlessly grazed the coals, unharmed by the intense heat felt, but not burned by.

I stopped and studied the crinkled edges of the thing that had caught my attention, shimmering green silk melted into skin. Male or female, I could not tell. Blood dripped down my legs. Mine or that of others, I did not know.

It was pitch black beyond the eerie blue light that spewed from a well in the ground. There were no stars, no moon, and there was no sound. As if the world I had known had collapsed in on itself and I was all that remained of it.

It was the way it had been, on that very first day, when God had said, let there be light. And I was given this gift of looking out at it through his eyes.

I jolted upright, heart thumping wildly, the heaviness in my chest making it hard to draw in air. It took a long time to shake the feeling that still clung to me. The feeling that I'd touched something divine, something absolute, all powerful, and as destructive and unmerciful as it was loving and forgiving.

By its nature it was balanced, of two opposing forces, impartial to either, and freewill could tip it in either direction. It did not care. It only observed.

Only after many cycles of deep focused breaths, was I steady enough to stumble to the kitchen for a glass of water to soothe my raw throat. I must have been screaming out in my sleep.

It was the third nightmare in as many days, ever since Lester and I had made the discovery in the woods.

Something about being in the energy there had triggered their return. Only they were much worse. They were an aftermath, a glimpse of an outcome I wasn't sure that I could change.

The unease and anxiety clung to me long after I awoke.

I had not been able to get in touch with Lester. I'd stopped by on my way back from my visit to the doctor, but he hadn't answered the door.

His voice mailbox was full and I had not been able to leave a message for him. But I had the uneasy feeling that Lester was not alright.

I quickly dressed, alarmed when I slid the stretchy fabric of the maternity pants over my belly. In three days, the size of it had more than quadrupled. I had been given paperwork at the clinic, and remembered there was a chart which showed a woman's belly at each month of development.

I frantically tore through them until I'd found it. I looked like the woman in the six-month diagram. It was impossible. What was happening to me? The ultra sound hadn't shown a tumor.

A prickle of fear tried to elbow its way in but I wouldn't allow it. I had to check on Lester.

I drove entirely too fast along the unmarked country road which led to his farm. Nothing seemed out of the ordinary until I reached the house.

I found Rogue scratching at Lester's front door. His whimpering only confirmed my fears.

It was unlocked. Rogue ran in ahead of me, up the stairs, leading me to a room at the end of the hallway. There I found Lester crouched by his bed with his hands covering his ears.

"Lester, are you alright?"

"It's too much. It's too much," he said.

"What is?"

"I hear everything. All of their thoughts, every wish, need, everything!"

"You're scaring me, Lester. Whose thoughts are you talking about?"

He glanced up, lowering his hands from his ears and gazing at me with pained bewilderment, "The town's folk, you, the child inside of you."

Had the encounter with the barrier in the woods triggered a psychotic break in Lester, the same way it had triggered the nightmares in me?

I treaded delicately as I searched my intuition around the situation, "How could you hear the baby, Lester? It doesn't even have a fully developed brain yet."

"It does. It's growing faster than a human child would. It knows things, Helene."

I slid onto the floor next to him and placed my hand on his arm, wanting to ground him back in reality, "What kind of things?"

"The man from the store, the white-haired man in the suit. He's coming for you."

I felt the blood drain from my face, "How do you know about that man?" I hadn't mentioned him to anyone.

And what did Lester mean by, it's not a human child?

"You think I'm losing my mind. But that child showed me the man you saw twice, once in Glenhaven and again on the day you saw the doctor. You felt that it wasn't a coincidence and it wasn't."

"Who is he?" I asked.

"A destroyer of worlds."

The words were chilling. An endless stream of carnage and blood curdling screams flashed through my thoughts;

all the things I had prayed would never come to pass. But to hear this, was a step too far toward the edge of doom.

I honed in on my feelings. Everything in my being told me that the danger was real, that we were about to clash with things beyond our understanding, and that something terrible was about to unfold in Glenhaven.

"What is this child?" I whispered.

"It's like you. Like everyone in this town. Part djinn."

Lester's words registered but it was as though I were hearing them from very far away. I felt a cold sweat break. The thing I had seen, the winged creature that had filled me with dread, Amsel had clearly tried to cover up its existence.

Suddenly, it was clear to me, or perhaps I'd known all along and just couldn't allow myself to believe it.

That being was Amsel.

And I was somehow like him. And my child was? What?

The shock of it slowly seeped into me, like a potent anesthetic, numbing me, until I was finally able to separate myself from it enough to speak, "Djinn. I don't understand. But why was this kept from us?"

I was startled by my cell phone buzzing from my back pocket.

"You should take that. It's the doctor's office," Lester said.

He was right. I immediately recognized the slow, Southern drawl of the nurse from the clinic, "I'm so sorry. This is highly unusual, but we need to schedule a follow up appointment to redo the amniocentesis. The results were inconclusive."

"Inconclusive? I don't understand."

The nurse cleared her throat and there was a long silence as she looked over the lab results. "It seems the sample we sent to the lab was corrupted somehow. The cells were not recognizable."

"I'll have to call you back." The nurse was still speaking when I hung up.

"Do you still think I'm having a psychotic break?"

"Maybe we both are."

This life inside of me was developing at supernatural speed. A nurse had just confirmed the cells they had taken from the baby were not even ones they recognized.

This chilled me to the core. What did any of it mean?

All this time, my parents had kept this a secret from me. Why?

"Please, Helene. You can't say a word to Mary. Not until I can get control of what's happening with me. I don't want her to see me like this."

"Alright, Lester. But you can't hide forever. At some point, she's going to suspect something is wrong."

He'd told Mary that he had the flu, but he was convinced she was going to show up on his doorstep at any moment. That's why I stopped by the diner and informed her that I needed chicken soup to take to him.

"Perfect timing. I was just about to head over there to check on him. In all the years I've known him, that man has never been sick. Not one time. How did he get the flu, anyway?" Mary frowned.

I simply shrugged. The less I said the better. I had on an oversized jacket and hoped she didn't look me over too closely.

"I don't want you to get sick too. Maybe I should take the soup over to him myself," Mary said.

"No! What would the town do if you got sick? Anyway, I'm pretty sure I'm immune to the flu."

The only reason Mary's built-in lie detector didn't instantly go off was that it was true. I had never had the flu, even after being cooped up with my parents after they both contracted it. And cushioning a big lie with a little bit of truth, had worked, temporarily, to appease her.

There was something else I'd been wanting to ask her about.

"Mary, the other day when I was here, I saw something happening in the back, something I was hoping you could explain to me."

Mary took the wet cloth she had in her hand and wiped down the counter. I felt like she already knew what I was going to ask and was simply buying time for herself, contemplating how she would answer the inevitable question.

But then she surprised me by leaning in close and looking me squarely in the eyes, "I'll explain that, if you can tell me how the hell you went from having a stomach as flat as a pancake four days ago to looking like you could pop a baby out at any minute."

"Touché, Mary. Touché." With effortless finesse, Mary had successfully turned the tables, out maneuvering me.

A customer saved me from this dilemma by calling for her from the back of the restaurant, "Miss!"

Mary snapped at her, "I'll be right there." Then instantly composed herself, offering up a smile so warm and dripping with kindness, it could have melted an ice shelf a mile wide. "I'll be right back with Lester's soup."

The Mary I knew and loved had returned and it was as if the verbal cage-fight we'd just engaged in, had never even happened.

Mary had totally gaslighted me. She made her rounds, filling water glasses, checking in to see what her customers needed. Then she went to the back and came out with a bag that she handed to me.

"I put an extra slice of pound cake in there for you. Please tell Lester I'll call and check on him tonight."

The way she had completely avoided the topic of the strange phenomenon I'd witnessed in the kitchen, led me to believe that there was no easy explanation for it, that maybe like myself, she was grappling with something she didn't really understand herself.

I left the soup in the car and stopped by the library, nothing, not one book dealing with djinn, amazing, in a town that was supposedly crawling with them.

The internet was spotty in this remote location at best, but I was able to connect to a few sites long enough to gather some information.

They were supernatural beings. Djinn and genies were one and the same. As in the tale of Aladdin and the Magic Lamp, they held special powers.

287

In Middle Eastern lore they were primarily spirits similar to what we would think of as fallen angels or demons. Like humans, they possessed free will. They could be extremely good, extremely evil, or somewhere in between, but there were certainly more negative associations with them than good.

Unlike humans, their abilities ran the gambit from casting magical spells which could help or harm, to shapeshifting. They were blamed for possessions and malevolent deeds, as well as being protective guardians of religious sites and of certain humans. They also, mostly remained hidden from humans, existing in space beyond human perception.

I had no way of knowing what information I'd read was fact and what was pure fiction. It didn't take long to figure out that my answers would not come from the internet.

So why the fuck were djinn in Glenhaven in the first place? And how could so many of us be related to them and not know that?

This part of me that I had always feared, was it truly evil? Was I evil? My head throbbed from all the questions swirling around in there.

Was my mother one of them? And if so, what did that mean for myself and my unborn child? Were there things I could do that I hadn't even tapped the potential of?

I found myself driving up the steep road to Amsel's house, stopping at the gate. Conveniently, it swung open and I pulled my Civic up front.

Through the glass panes of antique oak double doors, I could see into the foyer. One of the corners of the Persian rug was flipped over as if Amsel had dragged his foot across it on his way out.

I made no pretense of knocking. I simply turned one of the doorknobs and was surprised to find the door was also unlocked.

Now what?

The lack of locks and the ease at which I had accessed his property, made my actions feel a little paranoid. Would a person with so many secrets leave town with the house wide open? But then there *were* cameras everywhere.

What would I have done if the house had been locked up tight? Would I have broken in? I didn't allow myself to think about this. It was so counter to anything I would have done under normal circumstances.

But it wasn't like I was there to take things. I needed answers. And it wasn't like Amsel was around to ask. I wasn't the thief. I wasn't the one who had stolen his heart and disappeared into the night.

I moved through the house searching aimlessly through drawers and closets but paused in the doorway of his study.

I could feel his presence in this space, in the worn leather armchairs, the books scattered around, and there was the lingering scent of sandalwood.

It was a room he spent a lot of time in, and it felt like a betrayal to have stepped across the threshold.

Before I could talk myself out of it, I began pulling out documents. They were mostly, unimportant things, bills to be paid, correspondence to an attorney over a tax issue, a letter from a college friend lamenting the closing of a cherished restaurant they had frequented and the loss of all the things held sacred to them in their youth.

As soon as my hands touched the next page, I knew I had found something out of the ordinary. It was extremely old, parchment, made from the skin of some unfortunate animal. The writing was composed entirely of characters I did not recognize as any known language.

There was stylized letterhead with a brilliant blue orchid. It was familiar as if I had seen it before, so long ago, it was buried deep within my subconscious.

Then I remembered a detail of my father's funeral. The flower arrangement that had been sent, blue orchids of the deepest indigo. Everyone had commented on them, that they had never seen orchids that color.

And they were sent without a card, no writing anywhere, only this beautiful blue flower printed on the card.

"Do you know who these are from?" I'd asked my mother.

She'd reached out to touched them, her hand trembling. "It could have been anyone. What a shame we will never be able to properly thank them."

I hadn't believed her. She'd known. Like so many other things, it was something she preferred to keep in the shadows.

I hadn't heard anyone enter the room, but I glanced up to find the most stunning woman I'd ever seen, watching me. Her shiny white hair fell elegantly over her shoulders as she smiled serenely from across the room.

Her resemblance to Amsel was remarkable.

She didn't seem at all surprised to find me pilfering through her son's private papers. And I made no effort to explain my actions. Somehow, it felt unnecessary, as if she had acquired every thought in my head, every detail about me, in the span of a few seconds.

"Hello, Helene. I'm Lilian. We have a lot to talk about. Would you like some tea?"

I managed to nod and stumbled to my feet, following her to the kitchen in awkward silence. Where would we begin? She had to have noticed my pregnant belly. What would she have to say about the way her son had abandoned me?

What I sensed in her, I'd sensed in Amsel. Something that defied explanation, an energy that was both alarmingly foreign, and yet which drew me in like a flame on a cold day.

She wasn't human. She defied everything I'd ever known about the world. I should have been terrified, but I wasn't.

Lilian motioned for me to sit and I did so, taking the cup of chamomile tea she offered and sipping it slowly. It was her who broke the ice, not bothering with pretenses.

"The blue orchid, you recognized that image?"

"Yes. I saw something similar when I was a teenager. I didn't really understand its significance, but it felt like an important secret that I was never supposed to know."

"It represents an organization, the Order of the Blue Orchid, an arm of our royal crown. Its sole purpose, to weed out amalgam. That is what our people call people like you. People like your unborn child."

Amalgam? That was what the men who had attacked Georgia had called her. I shivered at how close they'd been to succeeding in that mission.

"Does Amsel know...does he know that I'm pregnant with his child?"

"Yes."

She must have sensed the way my stomach lurched into my throat. She must have seen in my face how much this hurt me.

He knew and yet he stayed away. That confirmed everything that I had feared, that he had never really cared for me, that he wanted nothing to do with me.

"It is not my place to make excuses for Amsel or to explain what is in his heart. That, only he can do. But the nature of your relationship is forbidden. The Order would see that you both were killed, Amsel for defiling himself with you, and you, for simply being what you are. We are, I'm afraid, in a pickle."

"What is this place? Why are so many like me, here?"

"Glenhaven was created to protect people like you from harm, but this place also holds a greater secret. There is a portal here that connects the human world and the primordial world. If opened, it could--"

292

"Destroy everything."

Lilian looked at me in surprise, as if she were seeing me for the first time, "We think so, but none of us truly know. A large portion of humanity could perish, or all of it. That is why this place has been shielded. It was never meant to be reopened. But now…everything is threatened."

"Then I'll just take myself somewhere far away from here. Amsel can forget he ever met me, and things can go back to the way they were," I stood up and began to head toward the door, but Lilian was already there, waiting for me. "How did you…You were in—"

It was difficult to wrap my mind around what had just happened. Lilian could simply wish herself somewhere else and poof, she was there in an instant. I reached for the doorknob but Lilian placed her hand gently over mine.

"I'm afraid it may be too late for that, my dear. The threat we've feared may already be on its way."

I froze. *The Destroyer of Worlds.* That man. He was part of this Order of the Blue Orchid. I was certain of that. I had to get Lester, Mary, Mark…everyone. They had to go far away. Somewhere safe.

Lilian read my thoughts, "There is no place that will be safe out there. I'm sorry, but I can't allow you to leave."

"So, I'm a prisoner?"

Lilian winced at the accusation. "Think of it as being in protective custody."

After many hours of working through my anger over being held against my will, I took advantage of being allowed free access to the property.

293

Times when Lilian was out of sight and sound, I tested the limits of that, seeing how far I could venture out. I made it as far as the ledge which overlooked the mining area before hitting a firm boundary that pushed back against me with a gentle jolt.

The boundary also obscured the view, a thin veil that caused everything to be hazy and out of focus. I now understood what lurked down there, and what they were protecting. The portal.

The stress of the day instantly, took its toll. I felt extremely tired. Perhaps a nap would do my body good and help me to think clearly about how to get out of this situation.

People would miss me. Lester was expecting me. He would wonder why he could not reach me. And Mary would wonder why I never delivered the soup to Lester.

I tried to send a clear thought to Lester, letting him know where I was and what was happening.

"He won't be able to hear you. I put a shield around the house to protect us."

Like before I had not heard Lilian approach and was startled to hear the sound of her voice, mere feet from me.

My hand flew to my chest. "You really shouldn't sneak up on people like that. It's unnerving."

"I'm so sorry, dear. When I'm at home or in private I feel freed from following all the necessary protocols we are restricted to when interacting with humans."

I nodded to let her know that I understood. Didn't I do the same? Pretending to be someone different when interacting with others, so that they weren't uncomfortable around me.

It had only been here in Glenhaven where I'd felt safe to be myself.

I tried to hold on to the anger and outrage over the situation I was in, but Lilian had such a kind way about her. I felt myself warming to her against my will.

"When Amsel Senior was alive, we spent a lot of time together here, roaming the property. He built this house, down to every little detail, from architectural pieces he salvaged from around the world. Through this house, he wanted to preserve and protect the past. I guess that is the reason I stay away. I miss him entirely too much here."

"How old is the house?" I'd always felt it was far older than what my logic told me was possible. Now I realized my perceptions about what things were possible, had been completely wrong.

"It's been over a century now. Amsel did remodel the kitchen when he moved back in, but other than that, it is the same."

"It's beautiful. So how was it that the land fell into the hands of the mining company?"

"You've done your research. There was a time when we left this place and traveled the world together. We thought we had taken enough precautions to keep others out. This area was so remote, we never dreamed anyone would discover any practical use for it. But the world changed on us. With the invention of modern transportation, the world became smaller, more accessible. It took quite a bit of finagling to get the deed to this land and keep the story of what happened here under wraps."

"What happened to those miners?" I asked.

"The energy around the portal is not compatible with human DNA. They could not survive the exposure."

"I was down there. I went beyond the force field. Will I meet the same fate as those men?"

"No. You are not human. You are part djinn and it doesn't have the same effect on you."

"And that little bit of horrific history kept on display for the public is a convenient way to keep them from getting too close to your secret."

"Yes. That is correct. But it didn't stop you, Helene."

"Why do you care so much about saving amalgam? Why do you protect us?" I asked.

"We had seen so many of your kind murdered. We could no longer stomach the genocide being carried out under our noses without doing something. So, we and other like-minded djinn, devised a plan using spell work that would lure as many of you here as we could, and keep you hidden from the outside world."

"But how could so many of your kind allow these murders to happen? Who started it all?"

Lilian gazed at me, intently. "When hate is conditioned into us, it's difficult for some to allow themselves to see the wrong in it. As far as who is responsible, I don't think you are going to like the answer to that question."

I pondered her words and my feelings around them. There was something there, so dark and unpleasant, and yet somehow connected to me. She was right, I wasn't sure that I was ready to know.

"You're tired and hungry. How about a bit of that delicious soup and cake I rescued from your car?"

"Sure. That sounds nice."

After some of Mary's food, I felt my disposition improve and with a full belly, could barely keep my eyes open.

Lilian insisted that I stay in Amsel's room, since it had the most comfortable bed in the house. I found myself clinging to Amsel's pillow. Even though he hadn't slept on it in over two weeks, it still smelled like him.

Tears welled up in my eyes, but I didn't try to hold them back or pretend that these feelings weren't there.

The fact that he did not love me, that he regretted our union, and that his life was in jeopardy because of me and our unborn child, filled me with sadness and fear about what the future might hold.

Knowing what he was, hadn't change my feelings. Somehow, I knew that whatever transformation he took in his true form, I would still love him.

He'd turned his back on me because he did not feel the same. I would make sure that myself and the child would never be a burden for him.

I wondered what lengths he would go to protect himself? What lengths would Lilian go to protect her son? It was hard to believe that I might matter in any of this.

It was late afternoon when I finally fell asleep, so exhausted that even nightmares could not haunt me.

CHAPTER TWENTY-EIGHT

HER ICY STARE

The sound of raised voices in the den woke me, voices I did not recognize. I proceeded as quietly as possible, hugging the wall so as to remain unseen.

"What do you propose we do? We've woven every protection spell we can think of but it may not be enough. Absalom has already taken control of as much of your army as he could round up, and you, my Queen, are in exile," the male voice said.

"Please everyone, call me by my first name. I know all of this, Conway, but there are still many who are loyal to me. And I will worry about that later. The pressing matter is finding a way to collapse the portal once and for all."

I leaned forward as much as I dared to peek inside at the woman who was apparently some kind of djinn royalty.

Her appearance was entirely human. She was tall and full figured, her movements as she paced around the room, entirely graceful and refined in spite of the fact that she wore dark jeans, a cerulean blue cashmere sweater, a simple strand of pearls, and wellies.

She was quite beautiful and strangely, familiar.

The raspy voice of another woman joined in, but when she came into view, I drew my breath sharply enough that I almost gave myself away.

Her skin was as black as ebony and her massive feathered wings filled the space, nearly stretching from one wall to the other.

"And how are we going to do that, shy of detonating a nuclear bomb large enough to destroy the planet?" she asked.

Her wing tipped over an expensive looking vase that Lilian caught, "Really Marie, could you take on a form that this house can accommodate, before you break another precious artifact?" She motioned toward scattered pieces of painted pottery that might have once been an ancient Greek bowl.

"Sorry! I just needed to stretch my wings for a moment." The woman known as Marie instantly transformed into a studious looking woman with medium length dark hair and glasses.

"Demetria may be onto something. A conduit could hold it open long enough to warp the space and force it to collapse," Lilian said.

Demetria. Could it be?

A sick feeling formed in my gut. It was the same name as the woman who had written the letter, the woman who claimed she was my birth mother.

"What is it, Alton? You're chomping at the bits over there," Marie said.

"That ain't no plan! A conduit? Why hell, that's a damn fairytale and everybody knows it. Has anyone in this room ever met a conduit powerful enough to connect to the primordial world?"

Was this man a djinni too? He had the beginnings of a beer gut that lapped over the enormous silver belt buckle holding up his skinny jeans, and he wore deep, burgundy, cowboy boots. The idea that this man was a non-human entity, made me want to laugh.

"My great-grandmother, Queen Calendula. She never made this public, only the family knew. Toward the end of her life, she locked herself in the tower and refused to speak. The gift was also a curse. It drove her mad."

"Remarkable, tell me more." Conway crossed the threshold and moved closer to Demetria, his soft-spoken voice incompatible with his enormous size.

I wondered how many more djinnis were in there when Penelope edged into my line of sight.

She looked as casually sophisticated, with her hair pulled into a low ponytail and in her corduroy jumper, as she had the day that I'd met her. The complicated knot on the silk scarf tied around her neck resembled a giant lotus flower.

"Unless we can conjure this grandmother from the dead, this is hardly helpful. And anyway, we have a guest in the hallway," Penelope said, ratting me out without even a glance in my direction.

With my position blown, I couldn't very well cower in the shadows. I stepped into the room and immediately locked eyes with Demetria.

The way she stared back at me with a confused mix of joy and sadness, only reinforced my suspicion that she was in fact, my mother. Also, we had the exact same nose.

It was instant recognition.

"Would you all be so kind as to give me and Helene a minute alone?"

The gentleman who was dressed as a knight and had been quietly taking everything in from the corner, made no move to leave.

"Sir Langdon, I am quite fine on my own. You can go," she said.

Once we were alone, we were free to size each other up awkwardly.

"Do the others know that you are my mother?"

She smiled, seeming pleased that I had figured that out already. "Some do. There hasn't been a great deal of time to explain this with everything devolving into chaos." She motioned toward a chair.

"I prefer to stand, thanks."

She accepted this without complaint and sat down on the same leather sofa where Amsel and I had cuddled together watching B rated movies.

Demetria was the reason Lilian had said I wouldn't like the answer to my question about who was responsible for the genocide.

"This is not how I imagined our first meeting would be," she said.

301

"Why, because you didn't think I'd learn about the hand you played in murdering innocent people?"

She snapped back as if I had physically slapped her, recovered, then leaned forward to position herself closer to me, "I had always planned to set things right when I took over the crown. My mother, your grandmother, was hard and cold, shaped by outdated views, and manipulated by the very institution we are up against now, the same one that only yesterday, murdered her. The Order wants to keep things exactly the way they are."

"And in the meantime, you sat back and let things take their course while people were being slaughtered right and left?"

"It's a bit more complicated than that. I did not have the authority to make a change. I worked against them in secret, connecting to people who believed the way that I did, that it was wrong and time for things to change. That is how I met your father, William Haim. Because of my brother, Prince Bertrand, the Order found out about my pregnancy and had William murdered."

I hugged my arms across my abdomen. I wanted to hate her. I wanted to tear into her and blame her for everything that I had lost. No, I would give her this. I would hear her out.

"I swore to Absalom that I would end the pregnancy, but instead turned to Lela and Howard for help. They were friends of mine and your father's. They were loyal to the cause. And they knew the risks of what they were taking on."

302

"My whole life was a lie, then. My parents took care of me because of loyalty to a cause? Did they even want me?"

"Helene! You know the answer to that. They loved you. Very much. You were their daughter."

"And now what? From what was overheard, you no longer have a kingdom. You are in the same position you were in before, when you did absolutely nothing."

"It is a cruel lesson. I must live with the choices I've made. I waited for the ideal moment, planned for a future when I could safely have you by my side. But now, the odds are still stacked against us, and I can no longer ignore the world as it is. My hand is forced. I have to fight the battle I should have fought long ago."

Helene unfolded her arms and laced her fingers together, "I'm happy you learned this important life lesson. It's just a pity it cost so many lives. Did you think I would just be accepting of this and that I would forgive your silence? That's too tall of an order, I'm afraid."

I walked to the doorway and paused for a second before turning back. "I would like to thank you, though, for turning me over to people who were much better parents to me than you ever could have been. But as far as I'm concerned, we have nothing more to say to one another."

Demetria's shoulders slumped forward and I thought for a second, I saw a tear escape from the corner of her eye. But I must have been mistaken. Her features were drawn into stone, a mask of calm and stillness as she watched me walk away.

I struggled to find my way back to Amsel's room, blinded by stinging tears. I escaped to the balcony and relished in the steady rain that quickly coated my face and soaked my hair and clothes, until my teeth were chattering from the bone chilling cold.

Lashing out at Demetria should have given me a sense of release, but I just felt sickened by my own behavior, essentially, kicking someone when they were down.

Demetria wasn't an evil person. I knew this. She did what she had to do to survive. She'd risked her life to save mine.

If I were honest, I had been harsher with her because deep down I'd always harbored a resentment over being abandoned by my birth parents that had never truly healed.

I'd suppressed this just like I suppressed my anger at Amsel for abandoning me.

Also, I was having a hard time reconciling my feelings over so many wild and unbelievable discoveries happening all at once. The world that I thought I lived in, didn't exist.

There was some comfort in knowing that I belonged to a tribe of others like me, that I wasn't as alone as I had always believed. Knowing these things, made it easier to forgive my own darkness.

But was there a path to forgiving Demetria or Amsel?

I knew that if this Absalom guy won, in the large scheme of things, none of this would matter anymore.

I heard someone enter the room and turned to see a petite woman with short, bleach blonde hair, holding a plate of tiny chicken sandwiches, "Wow, it's freaking cold in here."

She sat the plate down on the nightstand and grabbed a towel from the bathroom that she wrapped around my shoulders before ushering me back inside.

"Let's get you into some dry clothes," she said.

"Who are you?"

She held out her hand, "I'm Courtney Lazar, Marie's assistant,"

Before I could say anything else, she volunteered, "I'm not like them. I'm not even like you. I'm just a human."

This made me laugh. "Hello, human. A week ago, I would have sworn that I was just a human too. Now, I understand that I'm some kind of hybrid outlaw."

"It's a pleasure to meet you, hybrid outlaw. And can I just say, I know that all of this is strange and hard to wrap your mind around. At first, it was for me. But now I can't see the world without seeing the magic. It's a gift really, to be included in something like this."

I wondered if I would ever feel that way. Especially, now that I knew there was a target on my head and those like me. It felt more like one of my horrid nightmares. But I didn't say this to Courtney.

She was extremely likeable, and easy to talk to. Being in her presence, made me instantly feel more at ease. "Would you like to join me for sandwiches and maybe a movie of some kind?"

"Sure, but maybe you should change first." Courtney motioned to the sloshy carpet where I was steadily dripping.

"Right. Just give me ten minutes." I caught sight of myself in the bathroom mirror. I looked frightful. Thick streaks of mascara ran down my cheeks and encircled my eyes.

I turned on the shower and slipped in, grateful for the hot water. I ran my hands over my protruding belly. It was so distended that I had to lean forward to see my toes.

This wasn't normal. Each day my belly quadrupled in size and I had begun to walk with a slightly clumsy waddle.

What would happen to me? Would I survive this pregnancy? Would my baby? She was a girl, according to Lester.

There were other concerns too. Would she come out with huge wings? So different and strange that I had to hide her away from the world in order to protect her? What would I name her?

I clearly heard a voice say, Adelaide. I heard it, not spoken aloud, but in my own thoughts.

Could it be that my child was communicating with me telepathically, the way she had with Lester?

I said it out loud, liking the sound of it, "Adelaide…"

It was beautiful.

I felt a hard kick against my right hand. At first, it was disconcerting, this feeling of something moving inside of me. But a few minutes later I felt comforted by it, even reassured by it.

Looking down, I could see her tiny, round fist rolling across by belly and gently pressed back against the hard balled-up lump, an emotion bubbling inside that I hadn't felt in a very long time.

It was wondrous joy over this life that Amsel and I had created.

"I will always protect you, Adelaide. I will always love you. No matter what."

When I came out, Courtney was flipping through the channels, but stopped suddenly, "OMG. This freaking movie sucks me in every time. What do you think?"

The thought of watching a romantic comedy made me want to burst into tears again, but she looked so happy, I couldn't refuse.

We finished off the plate of sandwiches and later, a huge bowl of popcorn. I was glad for this break which made everything feel normal for a couple of hours.

It dawned on me that Courtney might have some inside information about what was being planned, but after questioning her, I understood she was as in the dark as I was.

With pent up nervousness, I wandered about the house like a phantom, lingering outside any door that hinted of conversation, but it was fruitless.

Whatever, lax state existed before my eavesdropping, was no more. They were obviously taking precautions to make sure that nobody would be able to sneak up on them again.

In a matter of hours, the den had been transformed into a makeshift command center. A map of Glenhaven was fixed to the wall with thumb tacks marking the locations where cameras had been stationed all over the town.

The enormous Conway manned the series of monitors, looking chill in his plush office chair, while Alton paced around the room.

"Something don't feel right." The twang of his Texas accent and misuse of subject verb agreement, made me smile.

"The perimeter is secure. None of the trip wires have been triggered." Conway said.

The rain had stopped falling and I couldn't help but notice how deserted the streets were, "Where is everyone?" I asked.

Alton stopped pacing. "Shit. Shit. Shit. She's right. It's too quiet. I'll go check things out."

"Keep a low profile, my friend," Conway said.

Alton slammed the front door and soon appeared on one of the cameras. Before my eyes, he transformed into a hawk and disappeared into the shadows.

The hairs on my arms stood at high alert and I found myself trying to convince myself that I had not just seen what I had seen.

But the shock was soon overpowered by my concern for the townspeople I cared about, Mary, Lester, the entire Houston family, Georgia, and Alexia.

And where exactly, was Amsel?

What would I do when we were finally face to face? It was almost too painful to think about. I didn't want to learn the truth about his feelings for me. The thought of a world without Amsel was nearly unbearable.

"If you are going to drive me crazy with all your worrying, you could make yourself useful by bringing me something to eat," Conway said.

The djinni sweated profusely, beads of it rolled off of his forehead and saturated his laptop. He looked as if he could have a heart attack or electrocute himself at any moment.

As if reading my thoughts, he added, "I'm healthier than I look. Snack cakes would be good, if you can find them."

I walked into the kitchen and realized too late to turn around, that Penelope was also there. She'd seen me.

"I fancied a bit of hot chocolate. I love the way Amsel makes it, but I can never make it taste the same," she said.

The mention of hot chocolate made me cringe. Was that part of his whole seduction plan, reeling us in with decadent hot beverages?

"Would you like some?" she asked.

"No, thank you," I had no desire to be around Penelope for any length of time, and I sensed beneath the friendly veneer, she felt exactly the same way about me.

"I do hope you aren't upset with me for calling you out for snooping, but there are some places where humans really shouldn't stick their noses."

"I'm not really human, though, am I? And I'll stick my nose in any damn place that I like."

I was relieved to have moved past the point of pretending to like one another.

"Of course, you can. I didn't mean to upset you. I know it must be hard carrying the child of a being that doesn't even see you as his equal."

"What's wrong, Penelope? Did that touch a nerve? That it's me and not you, carrying his child?"

Penelope flashed me with a condescending smile, "It must hurt, knowing that people you've cared about, people

309

who should have loved you, only did so out of duty. I mean, your own mother washed her hands of you when you were born, didn't she?"

Her insinuation that I was unlovable, that I was less because of what I was, cut deeply. It hit upon all of my insecurities with jaw dropping precision.

At once, a series of visions popped into mind, Penelope concealed right under our noses when I had words with Demetria, Penelope lurking invisibly in the shadows as she studied me, stalked me, Penelope with the man I knew to be Absalom.

The last image was of Penelope, behind the wheel of the SUV that had tried to run me over.

I froze in terror as all of these things sank in.

Stay calm, Helene. Think.

I attempted to steady my shaking hands and grabbed a box of crackers from the pantry closet as nonchalantly as possible, as if everything were normal and I had not just discovered that there was a snake in our midst.

But when I turned to leave, she was there, standing too close to me and smiling knowingly. "I can hear your heartbeat, Helene. You are afraid of me. Why?"

My pulse became lodged in my throat and I wasn't sure if I could speak. I managed to sound much braver than I felt, "It was you. You were driving the SUV that day. You would have killed me."

"Very clever that you figured that out. Not my greatest moment. But yes, I would have. Don't take it personally, I only did it to protect Amsel."

I knew this was a lie, the way I always knew when people lied, "No. You did it because you were afraid. Of what, though?" The moment I saw her expression, I knew the answer to that question and began to laugh. "Oh, my! You are afraid that Amsel is in love with me."

"He was infatuated with you and that was dangerous to all of us." She forced her words through gritted teeth, but then her face softened. "It's good he's over you now. In fact, he stayed away because he can't stomach the sight of you, reminding him of how weak he was. He was hoping you would just go away, but the pregnancy made things complicated."

"And how do you think Amsel will feel about you when he finds out you tried to murder me and his unborn child?"

She smiled, the way an opponent did in a chess game, the second they saw an opening. "You don't know anything about Amsel. Not really. Once upon a time, he was a Knight in the Order of the Blue Orchid. He rounded up amalgam and delivered them to their horrible fates."

I thought of the document with the blue orchid that I had found in a drawer in Amsel's desk. It sickened me to think that this could be true.

That Amsel might have directly taken part in this genocide, murdered people like me, made my blood run cold.

But then why create Glenhaven? Why put yourself at risk by protecting people like me?

"No. He cares about the people here. He's not a murderer," I said.

311

"Are you so sure about that? This town is a way for Amsel to atone for the things he's done. But he will never choose loyalty to a half breed over his own family. It's a good thing I am here to save him from the guilt of having to make that choice."

Her icy stare filled me with panic. Where were the others? If I screamed, would they hear me?

An alarm sounded, piercing my eardrums with its high-pitched siren. It distracted Penelope just long enough for me to make a break for the door.

I ran as fast I could, waddling off balance, slipping and sliding in my bare feet as they skimmed across the polished hardwood floor.

I glanced back, expecting Penelope to be fast on my heels, but she wasn't.

Why wasn't she chasing me?

I made it to the front door as it suddenly burst open and Alton stood there, his face white as a sheet. "The townspeople—everyone—they're all gone," he said.

I felt panic then. I tried to shove past him. I wanted to disappear into the trees. I needed to find them, to save them. I needed to save my child.

But Alton grabbed my arm.

"Let me go!" I screamed, trying with all my might to break free, but it was futile. There was no escaping his strong grip on me.

"You can't leave. The shields have been breached. The Order is all around us," he said.

He dragged me, hissing mad, into the makeshift situation room. Demetria was suddenly there, followed by

Marie, Lilian, and Courtney. There was also an elderly man in a wheelchair, who looked exactly like a photo I'd seen of Amsel's father. I realized this must be his uncle, Harben, Penelope's father.

But where was Penelope?

"How did they break through our wards?" Harben asked.

The simple nod and the look Demetria gave me, told me that she knew everything.

But how? Had she seen the fear in my eyes? Had she read my thoughts?

"They didn't break through. Someone let them walk right in," she said. "Isn't that right, Penelope?"

Demetria waved her hand and Penelope was suddenly made visible, leaning casually against the wall.

CHAPTER TWENTY-NINE

THE LIGHT THAT SHINES THROUGH THE CRACKS

"Did you really think I hadn't noticed you slinking about in the shadows of this house? I have been watching you as well and you had no idea. How does it feel when the shoe is on the other foot?" Demetria asked.

Penelope clapped. "You discovered my secret talent and I dare say, share it. I only wish we had met under different circumstances. But I had no choice. I made a deal with Absalom."

"What kind of deal?" Harben's words cracked the air like a whip.

"The townspeople, Queen Demetria, Helene, and the portal, in exchange for our family's safety."

Harben viciously scolded his daughter, "I hadn't realized I'd raised such a fool!"

Penelope winced at her father's words. "What else was I to do? Let them waltz in and take everything we have?"

"Penelope, where's Amsel?" Lilian asked. Her words very faint, as if she couldn't bear to say them out loud, as if she already knew the answer to that question.

"I sent a message. I said it was at your request and asked him to meet me. It was an ambush. But Absalom promised he would not harm him. He said there would be a matter of restitution, but that Amsel would be released in due time."

Lilian raised her hands to her mouth. She closed her eyes for a moment, but when she opened them, they were watery pools of deep purple, "You have consigned Amsel to torture. The only release he will know, will be death. Our family will never be free. You have sealed all of our fates."

The pain that punctured my heart was so sharp, I could scarcely breathe. Whatever Amsel had been. Whatever Amsel had done, I forgave him. I had no choice. I loved him.

That I might never get a chance to tell him that, even if he couldn't love me back. That I might never see his face again, that he might never hold the child we created, made my knees buckle beneath me. I felt myself falling.

And them my lifeforce, my essence, was outside of my body.

I reached out to touch Alton, but my hand slipped through. I tried to scream out his name, but he could not hear me.

I was astral, a shapeless form within a space that was just another layer atop another. My hands and arms were threadbare and shimmering, woven together with fine delicate light.

I floated above, and looked down upon my unconscious body. I saw a person I did not know or understand anymore. I saw a life I did not want if Amsel was not in it.

And just as quickly as that, I was sucked back into myself, and back into the excruciating pain that made my

315

heart feel it might explode, back into the hell that was our current reality.

Alton let out a relieved sigh when I opened my eyes again, "You're back, little lady."

I had left my body. It was what people described happening in near death experiences, only I hadn't died. The phenomenon was called astral projection.

Was this an ability that I had? Could I do it again if I wanted to?

I managed to stand up and Alton guided me to a chair close to the fire. I sank into it, silence falling over me as I pressed my hands into my belly feeling for any sign of movement.

But it was still. She was still.

Penelope was worked into a wild panic now.

"Absalom swore he wouldn't harm Amsel. He may be many things, but he is a man of his word," she insisted.

"Absalom's promise to you was purposefully vague. You, my dear, made the mistake of hearing only what you wanted to hear. He may not harm Amsel personally, but mark my words, no one here is safe," Demetria said.

The air around us began to crackle and hiss like a wet log tossed on a raging fire. The edges of the room were at once blurry and out of focus.

Two men stepped through the fuzziness. One wore the robes of a monk, and the other, wore a white seersucker suit with pale grey stripes and a bright green bow tie.

Absalom.

Sir Langdon moved in front of my mother, duty-bound to protect her.

"Demetria is correct. I never said no harm would come to Amsel. I only said, I would not be the one to do it. You didn't really think I would let your conniving family get off Scott free, did you?" Absalom asked.

Conway reacted instantly, moving so unbelievably fast, it hardly seemed possible for a man of his size. His dagger was instantly, at Absalom's throat.

But it never made contact, the blade flew from his hand and Absalom caught it without looking.

Confusion flashed in the large djinni's eyes. But the man in the red robe was already behind him. Conway hadn't seen the sword that sliced through his head with swift precision.

For several seconds, Conway stood erect, the two parts of him fitting tightly together. Not a drop of blood trickled out. And then he slid apart and fell, each half going in opposite directions.

There were shocked gasps. Courtney screamed but Marie pulled her aside and covered her mouth, casting a warning look at her. I was too shocked to do anything other than to acknowledge the nausea threatening at the back of my throat and the immobilizing fear that gripped me.

Penelope let out a piercing, high pitched howl and lunged for Absalom. With no effort at all, he took hold of her wrist and stopped her in her tracks.

"You are weak and selfish. Willing to betray everyone around you, for what, Penelope? The bank you own, your manor, your precious Amsel. You are no better than the humans, a blight on the fabric of time."

Absalom twisted Penelope's left arm until it made a grotesque pop that reverberated through the room along with the sounds of her shrill cries.

Her arm hung limply, as if every bone inside of it had been shattered and rendered into gelatinous flesh. She was so very pale and looked as though she would have collapsed had Absalom not been holding her up.

He spoke softly into her right ear, "Don't ever raise your hand to me again." Then he shoved her, and she fell onto her back with a hard thud.

Her father rolled his wheelchair over to her and Absalom made no move to stop him. With Lilian's assistance, they turned Penelope's scarf into a sling, all the while keeping watchful eyes on their captors.

Absalom straightened his silk bow tie that was already as straight as an arrow and glanced around the room. "What a motley crew of miscreants. We installed a floating iron fog over your whole operation with the exception of the clearing and the portal. Unless your clothing is charmed, I'm afraid your magic will not work."

"There was a reason our ancestors fought so hard to keep the portal hidden. It was closed according to the will of God. To open it, could mean the destruction of everything. No good will come of it," Demetria said.

"What do we have to fear? We are powerful djinn. We'll survive and all the humans will die. And another age will begin, the age of djinn."

I listened, horrified, just like in my dreams, all life destroyed. Bodies and ash piled up as far as the eye could see. The thing I had not been able to fathom as being remotely possible, was on the verge of happening.

318

And then I heard it, a whisper, a psychic voice coming from the small life I carried inside of me. Clear and unmistakable.

All will die, but you.

I thought of my last nightmare, standing at a well of light, all around me, complete destruction. I was alive. I was the only one left in a world of ruin.

And then it hit me, the shimmer of green silk. The fabric that had stood out in my dream. The person who had worn it, destroyed beyond all recognition.

That person was Absalom.

"I've dreamt this. If the portal is opened, no one will survive. Not djinn. Not humans. No one will survive. Except for me," I said.

I waited for Absalom to snatch me up the way he had with Penelope, to twist me and break me out of the hatred he held inside for me, for all amalgam. A hate that ran so deeply, he was ready to sacrifice our world to it.

But he didn't.

"And you think you are powerful enough to see my future, half breed?" He said with a sneer, his contempt for me dripping like a festering poison.

I answered him, without animation or urgency. It was true. It was something that I knew, the way I'd known many things in my life that came to be. I didn't want it to be true.

But wanting something wasn't enough. Without action, nothing would change. "Yes," I said.

Demetria watched me with the strangest expression. It was tender, as if she wished to say something but dared not.

Something was brewing in her eyes. I could almost see the cogs turning.

And then just as quickly, she was as cool as January rain, and I wondered, what it was she had wanted to say.

Absalom laughed. "Then you will be sure to get the best seat. Let's all go and find out if Helene, the amalgam, is right. Let's go find out if this is the end of the world."

I risked speaking again, hoping for answers but not expecting them, "Where are all the townspeople? Where is Amsel?"

To my surprise, he glanced over at my protruding belly before he said, "Your friends from the town were taken to a cave. The entrance has been sealed and when they run out of oxygen, they will all die. And as for Amsel, you shall see for yourself, very soon."

I felt as if the atmosphere had been suctioned out of the room. I felt dizzy again. Alton squeezed my arm gently to reassure me.

But how could there be any hope of saving them, when our fates were likely sealed as well? It felt so impossible.

When I was a child and unsure what to do about a particular situation, when things had seemed hopeless to me, Harold and Lela had comforted me by saying, "*Look for the light that shines through the cracks. And when the time is right, it will reach you and you will know what to do.*"

Yes, I would wait for the right moment. A break, an opening, an epiphany. And when it came, I would act.

The robed man shifted his attention to Marie. She stepped back, placing a protective hand on Courtney's shoulder, and said, "Sergi, it's been a while."

His smile did not meet his cold black eyes and the absence of emotion was chilling. Without warning, a chain spun out from his right hand, wrapping Marie in a cocoon of iron.

When he tugged it sharply, Marie collided so violently with the wall, a projectile of blood sprayed from her split lip. Some landed on Sergi, all but disappearing as it blended in with color of his garment.

Courtney, who was also covered in Marie's blood, began to tremble, staring back at Sergi with unwavering hatred.

"How did you do it?" Sergi asked her. "How did you survive what I did to you?"

Marie spat out blood before answering, "It was divine intervention that spared my life."

Sergi sneered, "You weren't important enough to matter, let alone to be saved. You're nothing. That's ok. I have all the time in the world. You'll tell me the truth, sooner or later."

Absalom smiled serenely as he took in this scene. He looked charming and utterly harmless, which made him even more dangerous. "It's a good night for a walk. Shall we?" he asked.

We were all led outside where more of his men were waiting. They had not bothered to bind us. There was no fear that we had any chance at all of escaping.

Absalom led the way, looking like a gentleman who was simply out for an evening stroll instead of leading a doomed processional to the end of the world.

Courtney whispered to me, "Someone should tell that asshole that nobody wears a white suit after Labor Day."

Absalom glanced back and with the flick of his fingers, Courtney's head snapped to the side as if she had been slapped, "Tsk, tsk, tsk…mind your manners," he said with a disappointed finger wave.

Her features contorted into an unveiled fury, but she said nothing.

Holding up the rear, was Sergi, who with a rough jerk upon the end of Marie's chain, landed her flat on her back. He dragged her behind him, her skin tearing from being drawn through the muck, across sharp twigs and rocks.

It was sickening to watch.

The look on Courtney's face told me that she would like nothing better than to tear them all apart and hand feed them to a flock of vultures. Her helplessness to stop what was happening, fueled this rage even more.

There was something ominous, glistening, and otherworldly about the fog draped across the sky. It was like billions of tiny specks of silvery starlight illuminated the landscape. My mother's skin glowed milky white beneath it.

She moved gracefully with her head high, perfectly composed and unafraid. She looked like a warrior going into battle. She was beautiful.

I watched her, trying to make sense of this being that had given birth to me and then disappeared from my life, a djinn from a long line of queens.

My mother was royalty.

None of this seemed real. I expected to wake up to someone telling me I'd been in a coma for weeks and that I had imagined everything.

If I could forgive Amsel for taking part in the evils of the Order and for not loving me back, why couldn't I forgive her?

The slippery leaves and deep holes concealed by puddles, made the trek treacherous for me in my condition. My bare feet were already full of scrapes and nearly frozen. I slipped several times but Courtney was right there, ready to steady me again. I was grateful.

The instant we crossed the force field surrounding the clearing, all of the djinn prisoners were bound in iron chains, but they hadn't bothered with Courtney or me. They hadn't perceived either one of us as threats

I'd felt its energy before we even reached it. A high vibration that coursed through my body, energizing me in a way that I did not understand.

Darkness fell over us and I knew it was because we were no longer underneath the glimmering iron fog.

Now, our only light came from the waning moon and a bonfire up ahead.

As we approached, I gasped at the sight of the bloodied being that waited for us there. He was hardly recognizable and my heart sank.

CHAPTER THIRTY

PURE BLUE STARLIGHT

He was enormous, 8 feet tall, with wings covered in pale white feathers that were speckled with grey. They fanned out behind him. His face and skin had the appearance of an albino reptile.

But his eyes, I recognized them. They were not exactly the same. The pupils were vertical slits floating inside violet, but those eyes. They belonged to Amsel.

I began to sob.

That night I'd encountered him in the woods, he'd been only a silhouette framed in shadow. I'd been terrified of him.

Seeing him clearly in the light of the fire, he was giant and strange, the thing of nightmares. But not to me. Looking at him, I only saw Amsel. I only saw the man I loved, helpless, and in pain.

His hands and feet had been driven through with iron spikes. He hung from an enormous wooden cross. Almost every inch of him was covered in blood, the skin on his arms and abdomen marred by deep lacerations that told me he'd been whipped.

I vomited onto the ground, putrid sour mixing with the scent of decaying leaves. I felt wild and angry, and reckless.

Courtney must have sensed this. She dropped to my side and stroked my hair. She leaned in to rest her lips upon my ear, whispering so softly that I could barely hear her, "Be strong, Helene. We need you to be strong…and focused."

She was right. This wasn't the time to do something stupid. This was the time to find the crack.

What had been done to Amsel was grotesque. And the cross was nothing short of sacrilege, meant as a mockery to humans, to anyone who felt affinity with them, or with their institutions.

It was the same reason Sergi wore the robes of a monk to lure in those he intended to betray.

They believed in nothing, only power, and hate. They'd lost their souls. And like all who go down the wrong path, were indifferent to the wrongness of it, their minds corrupted by their own propaganda.

"I expected Prince Bertrand to be here," Demetria said.

"He's probably somewhere sleeping off a night of debauchery. We really don't need him. You leaving the way you did, created a crisis, and when the crown is compromised, our Order takes power to hold the peace," Absalom said.

He reached out and gently touched her cheek. "It was quite a stunt you pulled, hiding an entire kingdom and its assets away somewhere. But before this night is over, your suffering will be so great, you will not be able to restore them fast enough."

Demetria was not fazed by his threat. She motioned toward Amsel. "Is that really necessary? You have everything you wanted. Why all the showmanship?"

Sergi stepped forward and took my mother by the hair, "That man betrayed and murdered my father. Don't think he doesn't deserve every bit of that and more."

"You betrayed and murdered my mother. Is that what I should do to you?" she asked, her eyes daring him to do his worst.

His expression changed, a momentary hesitation as he remembered what had happened last time, he'd thought he was in control of Demetria.

He let go of her and whirled toward Amsel, glaring at him with pure hatred.

Amsel's voice was weak, cracking mid-sentence, "I didn't kill him. Your father sacrificed himself to save me."

"I should cut out your tongue for that, traitor," Sergi said.

"Look around. You hold all the cards. I have nothing to gain from lying to you. Deep down, you're afraid that what I say is the truth."

Sergi balled up his fist and punched Amsel in the gut. "I. Fear. Nothing." He held his right hand against Amsel's temple and a thin blue light streamed out and slipped inside of Amsel. "Tell me what happened that night."

"We rounded up a group of them. There was a mother, a small girl, and a few elderly amalgam. Sir Benowin walked in on me cutting them free. He went mad. Threatened to turn me in as soon as we returned. And then he began to cry and asked me why I had done what I had done."

"And is the part where you stabbed my father in the back?"

"No. I told him that I was repulsed by what we were doing, that the Order was wrong, and that I hated everything it stood for. I told him I would accept my punishment without a fight and would not deny what he had witnessed."

Sergi hissed, "Enough with the soliloquy, already. Spit it out, Amsel."

"He bound my hands and ankles in iron. Then he went over and finished cutting the prisoners loose. He handed the older man his own meteor dagger and turned his back. The man stabbed him and ran away."

"You poisoned his mind."

"Your father despised the monster that you had become. He loved me and I loved him. He couldn't live with betraying the order and he couldn't live with turning me over. I'm sorry, Sergi. I am responsible for Sir Benowin's death."

Sergi struck Amsel with the dull edge of his sword, splitting his temple, blinding him as blood poured into his eyes, "You will never disgrace my father's name again. In a few hours, you will exist no more. And after we have killed you, we will kill every one you have ever loved, until there is no one left to remember you."

Absalom stepped forward and leaned over an opening in the ground. Faint orbs of light zoomed out, lifting up into the night sky where they were displaced by the force field, creating an aurora like effect. He pulled a small book from his breast pocket.

He flashed us with a brilliant smile, "I found this centuries ago, written in the language of the ancient ones. It took a long time to translate the text. It turns out all we really need to open the portal is a good old-fashioned sacrifice, any part of a pure blooded djinni will suffice."

Sergi pulled out a knife and held it in front of Amsel's face. "I'm sure you recognize this. Only appropriate that I shall use the same blade that killed my father to cut out your heart."

The sound of my shrill, gut-wrenching screams broke the heavy silence, swelling inside of it, until my voice failed me and I sank my knees into the mud, until what was left inside of me, wasn't rage anymore.

It was a dangerous calm.

Lilian glanced around at her fellow beings, a hodge podge of unlikely soldiers, underdogs dealt impossible odds. And when she landed on me, she smiled reassuringly. It was the kind of smile that said, *Brace yourself! Shit's about to get real.*

Sergi took his time, shoving the very tip of the blade into the first layer of skin and muscle in Amsel's wide barrel chest.

Amsel didn't budge. He hung there as if he were made of the same quartz stone as the gargoyle resting upon his family's crypt. He watched Sergi do this with empty acceptance. He watched this thing being done to him without any fear.

Sergi paused long enough to twist the knife. But even this did not provoke the reaction he wanted from Amsel, and his anger over this was laid bare for everyone to see.

Marie shouted out to him, "Hey, Dalai Lama. He's not going to give you what you want. He's not going to beg and plead with you, the same way, I didn't."

Sergi pulled the knife out and turned toward Marie. He tugged the end of her chain and spun her, unwinding Marie from her cocoon. She was inches from him now.

Sergi leaned over her, "Don't worry. I promise you, this time, I will break you."

"You can't break the light," Marie said.

She let go of her chains, chains that she had merely been holding, chains that weren't even attached to her.

When Sergi realized this, a dumbfounded puzzlement furrowed his brow.

Marie transformed, standing defiantly with her wings stretched wide. Her body began to glow, a brilliant, shiny hue, a golden light that was almost too painful to look at.

Sergi stared at her in disbelief, words for the first time in his life, escaped him as he was met with Marie's smug grin.

She flicked her wrist and the chains fell off of the other djinnis. Marie wrapped her body, one that seemed to be composed only of golden flame, around Amsel and he was absorbed within its protective sphere.

Sergi lunged at her and the blade he held disappeared into the middle of her back. The light jumped from the gash and entered in through his hand.

For a moment, Sergi too, was composed of this same splendid golden light, light that looked as if it had spilled out of heaven itself.

Slowly, the light began to fade and Sergi became a void of inky blackness. He wasn't there anymore. He wasn't anywhere.

He was simply, *gone*.

Knights of the Order moved in around us with their swords raised. Sir Langdon and Alton held them off while Demetria set her sights on Absalom, but then her face fell and she just stood there looking out in suspended animation.

Absalom was at the portal. During the chaos, he had taken Penelope. He chopped her head from her body. It tumbled, disappearing down the deep hole of the portal.

He let her lifeless body fall and it hung over the edge of the well, half in and half out. It was an atrociously heinous act.

Penelope was dead.

The sacrifice was complete. It was too late.

All the people I cared about would be consumed until only ash remained. The world I knew would be gone.

The ground began to rumble and shake with tremendous tremors. Beneath our feet, it rolled and undulated like ocean waves.

A flame made of pure blue starlight broke free from the well. It was blinding and disorienting.

I could not tell which was sky or which was ground, or where I began and it ended. I was floating weightless, part of it somehow.

And then I simply knew. The way I understood things without knowing how. It was the moment I'd waited for, the light that shined through the cracks.

I knew what I had to do.

CHAPTER THIRTY-ONE

NOT FOR US TO KNOW

I moved toward the portal. The air was viscous. I could taste it on my tongue, salty and bitter. I could smell it, the dust of ancient lands, laden with spices and ions, the primordial soup of life, beginnings and endings.

I could feel it, the frequency hummed through me, connecting to every nerve cell in my body, a vibration which was a language of its own, a language I understood,

It was encoded inside of me, locked away in my DNA, and it beckoned to me.

In that moment, I knew. I was a conduit for this power.

Near the edge of the well, I closed my eyes and allowed this stream of pure energy to draw me inside of it. It stretched me, twisted me, and consumed me, until there was no Helene left. And I was the event horizon.

There was a sudden and distinct calmness to everything, a stillness to it that no words that existed could accurately convey.

I could see the whole of everything tied together with strings of blue fire, the past and future, interwoven. I could see alternate histories where different choices were made, connecting to alternate futures, and yet they were all still connected to each other.

It was like being submerged in pure love and acceptance. There was no fear. Time would stretch on in multiple dimensions of space and time. There would never be an end. Only cycles of change and transformation.

We were all connected, djinn and humans alike, and our destinies would always be linked. We were of the same source, of the same creator.

I saw the future where I stood alone in a world destroyed. And it was exactly as it had been in my dreams. But there were other possible futures where the world went on, where I collapsed the portal and saved the world.

I alone had the power to choose.

It was a destiny that had been pre-set, a destiny that I had never had the power to stop.

From the multitude of possible outcomes, I plucked out a string and bound it to myself.

It wasn't the best-case scenario. The world did go on, but it was not a utopian version of it. It didn't necessarily have a happy ending. It was fraught with suffering and all the failings that went along with living.

But it was the best choice for the evolution of life itself.

I snapped the cord which connected me to the all of everything, and it broke. Its frayed edge floated weightless in front of me. And then the light began to disappear, rushing into the hungry blackness of the portal.

Only a final ring of light, no brighter than a candle's flame, flickered briefly at its edges, and then it too was no more.

I stared up into the sky. The clouds had cleared away, and I could make out the constellation of Orion, the Hunter. I felt the knowledge ebb away from me, the details already fading from my memory.

It was then I understood. I would live my time in this life without the benefit of knowing what my choices would bring. One could only know these things while in the presence of this source energy. We could not take it with us.

It was not meant for us to know.

For a second, I lingered in the hazy fog that came after a dream. Someone had wrapped me up in blankets. I turned my head slightly, enough to see Absalom's men, naked and shivering, huddled together under a giant iron dome that looked like an enormous fishing net.

The cross that had held Amsel blazed brightly on the bonfire next to them.

All the barbarity of the night came rushing back to me.

"Where is Amsel? The people of Glenhaven, we have to get to them quickly."

I struggled to sit up and realized I was being cradled in someone's lap. Amsel's lap.

"Marie and Lilian are on their way to them. You were out cold for a good thirty minutes. You had me worried," Amsel said.

He gazed down at me, no longer in the form of the winged being. This was the version of him that I'd fallen in love with, the sexy hulk of a man with white hair and intensely, violet eyes.

I reached up to touch his blood-stained face. The cuts on his head and chest had been stitched up, and he was covered in black and blue bruises that would take time to fade.

I sank into him, wrapped my hand around his neck, and pulled his lips down to mine.

He kissed me tenderly and everything else faded away. Nothing else mattered. He was alive. Amsel was alive. The world was alive.

When he pulled away, I smiled gently and said, "You look like hell."

He laughed, but this only caused him to wince in pain "You look beautiful," he said.

All the humor faded, and he searched the depths of my eyes, worry pulling his well-defined eyebrows together. "I was afraid you would be terrified of me after what you saw. I was afraid you might hate me for not telling you the truth, and for this…"

Amsel's palm slid over my swollen belly. "What must you think of me?" he asked.

I sat up fully and took his cheeks between my palms, "I don't hate you, Amsel. I am grateful for this child. I was hurt and confused when you ran away from me. Why did you leave?"

Amsel stood, pulling me with him. I gasped at the shocking extent of his wounds that were already beginning to heal, thanks to Marie, and felt the stinging tears at the memory of what the Order had done to him.

A wooden box appeared and he handed it to me. It was gorgeous, with inlaid lapis lazuli, malachite, and gold. I opened it and saw the gold ring with sparkling blue diamonds around its band, and on its face, the raised image of a crane taking flight from a field of orchids, balanced inside, as if by magic.

"This belongs to you. It was in a safe in your family home. Your mother always planned to reveal your identity, and this was the proof. It's a signet ring, from the royal house of Courtenay."

I looked back at him, confused.

"But we didn't have a safe."

"It's there, hidden in a closet, very cleverly disguised, I might add. I needed answers. I was afraid of what I felt for you. I wanted to see where you came from. What was so different about you, that made me long for you with every fiber of my being."

"And did you find the answer?" I asked.

"Just a realization. I love you, Helene. For better or for worse, you are what I choose over all else. You and this child are what give me hope for the future."

"And you are sure about that? That you can love an amalgam?"

"Yes. And what about you, could you ever truly love a monster?"

I slipped my hands into his. "You're no monster, Amsel. I love you."

The tender moment was interrupted by warm liquid gushing down my inner thighs. I touched the wetness and brought my hand up to the light. It was clear, not bloody.

336

My water had broken. And that wasn't good.

"No! It's too early," I cried. Tears streamed down my face, the culmination of all the stressful events leading up to now. I was afraid. More afraid than I had been before.

I couldn't lose this child. She had a name, she was Adelaide. Little, precious Adelaide.

CHAPTER THIRTY-TWO

ITS OWN SET OF CHALLENGES

Amsel carried me up the steep hill to the house. He turned on the hot water in the shower in the master bathroom and pulled me into it with him. He was calm, which helped me to be calm.

We bathed each other. Me trying to be gentle with his newly stitched wounds, and him trying to soothe me with the sway of his soapy hands over my body.

When the contractions hit, he held my hand while I squeezed his with all of my might. It was the most intense pain I'd ever known. It held on until I thought I couldn't stand another second, then it eased, only to return three minutes later.

Amsel dried me off, dressed us both in warm robes, and led me to the bed. He pulled the covers up over us and we remained like that, folded together, until the contractions intensified, becoming more painful and frequent.

He checked me. "You are already fully dilated, Helene. You need to push the baby out."

"No! I don't want to! Can't you do it for me?"

Amsel began to laugh and I considered punching him squarely in the nose.

"If I could my dearest, I would," he said.

Desperate to ease the discomfort and the intense pressure on my cervix, I prowled about the room, casing its walls like a trapped thing, desperate to break free.

The pressure became so great, that I rushed to the bathroom, mortified at the prospect of possibly having a bowel movement on the floor and in front of Amsel.

As soon as I made it there, I reached down between my legs and grew faint with panic when I discovered that I could feel the top of a head there.

Amsel held me securely as he squatting next to me, "Breathe, Helene. You're alright. You're doing great."

I pushed and our daughter's tiny form slid out into Amsel's right hand.

I stared down at her in shock and amazement.

She was long and pink with a nest of matted, dark brown curls. Her eyes were a dazzling shade of the palest blue lavender. She was perfect. The loveliest thing that I had ever laid eyes upon.

Amsel handed her to me and I cradled her in my arms. She curled her tiny fingers around one of mine. And then she began to wail like a banshee.

"I think it's safe to say that her lungs are fully developed," Amsel chuckled.

Courtney appeared in the doorway, saw my naked body, and turned bright crimson with embarrassment, "I'm so sorry. I heard screaming and thought something was---Oh, my God! Right. I'll just go boil some water, get some fresh sheets, and find some cigars."

Her panicked voice trailed away, and I called after her. "Don't forget about diapers…"

"I don't think she heard you," Amsel said.

"I think she wants us to call her Adelaide. What do you think about that?"

He mulled over this for a moment, then kissed me on the forehead. "I think she looks exactly like an Adelaide."

After I'd bathed, I felt surprisingly fabulous, considering what had transpired.

Amsel left and returned with a gorgeous, vintage white Christian Dior gown for me to put on that still had the tag on. Before I could question why he had a gown in his possession, he said, "It's Lilian's. She still keeps some of her things tucked away here."

"It's beautiful, but I'll ruin it in my current state."

"Nonsense." He slipped it over my head and I brushed my hair in the vanity mirror. I didn't recognize myself.

There was a brightness to my hazel eyes which made them appear even more green. My skin glowed with health, and my hair was unnaturally shiny, falling perfectly over my shoulders.

"Do I look different to you?" I asked him.

"I had noticed you had this new goddess quality about you. Maybe it has something to do with your abilities opening up or coming into contact with the portal."

There was a knock on the door. Lilian walked into the room, holding a swaddled Adelaide, followed by Demetria,

"I think she misses her mother's smell." Lilian handed her to me and she snuggled in, immediately searching for my breast.

"I am happy to have you in this family, Helene. And thrilled to finally have a grandchild."

"Thank you, Lilian."

"Now, I must get back to shopping. This child needs many things, and they are not going to order themselves."

Amsel followed behind her. "If you will excuse me, I think I will try to keep my mother in check. There are only so many things this house can hold."

Demetria stayed behind. "I just wanted to say, thank you. You were so brave. I am proud to know you."

"Please, don't thank me. I'm not even sure how I did what I did. And what of Absalom, any news?" I asked.

"There are wanted signs posted for him and my brother in every realm from here to Timbuktu. We will find them. Now that the kingdom has been re-established and the Order of the Blue Orchid disbanded by royal decree. All involved will be tried for treason the moment they are apprehended. And thanks to my list, we know the names of most who were loyal to Absalom. Sir Langdon is away seeing to this."

"And do you think the djinn world is ready to accept amalgam?"

"That's the wonderful thing about being a Queen. You get to make the rules."

Demetria wore a well-tailored jacket and matching skirt. She looked dignified and formal. Almost unapproachable compared to the woman from yesterday.

"And you aren't worried that your actions might cause others to rise up against you?"

"These changes won't be easy. Many will push back against them. But I've displayed real power and few would be fool enough to challenge me. In time, they will learn to accept you."

Demetria clasped her hands together, looking characteristically uncomfortable, "I hope that you might be able to someday find room for me in your life. I would like to get to know you better, and Adelaide. There is also the matter of preparing you for succession to the throne. You are the next in line."

"Absolutely, not. I have no desire to sit on a throne or to rule over a kingdom."

"You are born of a priestess class. We walk closer to the creator. We have duties to the world that others do not have. In many ways, our lives do not belong to us."

Adelaide began to fuss, "I think she's hungry again."

"Of course, you should tend to her. We can talk about this later." Demetria turned to leave but then paused. "Helene, the ability you possess is rare. It comes with its own set of challenges. You must gain control of it, or it will gain control of you…" her voice trailed off.

I nodded. I knew that once things had settled down, it was something that I would have to face. "Demetria, I would like to get to know you better. I'm very sorry for what I said to you before. I was harsher than I should have been. Maybe sometime you could tell me about my father?"

"Yes, I would love to do that." When she smiled, her face softened. She looked more youthful and even more breathtakingly beautiful. "Oh, I almost forgot. You have some visitors that would really love to pop in for a second to pay their respects."

"Sure, send them in."

Mary, Lester, Mark, and Sadie tiptoed inside. The instant I saw them, tears of relief began to pour down my cheeks. I was surprised when Rogue pushed past them, propped his front paws on the bed, and licked my nose.

I laughed, "I missed you too."

Rogue glanced down at Adelaide briefly, before sprawling out at the foot of the bed where he kept a watchful eye over me and the baby.

"We don't want to disturb that precious one," Mary whispered.

"Get in here," I said.

Mary also had tears in her eyes when she hugged me gently and leaned back to look at me, "How do you look so fabulous? I mean you have been through pure hell in the last few hours."

"It isn't a night I would care to repeat anytime soon, but I feel pretty good. How are you all holding up?"

Mark peered over Mary's shoulder, "I'm not going to lie. It was damn terrifying. And I'm a little freaked out to learn that nobody in Glenhaven is fully human and that you suddenly have a fully developed baby, a beautiful baby, maybe the most beautiful baby I have ever seen, but I'm grateful to you, Helene."

"Stop. Any one of you would have done the same for me."

I was embarrassed by all the attention. The truth was a little more complicated than I wanted to go into until I had time to process. The force that I came in contact with in that clearing, had taken me over. I wasn't really me in there. I became someone else.

Sadie waved shyly, "Hi. I want to apologize for all the dirty looks I shot at you. Mark told me about how he conned you into helping him. I'm thankful to you for that, for helping me see him. And I hope we can be friends."

"We are going to be fast friends, Sadie. We have a lot to learn about ourselves. We can all lean on each other to heal from this."

Lester hovered close to the door. I wondered if he was alright, if he was still being tormented by the voices in his head.

"We should probably let these two get some rest," Lester said. He approached me, dropped a kiss on the top of my head, and whispered so that only I could hear, "Don't worry about me. You weren't the only one to come into your power last night. I got my sea legs in that cave."

I took his hand and squeezed it tightly, "I'm glad."

It was hard to keep from pushing him for more information. But since he was still being rather secretive, I had a feeling he had not yet shared this with anyone else.

When everyone had gone, Amsel carried in a cradle.

"It's gorgeous," I said.

"The Brenner's dropped this off as a gift. Seems they have had this in their store for a very long time just waiting for our little princess. Apparently, it's 19th century Gothic Revival."

Made from walnut and with caning, the craftsmanship was exquisite. Inside there was a perfectly fitted mattress, and white eyelet bedding that looked very new and extremely expensive.

"And I suppose the mattress and bedding are from the same period too?"

"No, that required a bit of magic," He took Adelaide who was fast asleep and placed her inside.

She did look like a little princess. Of course, technically, she was a princess.

Amsel slid into bed next to me and was suddenly, very serious, "No matter what, I will always protect you and Adelaide. I never directly killed one of your kind. But I did turn them over to the Order when I had no other choice. It was the darkest time of my life, and I am not proud of the part I played. I have not forgiven myself for what I've done. I didn't think I deserved happiness, so I did not allow myself to think I could ever have what I have now."

I laid my hand on his arm, "Amsel, I forgive you. You must forgive yourself. You are not an evil person. You were willing to die to protect people like me. Yesterday doesn't exist. The present is the only thing that matters."

"Someday, maybe, with your help, I can do that."

Exhausted, we fell asleep with the light still on, with Amsel spooned behind me, his hand buried in my hair.

CHAPTER THIRTY-THREE

FINALLY, HOME

Penelope and Conway's memorial service was held at Harben's estate.

The house was immense. Done in the French Provencal style, it was situated among sprawling acres of countless formal gardens. The scale of it was grand, awe inspiring even, but there was a coldness to it, a complete absence of any semblance of coziness or intimacy.

I couldn't help but think it was an outward reflection of this branch of the Richter family, that they were uncomfortable wading in emotions that ran too deeply, always denying them proximity to their hearts.

An abundance of white lilies flowed through every room saturating the air with saccharine sweetness. There was a table covered over with photos of her, Penelope on horseback, twirling on pointe, graduating from Harvard, surrounded by friends and family.

There was also a table draped in white velvet and covered in gorgeous blue orchids, dedicated to Conway

Spizzeri. His sword was displayed, along with a plaque from my mother. It read:

In honor of his bravery in the face of adversity and sacrificing his own life for a moral cause, I hereby posthumously dub Sir Conway Spizzeri, Knight of the United Kingdom Between.

Someone had stacked a tower of assorted boxes of snack cakes nearby, and I was pretty sure that Marie was behind it.

When it was time to speak for him, Alton stepped forward, "He was a bull-headed, soft-spoken tyrant. Most days I just wanted to put my boot up his butt. And I ain't even gonna get started on the wrappers that he left all over the goddamn place. It was crazy making. But he was also a good friend. He always had my back. And inside that giant, hairy, ugly, beast of a man, was a heart that was even bigger and purer than you can imagine. I speak for all of us when I say, this world has lost a beautiful soul in disguise. We will miss you."

Alton threw up his hands as he began to tear up. Courtney, seeing this, walked up to the podium and gently led him back to his seat.

As heartbreakingly sad as the ceremony was, it was also full of so much love and compassion, reminding us all of the power of forgiveness.

Many people came forward to speak of the charity and kindnesses Penelope had shown them in their years in Glenhaven. I did not recognize any of these different accounts of her. It was a side of Penelope I had never been given a glimpse of.

Her actions led all of us all into harm's way. An obsessive love and clinging, led to her own death. It was a lesson for us all in the destructive power of hate, and the way fear could steer us all off a cliff if we weren't careful.

But her actions also brought us closer together. They illuminated what was important to all of us, what we would fight for, what we were willing to sacrifice to save the ones we loved.

Almost everyone in the town attended. Many faces I knew, but most I'd never seen before. And I did not see Georgia or Alexia, which was not surprising.

I could understand why Georgia would want to shelter her daughter from the gory details of what happened to Penelope and Conway.

Harben could not contain his gratitude to everyone there for showing up to pay their respects to his daughter.

He hugged me and Amsel, "Thank you both for coming. There are no words to express how deeply sorry I am over the actions of my daughter. I hope you can find it in your hearts to forgive her." Harben wiped away his tears with a monogrammed handkerchief.

"We are so sorry for your loss. I didn't know Penelope long, but I feel like if she'd survived our ordeal, we would have been able to smooth things over and find common ground between us," I said.

"Helene is right. It's water under the bridge. We are family, always, and you are welcome in our home anytime you like," Amsel said.

Harben was deeply moved by this, lifting a finger to buy himself a moment before he completely broke down, "I would very much like to meet Princess Adelaide. And your mother was gracious to invite me to her upcoming coronation. It's an honor I never expected. Please express my gratitude next time you speak with her," he said.

"Certainly, I will do that."

At some point Amsel and I became separated and I wandered through the enormous house, studying the paintings which hung along the walls of a grand hallway.

I was amazed by the extent of the collection, Salvador Dali, Picasso, Matisse, Georgia O'Keeffe, and many more recognizable works.

There was a rough drawing in pencil of a winged being. Most would look upon it, see the wings, and assume it was an angel. But if you looked closely, you could make out that the features were more serpentine. Without a doubt, this was a djinni.

The signature of the artist gave me chills. Leonardo da Vinci. Was this purely speculative on his part? Or had he been in contact with one?

I sensed Mary and Lester approaching, but didn't turn around. I just knew it was them, "Do you think Leonardo da Vinci could have been one of us?" I asked.

"Wouldn't surprise me one little bit," Lester said.

I turned to see Mary staring up at the sculpted molding on the ceiling of the grandiose hall. "This place is something else, like Buckingham Palace got dropped smack in the middle of our little town. We've been looking everywhere for you," she said.

I was happy to have some time to speak with them away from the crowd. Mary looked toward Lester, as if siphoning courage from him before she spoke.

"The other day, you asked me a question about what you saw at the diner. And I…well…I didn't know how to answer without you thinking I was some kind of a freak. But while we were in that cave, I realized I could help people. We thought we were all going to die in there, so what would it hurt to use my natural gifts to ease the suffering of people I love."

Seeing Mary falter, Lester stepped in. "She filled that entire cave with light, suspended hundreds of chandeliers above us. It was the most beautiful thing I'd ever seen. Moved us all to tears."

"The thing is. Nobody tried to tie me up and burn me at the stake. They were so happy about it, they didn't even question how I was making that happen. It didn't matter to them. I was still Mary. Helene, I can make things appear simply by thinking about them, I can control objects with my mind, and I'm two hundred and fifty years old. I've been called a witch and driven out of more towns than I can count. I've been alone my entire life, and until now, I didn't have any idea why I am the way I am."

I wondered, if she had confided in me that day at the diner, how I would have reacted? These weren't confessions you heard every day. And if this last week hadn't happened, I would have had a hard time believing it, even after seeing evidence with my own eyes.

"I can't imagine how lonely that must have been. And how do you feel now?" I asked.

"Like I've been given a new lease on life. Like the burden of this secret is no longer bearing down on me. But also, anxious about how it might change my relationships with people."

"Mary, I can't speak for others, but this changes nothing between the two of us. The truth is, none of us here are conventional. I do have questions, though. Lots of them, that I hope you will humor sometime."

Mary exhaled and clasped her hands together, "Yes. Of course. Thank God! I was so worried."

Lester wrapped an arm around Mary's shoulders and gazed at her with pure love and adoration.

"Lester, you said you had gotten your sea legs in that cave. What did you mean by that?" I asked.

"I was a wreck when they came for me. I didn't have enough strength left in me to fight back, not that it would have mattered. But now I understand that being in that cave was a gift. It forced me to surrender to it. Instead of fighting to keep everybody's thoughts out, I just let them all come rushing in. The moment I did that, something clicked in my head."

"And everything is OK, now?" I asked

"Better than OK. I stepped into myself. I know you understand what I mean."

I did. Completely. We had all been forced into a sudden reckoning about ourselves. It was just a matter of accepting these things and moving forward.

"Should we start a support group?" I was joking, but Lester's face lit up at the mention of this.

"Wouldn't hurt. Listening to people's thoughts today, most of us are confused, and still reeling from what has happened. I would say all of us have some degree of PTSD. It might make it easier for others to come forward and fess up to things they've kept bottled up for years."

"Oh, I like that. We could do it at the diner. I'll handle everything," Mary said.

"You will do no such thing. I know you think I'll probably just get in your way. But let me help you. Please. I want to," I said.

I knew how much Mary hated the idea of help. She'd only had to depend on herself for so long, she was poorly equipped to accept it.

Mary pressed her lips together and studied me. I could see her playing over scenarios in her mind of how it might not be a good idea at all.

"I suppose that would be alright. But if I get all snippy with you, please feel free to put me in my place. I was born with a short supply of patience and no filter, just ask Lester."

"She's mean as a rattlesnake sometimes. But she has never failed to apologize when all is said and done," Lester said.

"Then that settles it," I said.

And just like that, the Glenhaven Friends of Djinn support group was formed.

After the service, Amsel and I walked out to say goodbye to Courtney and Marie. A pearlized red convertible waited for them in the driveway.

"Where to now?" Amsel asked.

"I like this place. Maybe somewhere similar, filled with mountains and splendid views. And of course, Courtney demands that this place must have a Waffle House nearby."

"I won't go there if it doesn't," Courtney shouted from the passenger seat.

"You know you could just stay here. We would love to have you as permanent residents," he said.

"As tempting as that is, I feel my services will be put to much better use out there." Out there, being the human world.

"Are you sure you aren't going to go traipsing around the world looking for Absalom?" he asked.

"Oh, I never said I wouldn't do that. And anyway, Queen Demetria is offering a sizable bounty to anyone who brings him in." She motioned toward Courtney. "Have you seen how much this woman eats? It takes a fortune to feed her."

Marie handed me a business card. It was stamped with a golden winged angel and read:

If you are ever in trouble, if you ever need anything, you will know what to do.

"Thank you. For everything. We are forever in your debt," I said.

"Nonsense. I only facilitated it. You're the one who saved us all."

I was gearing up to argue about this, but she had already slid behind the wheel and revved up the powerful engine.

The odd pair of friends disappeared into the sunset, the Fugees version of *Killing Me Softly with His Song*, drifting on the wind.

"I rather like that song. Makes me want to dance," Amsel said.

"You don't strike me as a dancer."

"There are many things about me that will surprise you," he said.

I smiled. The prospect of uncovering all of his secrets tugged at my heart, "I can't wait."

He kissed me then, and everything in the world seemed right. I was where I belonged. I had stumbled into an enchanted land, fallen in love with a djinni, had a magical baby, and discovered I was the heir to a royal empire.

It was the stuff of a dark fairytale, with all of its sadness and darkness, sweetness and light.

But what would life be without a balance of those things. And in learning how to accept the essential nature of both, I could finally accept myself.

I was finally, home.

THE END